DEAD
in
5
Heartbeats

RALPH "SONNY" BARGER
» with Keith and Kent Zimmerman «

WM

WILLIAM MORROW
An Imprint of HarperCollins*Publishers*

HarperCollins books may be purchased for educational, business, or sales promotional use. For information please write: Special Markets Department, HarperCollins Publishers Inc., 10 East 53rd Street, New York, NY 10022.

PATCH KINKADE is a trademark of Sonny Barger Productions. SHARPFINGER is a trademark of Imperial Schrade Corp.

FIRST EDITION

Designed by Adrian Leichter

Printed on acid-free paper

Library of Congress Cataloging-in-Publication Data
Barger, Ralph.
    Dead in 5 heartbeats : a novel / Ralph "Sonny" Barger ; with Keith and Kent Zimmerman.— 1st ed.
        p. cm.
    ISBN 0-06-053251-3
        1. Motorcyclists—Fiction. 2. Motorcycle gangs—Fiction. 3. California—Fiction. I. Title: Dead in five heartbeats. II. Zimmerman, Keith. III. Zimmerman, Kent, 1953– IV. Title.
PS3602.A833D43 2003
813'.6—dc21   2003051250

03 04 05 06 07 JTC/RRD 10 9 8 7 6 5 4 3 2 1

For Sharon and Zorana,
my first and last loves

» «

»» Acknowledgments ««

THE ZIMMERMEN" ACKNOWLEDGE THEIR WORK ON THIS NOVEL to singer/songwriter David Broza, jazz pianist Michel Camilo, and author Harlan Ellison, three friends who inspired us to live for our art. Love, as always, to our wives, Deborah and Gladys. Propers to Fritz Clapp, James Fitzgerald, and our editor/partner in crime Michael Shohl.

1

Incident
at Trader's

Trader's Roadhouse was bike-friendly and colors-welcome, a neutral hangout for riders of all stripes. It was a gigantic rectangular Quonset playground that sat on the dusty city limits of Hayward, California, a small blue-collar town a dozen miles southeast of the Oakland flatlands.

The joint was shaking wall-to-wall, shoulder

to shoulder at Trader's Thursday Bike Nite. Topic A screaming over the cavernous din among the men propping up the long mahogany bar: Which Johnny Cash "prison" album kicked it more? *At Folsom* or *At San Quentin*?

An assortment of barroom anthems played as customers jammed the jukebox and voted with their quarters. A wide variety emerged: Willie's "My Heroes Have Always Been Cowboys" followed by Kid Rock's "American Bad Ass." Arthur Conley's "Sweet Soul Music" flowed into "Sweet Child o' Mine" by Guns N' Roses. No logical pattern, just a mishmash of rock, soul, and renegade country. Sweet musical chaos. Since this was California, the only missing barroom ingredient was the stale smell of cigarette smoke.

The loud *crack* of the opening break of a rack of pool balls pierced the bar's ambience, followed by the unmistakable deep *thunk* of the first cluster of balls rolling toward their not-so-final resting place below the green felt playing surface.

A muted television set mounted up behind the bar broadcast an A's–Tigers game but was roundly ignored. Motorcycle memorabilia was plastered throughout Trader's, with *Easyriders* pinups, a mural-sized David Mann painting, tools, wrenches, and scooter parts hanging from the walls. Entire bikes were suspended from the ceiling.

The blonde behind the fryer was doing bang-up business. She handed out red plastic baskets of deep-fried zucchini, jalapeño poppers, chili bacon burgers, and cheese fries to the waitresses as fast as they came off the grill and out of the grease. Popular American brews, assorted premium lagers, and Mexican beers were sold on tap. Top-shelf whiskey, single malts, and Mexicano tequila brands moved briskly off the back line while fancy liqueurs gathered dust behind the plank. Suicidal mixed drinks were served in Ball mason jars. Customers ate peanuts and threw the shells on the floor.

The "male–female ratio" was impressive for a weeknight, close to fifty–fifty. There were more than enough eye-catching, mostly divorced, Chardonnay-chugging honeys with their 2.2 kids back home sleeping. They were the bait that lured the many buff bad boys on motorcycles to Trader's. These guys figured they had a better–than–fifty–fifty chance of scoring some decent tail before the weekend hordes invaded the place. The closer the clock came to striking two A.M., the stiffer and wetter the talk progressed, and the more coinage the condom machines in the men's room took in. After all, Trader's was "pro-choice." Ribbed, regular, and whiskey flavored were the most popular.

A dozen miles away, down a darkened road, a lone motorcyclist was headed in Trader's direction. Wearing his beanie helmet, he looked up from the darkness of the roadway and watched the stars punch their sparkle through the sky. Marco was supposed to meet up with a couple of his club brothers from the Infidelz MC. One by one, each rider had opted out. Marco made the trip anyway. He'd earned his Infidelz patch less than three weeks ago. He was in "any excuse to ride" mode. Nothing was going to stop him from throttling his FXR through the wind and enjoying a cool summer breeze on two wheels.

Marco was glad he hadn't stayed behind in Oakland. He needed a putt away from the ball and chain and the screaming kids. How could his brothers miss riding on such a night? The patch on his back, orange and black on a clean white background, seemed to add power to his glide and pride to his posture. After a few pops, maybe he'd head back into Oakland to the Infidelz clubhouse and drink beer with his buddies until dawn.

Thursday Bike Nite at Trader's, for better or for worse, was primarily a "1%er" night out. Depending on who you asked or how you looked at bike riding, a 1%er was either the baddest of the bad bikers, the cream of the riding world, or the 1 percent that gave all motorcyclists a shady rep. One thing was true—1%ers didn't give a shit about the reputations of the other 99 percent who rode. The remaining 99 percent of the area's bikers—law-abiding Rich Urban Bikers (RUBs), rice rocket daredevils, and weekend Harley riders—were safe at home in front of their TVs watching late-night *CSI* reruns.

The crowd at Trader's was divided mostly into four 1%er factions: patch-wearing MC (motorcycle club) members, their prospects (would-be members), supporters (friends and family), and hang-arounds (those thinking about prospecting for an MC). The three clubs drinking that night were the 2Wheelers, the Gun Runners, and Soul Sacrifice, the latter a racially mixed club. A leather-clad group of independent riders and a few HOGs (Harley Owners Groups) hung around the bar and minded their own business.

In theory, everyone got along. In practice, it didn't always work out that way.

It all started when Too Tall from the Soul Sacs smacked into Shadow from the Gun Runners. Both had been drinking steadily since early evening. Shadow's temper was short-fused enough so that when Too Tall trod on Shadow's expensive footwear, spilling beer, their tempers flared.

"Watch yer black ass, boy," muttered Shadow the Gunner. He brushed the beer off his pants, then gazed down at the silver-dollar-size droplet as it seeped into his brand-new light tan Tony Lama ostrich-skin cowboy boots.

"Motherfucker!" Shadow seethed and shouted.

Shadow was much shorter than Too Tall; he was built like a fireplug, solid and low to the ground. Too Tall was lean and wore his hair in cornrows. Described in script on his gas tank as *Slim, Sleek, and Deadly,* Too Tall stiffened at Shadow's insult. He might have been called a motherfucker ten times that night, but not with the disrespect Shadow's curse carried. Too Tall walked back toward Shadow and faced off with an evil sneer.

"Hey peckerwood! Who you callin' 'boy'?" barked Too Tall.

The fuse was lit. Shadow was poised.

The two bodies came hurling out of the back hallway, tumbling like a pair of loaded Vegas dice. Each man seized the other in a death-grip headlock, and they rolled around frantically on the floor flailing their legs, each trying to break free. Too Tall wrestled himself loose first and jumped to his feet. As Shadow got up from his hands and knees, Too Tall kicked a size-twelve Timberland into his head and leveled a three-inch gash across his forehead. It was the sound of a mule kicking in a melon patch.

The blow knocked Shadow on his ass. But before Too Tall could jump in and finish him off, Shadow rolled over on his stomach and bounced back up off the hardwood. In a single motion he spun around and yanked a stubby Buck knife out of his inner vest pocket. With a deadly clicking sound, the serrated combat blade locked into stabbing position. A split second later, he plunged the saw-toothed shiv into Too Tall's gut. A pocket of air inside Too Tall's stomach made a wheezing, farting sound as the blade left his body. Blood spurted out of the wound and splashed onto an onlooker's blouse. Too Tall reacted and connected with an adrenaline-fueled punch to Shadow's jaw that knocked him cold.

By then, all three MC factions in the bar jumped in, the Gunners and Wheelers taking sides against Soul Sacrifice. The main area was now a sea of patched and jackbooted brawlers. Unfortunately for Soul Sacrifice, the pounding and punching and pushing and gouging and shoving and name-calling deteriorated along racial lines. Knives, home-made prison-style weaponry, and chains that were once concealed now swung free. Fists flew everywhere. Broken ribs. Broken arms. Broken bottles. Broken teeth. Broken pride.

Although the Sacs stood up for themselves, the Gun Runners and 2Wheelers and their hang-arounds easily outnumbered the club. But the Wheelers and the Gunners were not without casualties. A 2Wheeler named Cutter caught a poke in the stomach from a Craftsman screwdriver. Another Soul Sac member, Julio, wielded a rubber-headed carpenter's mallet, for those "nonmarring" blows on wood surfaces— which was anything but nonmarring on the top of some Gunner's thick skull.

The bouncers at Trader's, sorely outnumbered, were caught flat-footed. They could only stand aside and watch. The slugfest went down quickly. The entire incident didn't last more than a minute. It was a senseless, brutal wrinkle in time.

Then somebody fired two gunshots, both of which ricocheted into the metal ceiling. A handful of patrons dived under tables for cover. One shot was ordinarily all it took to clear out the average barroom. But not Trader's. The regulars thrived on the lethal thrill-kill combination of biking and shooting.

The MCs continued their combat. A few more Sacs were sliced up and went down bleeding. Women screamed. Beer bottles bounced off men's heads. Chairs were hurled twenty feet. The mirror along the south wall was cracked and distorted, smudged with blood from some poor bastard's mercilessly pummeled head.

A Soul Sac patch was cut and pulled. Pulling patches was the ultimate MC humiliation, signifying dominance on the part of the puller. Members would rather die than have their patch pulled, and that's why it often took a small army to hold down a resistant member long enough to cut off his colors. It was an unwritten law in the 1%er bike world: Lose your rags, turn in your membership card.

As the brawl wound down, Lock N Load, the Gun Runners' MC prez, wiped the blood from his nose and drew his weapon, a short-barreled, blue steel Colt Python six-shooter. Surrounded by four armed bodyguards, his so-called Ring of Fire, he figured it was high time for the Gunners to bolt for the front exits. The Gunners backed out of the barroom Billy the Kid style. Chino, president of the 2Wheelers, and *his* gun-toting mob took Lock's cue and followed not far behind.

There were no cops. No sirens screaming in the distance. Nobody knew for sure if anybody had even called John Law, since the pay phones had been ripped off the walls and cell-phone reception in outer Hayward was for shit. But bike riders don't usually call the cops anyway.

7 «

A few men groaned loudly, sprawled across the floor, their faces bleeding and swollen like Halloween masks, their arms and legs nicked, contorted, and fractured. Some of the injured hulks would never ride motorcycles again.

As bar brawls went, it was a mini-massacre at Trader's. On a scale of one to ten, the fight ranked a hard eight, partly for its severity, partly because it had been over a year since the MCs in Oakland fought one another en masse.

Up to now, there had been peace. While members fought each other occasionally one-on-one, or more accurately, two- or three-on-one, there were no blatant incidents of clubs at war. Thanks to an alliance among the local 1%er MCs, riders were instead united against a more common enemy—the cops.

While chaos reigned inside, outside Lock's Gunners and Chino's Wheelers revved their Harleys, ready to hit the road just as Marco arrived in the parking lot.

The Infidelz MC was *the* dominant Northern California bike club. Marco, one of its youngest members, rode his smoke-gray 1992 FXR into the lot. As he approached the long row of parked cycles, he hit the kill switch and brought the FXR to a dead stop. Then his profile filled the red-ramped sights of a pistol. A trigger finger twitched. Marco had just got the kickstand down when he heard blasts from behind.

Pop. Pop. Pop.

Marco felt sharp burning pains sting and sear his side. His inner organs shifted, and blood seeped through his T-shirt and denim cuts. Red stained his black jeans and the FXR's gas tank and handlebars. More stray gunshots bounced off the frame of his Harley. Still straddling the bike, Marco tried to stand and draw his pistol. He felt light-headed as his legs turned to rubber. Three seconds later he was slumped over his handlebars, clutching his gut. The FXR fell on its side with Marco on it. He heard the sirens in the far, far distance. It was the last sound he'd ever hear.

HAYWARD POLICE AND ALAMEDA COUNTY DEPUTIES ARRIVED in force, sirens wailing and lights flashing, their revolvers and shotguns drawn. They stormed Trader's in military SWAT formation, but without incident. With nothing else to do, they gathered and cuffed the remaining unlucky members of Soul Sacrifice, since the perpetrators had already scooted away. A beige police van backed up to the entrance as the members were herded, one by one, into the wagon. By the time the blond reporter arrived with her television news crew, the Soul Sac members had already been whisked away to jail, leaving behind a squad of investigators questioning patrons. Most of the lingering witnesses were blinking their eyes in shock. There was no sign of a single Gun Runner or 2Wheeler, but plenty of onlookers from which the cops could take statements. Or so they thought.

9 **«**

Two ambulances pulled up to take away the remaining wounded. Marco lay collapsed in a lifeless heap, his legs tangled in his bike, surrounded by a circle of police officers filling out forms.

"Guess we won't be hearing anything from this one," said a plainclothes cop wearing a gray suit. "He took a few rounds in the ribs. See if you can't get an ID or something. Try his jacket, then bag him."

Inside Trader's, the emergency floodlights cast a caustic

halogen brilliance on the bar's interior. Aside from the shattered mirrors, the evidence of a battle was vanishing. As the cops cordoned off the crime scene, the bar's staff restored the tables, chairs, and bar stools to their original upright positions. Only a fourth-rate PD would have tolerated seeing their crime scene corrupted so flagrantly—but the Hayward cops were hardly considered the nation's elite. Broken glass and a few broken teeth were quickly swept up off the floor. The cops interrogated the patrons, but it was impossible to piece together a consistent version of what actually happened or who started what. Witnesses and victims were tight-lipped, and since Trader's had no video surveillance system, the police netted only hazy accounts and evasive shrugs. Between the alcohol-addled, the meth-paranoid, and the confused, the cops got nothing.

» 10

After a couple hours, the law wrapped up their investigation for the night, gathered up their paperwork and blank arrest forms, and cleared the house.

A rookie cop waved his nightstick with the clichéd announcement. "All right, everybody. Fun's over for tonight. Let's all go home."

THE NEXT AFTERNOON, TRADER'S ROADHOUSE WAS ROCKIN' again. Despite the fracas, the bar barely missed a beat. Trader's was a resilient dive. Not a nickel was missing from the till. Outside of several dozen broken glasses, a few busted chairs, smashed mirrors replaced early that morning, and a few bloodstains on the wood floor, the place was completely back to normal.

Except for one local-TV news report, the incident was over and done with. Marco's death went unreported in the East Bay Oakland editions of the San Francisco papers. Outside, there wasn't a trace of combat anywhere, except for a large dark stain, a mixture of oil and blood, in the gravel parking lot.

A circle of five members of the Infidelz MC surrounded the stain. They stood dead silent, communicating with furtive glances and clenched fists. They shook their heads. It was clear that the burden to find out who whacked Marco that night, and why, fell on them, and them alone. As far as the Infidelz were concerned, the shit was on. Out of respect for a fallen brother, payback was imminent. A body for a body. A life for a life. Even if it meant all-out war on the Oakland Infidelz' home turf.

11 «

2

Anything
but Carefree

Serious moonlight illuminated a green road-weathered Harley Road King parked outside a remote Arizona ranch house. The bike, its pipes still warm, stood sentry outside the modest residence located off Arizona's dusty Carefree Highway.

The house sprang to life when a sudden jolt of electricity surged through its wiring. Two lights, one in the kitchen and another down the hallway, lit the previously darkened interior. The refrigerator, housing two cans of warm beer and a half-drunk plastic bottle of blue Gatorade, whirred into operation. A portable air conditioner wedged in a side window let out an abrupt, rattling blast of humid air.

A shadowy figure sat slumped, semiconscious, on a wooden straight-back chair. A black cat was sprawled across his lap. Next to the chair was an upright half-consumed bottle of Wild Turkey. The man in the chair responded to the room light with a slight shudder and started to stir. His arms were leathered and tanned, covered with timeworn tattoos of skulls, gargoyles, fiery crosses, tombstones, thunderbolts, and, even more horrifying, the names of ex-girlfriends. The man's greasy, road-dusted hair was full but closely cropped, a mixture of dirty gray and dark brown.

He wore baggy camouflage fatigue pants and a sweat-stained gym-rat sleeveless T-shirt bearing a demon skull. If a "citizen" were to be caught wearing the identical forbidden emblem, he would surely have it ripped right off his back, either by an enraged member of the club or any number of their bitter rivals.

13 **«**

The black cat on the man's lap flinched into an alerted state. Its green eyes darted around the living room and surveyed the short stack of cardboard moving boxes in the mostly vacant room. As the man rose gradually and uncertainly from the chair, he gently set the cat down on all fours, allowing it to skitter off into the direction of the light.

Patch Kinkade shoved the chair aside and regained his balance. Then he stretched out his brawny arms, arched his back, and groaned a measured yawn.

Let there be light.

Patch staggered a few more steps. Then he bent down and picked up a phone receiver situated next to the boxes. He listened for a warm dial tone but instead heard silence from the cold hard plastic touching his ear.

"Shit. Still dead," he said out loud, as if the stray cat understood English. *We got electric. Gas. No phone.*

Patch turned on an overhead light and sat on the carpet, rooting through one of the nearby boxes. It was filled mostly with congratulatory plaques from his motorcycle club: *Love and Respect: Everett John Kinkade. President. Ten Years. Oakland Infidelz MC.* Another piece was a handsome polished metal sculpture that once sat on his fireplace mantel back in Northern California. It had the same demon skull of the Infidelz in orange and black, the club's colors. Below, inscribed in silver letters, it read *Patch Kinkade. Twenty years in excellent standing. Love & Respect, the Oakland brotherhood.* Patch had already spent twenty-three years in the club, over half his life.

A framed eight-by-ten photograph peeked out of another box. Patch reached over and grabbed it. He drew a line along the dust-covered glass with his finger. It was an early lineup of the 187 Crue, an elite group within the Oakland Infidelz chapter. The "187" was short for California Penal Code section 187, the murder statute. It was also inmate slang for someone "marked for death."

The 187 Crue were hit men, some whispered, or else bodyguards, peacekeepers, enforcers within the Infidelz. Each member who wore the brass 187 Crue pin directly over his heart had murder or attempted-murder beefs included on his arrest record.

To join the Crue or to be "187," you needed to have accomplished something "extra" on behalf of the club. "Law enforcement experts" suspected murder. Publicly, the club always denied this. During the mid-1980s, Patch settled a grisly score involving an Oakland drug dealer, so when the "187 vote" came around that year, Patch's nomination and induction ran unopposed. Patch earned the right to wear his badge forever, so he did.

There were four other wily faces posing with Patch in the photo, their bodies a little bit slimmer, each face a decade and a half less wise and weathered. Patch grinned as he studied each character: Montgomery "Ahab" Haywood stared grimly at the camera as if he had a serious bone to pick with the lens man. Ahab was the current prez of the Oakland Infidelz, serving his umpteenth term, having taken over from Patch, who resigned the presidency before serving a stretch in prison. Next to Ahab was an enforcer in the club called Brutus, and leaning next to him was Big Jab, an ox of a man, an Infidelz sergeant-at-arms who first stood up and sponsored Patch into the club.

Big Jab was killed while racing his chopped customized Knucklehead with another club member. The bike careened into a freeway guardrail. That happened four years after the picture had been taken. Jab had been dead for over ten years. Patch reached over for a swig off the Wild Turkey bottle in his honor. He loved Big Jab. The two of them often rode side by side in the Infidelz pack on annual runs to Lake Berryesa.

To Big Jab. Patch tipped the bottle and took a long burning slug.

On the far end of the photo lineup was the youngest

member, in his early twenties, 220 pounds, shoulder-length sandy-blond hair and several days' growth on his face. Angelo Timmons was named after San Angelo, the Texas town he was born in. Oklahoma was where he was raised. Only a few people were foolish enough to call him "Angie"—Patch didn't—and he could soak up more brew than any other two-fisted inebriate at the annual St. Patrick's Day bash. Ahab had ordered him around mercilessly when he was a lowly prospect. Angelo the prospect was delegated the task of setting up the tables, food, and coffee for the monthly OMs, officers' meetings. Then he had to stand outside in the pouring rain to "guard" the bikes. Ahab and Patch laid it on thick, just to see if the kid had the 'nads to hang on.

And Angelo hung on. He grew into one of the club's most popular members. He was responsible for organizing and shaping up four new Infidelz chapters in Sonoma, Mendocino, Redding, and Lake County in Northern California and once served with Patch on Ahab's Oakland war council. His latest title was sergeant-at-arms, taking over after Big Jab died.

Alongside Patch, President Ahab rarely conducted club business without Angelo Timmons as his adviser and associate. As he swiftly rose from the rank and file, Angelo could be counted on to lead as an officer and a fighter. Cops were terrified of him. If they had to take Angelo into custody, their hands trembled and shook when they pointed their guns at him. Angelo had no fear of pain. His body was a mass of tattoos and scars from knife fights, skirmishes, and bike spills. He plowed through a harem of women, large, small, white, black, brown, beautiful, and butt ugly. The club's inveterate ladies' man, before he married, Angelo had lived with two, sometimes three, girls at once.

Patch carefully replaced the framed photo back inside the box, got up, and walked down the hall to the john to take a leak. He studied his own leather-faced image in the bathroom mirror. His driver's license said forty-one, but from the neck down he looked younger. He'd kept in shape. He hated weakness and excess body fat. He was under six feet tall, which meant he stood a head shorter than most of his club brothers, but could still bench his two-hundred-pound weight and then some.

When Patch rode, the fringe on his leather jacket flapped briskly in the wind like a freedom flag. On his back was his sacred orange-and-black patch, dutifully stitched on by one of the club's old ladies. Patch wore no businessman's haircut. The wind was his stylist. He sported a couple days' growth on his angled jawline, giving him the rustic and timeless look of an outlaw. At quick glance, he resembled a Wild West gunfighter, except that his status as a convicted felon forbade him the privilege of packing a pistol. Instead, his lucky knife, Sharpfinger, a seven-inch Schrade, hung from his leather trousers.

The Schrade Sharpfinger was the knife of choice for the Infidelz. Most of the guys carried them. They were perfect for skinning and stabbing. Sharpfinger was a fixed blade as opposed to a folder. The upper contour of the four-inch blade had a pronounced curvature and a thin deadly point that curled upward. Patch must have owned four or five of them. They were sturdy enough to be all-purpose and cheap enough to leave stuck in some unlucky victim.

As for women, on more than a couple occasions, in public places, Patch had found himself on the receiving end of a few female glances. Last week at a traffic intersection, a lady motorist, dressed for work, eyed him as he revved his Road King, "the Mean Machine," at the light. She looked him up, then down, checked out his MC colors, worked up the courage, and waved. Ordinarily Patch would have motioned to her and pulled over his bike. Instead, he throttled the Mean Machine down the road as the woman pulled her car into an office complex. Patch had places to go. She was probably chained to a desk.

"Fuck, man," he warned his buddies later over a beer at the clubhouse, "there was a time when Infidelz terrified women like that. Now these broads damn near scare the hell out of me."

PATCH HAD MEANT TO PHONE EVE, HIS EX-WIFE, WHEN HE got to Phoenix, at least to let her know that he had arrived in town. *As if she still gives a rat's ass.* Patch couldn't blame her for her indifference. He tried to gauge her mood when they spoke last, early in the day from a pay phone at a Denny's when he gassed up in Blythe on the outskirts of the Palm Desert. Eve told him not to worry, and then let it slip that the feds were already scouting the neighborhood. Two guys in white shirts and sunglasses lurked in a nondescript silver Pontiac parked down the street from Patch and Eve's humble two-bedroom Dimond district home in Oakland. One agent had a tiny earpiece jammed in his right ear. His mouth moved as if he was conversing, but he made no eye contact with his associate who sat next to him, bored behind the wheel.

"It's kind of weird," she had said on the phone. "They don't seem to care whether I notice them or not."

"Damned vultures. I warned you," Patch had replied.

The feds had sent someone over after word leaked out on the street that he and Eve had separated after twelve years. But that's how it was with the cops and the Infidelz. It was a game of wills; just another common tactic from the "gang squad" boys downtown: drop in on bitter ex-wives or pissed-off girlfriends dumped by Infidelz club members, in the hope that they might "turn" and try to get one over on the guy.

Patch felt guilty that he'd run out on Eve.

IT WAS WAY PAST MIDNIGHT, CLOSE TO MORNING LIGHT. Patch flipped on the light in the bedroom. Time to crash. A mattress was leaned up against the wall next to the switch. He let it plop flat onto the bedroom floor. Then he threw down a frayed blanket. Patch kicked off his cowboy boots. The moving boxes could wait till morning. With the little he brought down from Oakland, it wouldn't take too long to settle in.

19 «

In the arid night, Patch lay across the lumpy mattress, distracted, dredging up things to worry about. *There is no possible way Eve would give in to those motherfuckin' feds.* He knew that. He'd swear as much on his patch.

He thought about how he ended up in Arizona. At an OM the year before, Patch had stood up.

"As per our club rules, I officially request a transfer. Phoenix chapter. Arizona. Can I get an immediate vote?"

President Ahab was stunned. "Are you sure you don't need more time to think on this?"

"I've more than thought it over."

"Okay, brother. All in favor of granting Patch his transfer, raise your hand."

Because he was a member in good standing, the vote was unanimous. The Oakland mob let him go. What else could they do? The look on Ahab's face reflected surprise and regret. Patch was a high-profile member throughout all the Infidelz chapters. Phoenix gladly accepted him, and after a year spent tying up loose ends, here he was, lying in the stifling heat of the Arizona desert.

Patch's move south had much to do with Eve and especially with her little brother, who was like a son to them. They were Patch's family, and he felt very protective of them. But instead of keeping them safe, he had let something happen to split the relationship apart.

I thought I was keeping someone from being harmed when actually I ended up making sure they got hurt.

As a result, Patch's family life had imploded. His time in California had drawn to an end. So Patch left the Oakland chapter behind and joined up with his brothers in Arizona, not as an officer but as a member. He had transformed from leader to loner. Patch needed distance and Arizona offered him the solitude that he no longer had in California. He closed the book on the Golden State. Arizona was his new land of opportunity, where men rode hard and raised hell harder.

Even before Patch planned his transfer, the Arizona Infidelz had shown an urge to expand. Why not move into Colorado, New Mexico, and Utah? Patch liked their attitude, their recklessness and their restlessness, and it didn't hurt that sometimes they rubbed the other chapters the wrong way.

Patch had become a little too settled for his own good, and maybe a little too willing to share the streets with so many other clubs. California was now the land of "three strikes," helmet laws, gun control, and no-smoking-in-the-bar. In Arizona, on the other hand, you were careful whom you pissed off lest the guy shooting pool next to you reached for his concealed piece. Patch kinda liked that uncertainty.

THE AIR CONDITIONER SUCKED A FEW MORE DEGREES OUT of the stuffy house. Patch stared up at the ceiling and studied the cracks and cobwebs like he used to do from his prison bunk. But there wasn't that incessant yammering and yelling, the rattle and hum of ventilation and clanking machinery you heard 24/7 in the joint.

He now lived on the quiet Carefree Highway, but he was anything but carefree. He thought about his estranged wife.

Patch missed Eve's long, thin arms wrapped around him in bed. The day before he left her, he had sent his stuff off with a couple of Arizona-bound members in a pickup truck. As he was packing a single gym bag for the ride down, Eve walked into the bedroom for what would be one of their last moments together.

He was dejected to see that she had cut her long brown hair. It was now short and spiky, dyed blond. Patch tried to compliment her new look, but the words just died before they left his mouth. It was a twist of the knife. She looked strange. He hated it. But Eve wasn't angling for his approval anymore. By sundown, he was gone.

Patch found it strange trying to sleep in the desert silence.

He was used to hearing speeding cars, booming hip-hop bass, and the sounds of the city outside his bedroom. Their bedroom.

The stray black cat poked its head back into the doorway and prowled around the bedroom. It sensed Patch's body settling into motionless slumber. That's when the stealthy animal tiptoed onto the mattress, curled itself next to Patch's shoulder, and fell asleep, too.

Sharpfinger

Day two in Sun City. Patch couldn't sleep. Restless again. He tossed and turned on the lumpy mattress. That was futile, so at 3 A.M. he got dressed, slammed the front door and hopped on the Mean Machine for a late night ride. Patch needed an all-night coffee shop. He would check in with Groover and the guys at the Phoenix clubhouse first thing in the morning.

The phone line at Patch's pad wasn't connected yet, so earlier that day he followed modern fashion and bought himself a cellular phone. The guy at the store promised that the service would be activated sometime before dawn. Looking up at the nearly full moon and bright constellations, Patch knew he'd be hooked up soon. Then he'd be one of those "phone guys."

Patch roamed along the deserted freeway for a few miles before spying a coffee shop. The large windows revealed a nearly full house of patrons lounging comfortably in overstuffed Naugahyde booths. The furniture and countertops were yellow and red, the colors of desert sunset. Energetic waitresses patrolled the counter and booths with steaming pots of coffee, brown-handled regular in one hand, orange-handled decaf in the other. Inside were welcome sights and sounds, bright lights and the clink of cups and dishes. People chattering.

Forty-five minutes later, Patch ambled out of the diner, full from an early breakfast and ready to head back home for daylight, then off later to the clubhouse to meet up with the new crew. Across the street was a convenience store. In the dusky darkness, the temperature outside "dropped" into the high eighties. Patch putted across to the Speedee Mart to pick up a cold bottle of *agua* before heading back home.

The Mean Machine roared across the intersection and pulled up to the store's front door. Patch strolled inside as a young Latin couple stood outside the door yelling at each other. Both were in their late twenties, dressed up for a party or a nightclub. She wore a thin, short white dress. He was attired in T-shirt, a dark cotton sport coat, tight blue jeans, and boots.

"Enrique," the woman screamed, "don't you fuckin' touch me!"

The man stumbled toward the curvy young woman. His words came out slurred. "Listen, lady, as long as you're out with me, I'll touch you wherever, whenever I want. Wait till I get you back to my place . . ."

"I'm not going back to *your* place. Take me home. Right now."

Patch stood in the checkout line inside and watched the altercation between the couple heat up outside. He walked back to his bike and placed the cold plastic bottle inside his saddlebag. The exchange between the pair grew fouler.

"Listen, *puta,*" the man yelled, "it's either back to my place or you'll fuckin' walk home. You hear me, bitch?"

"I hate you," the woman screamed. "You're a bastard. You're drunk. You're mean, and you embarrassed me in front of all my work friends."

Patch saw the man grab the woman roughly by the arm, open the passenger door of his late-model pickup, and try to push her into the front seat. She resisted and cried out again. Patch shook his head in disgust and dismounted his bike. He approached the battling couple.

"Excuse me, you two." He spoke calmly. He'd seen it so many times, drunken craziness in the wee hours. "Look, ma'am, are you okay? Is this guy hurting you?"

The man reacted angrily. "Hey dude, mind your own business? This has nothing to do with you. Fuck off."

The young woman started sobbing again. "He called me a slut."

Patch stood between the couple and asked the woman again, this time more emphatic.

"Is this guy *hurting* you?"

"I told you to keep out of this," the man said behind Patch's back. "Get on your cycle, biker boy, and just ride outta here. This is between me and her."

Patch turned around, faced the irate man nearly half his age, and raised his finger.

"I was talking to her. Don't mess with me."

Enrique ignored the warning and pushed Patch aside. He lunged at the woman. "You whore! Get in the fucking truck. Now!"

Patch moved in closer toward the red-faced man until he could smell a combination of aftershave and the booze on his breath. Still facing the man, he spoke to the weeping woman and pointed to his bike.

"Go ahead, sweetheart. Walk over there and stand next to my bike. I'll be there in a minute."

"Who the fuck do you think you are?" Enrique asked. He raised his fist for the first swing, but with lightning reflexes, Patch stepped to his left and watched the guy fall forward, swinging at air. Patch grabbed Enrique by his neck, eyeballed him, and shook him forcefully. He smashed him on the forehead, Chicago Bears–style, with a powerful head butt. The collision threw the guy off balance. Then Patch tripped Enrique with his right foot and watched him fall backward and hit the asphalt next to his truck, tailbone first.

Patch reached down, picked up the shaken man, set him back on his wobbly heels, and pushed him against the cab of his pickup. Patch's eyes were now red with rage and lack of sleep. His breathing grew heavier. Then he said firmly, "Don't say shit to me or her."

As Patch released his grip, Enrique swung another punch.

Patch dodged it, then buried his fist in the man's gut, caus-
ing him to crumple to the ground. Patch left him sitting
dazed on the blacktop.

"Go home and sleep it off, amigo."

Patch walked back to his bike. *Now what?* He had just
decked the girl's inebriated boyfriend and here she was, crying. Patch pulled the red bandanna from his back pocket
and handed it to her. As she dried her eyes, he noticed how
beautiful she looked in spite of the tears that smeared the
makeup on her sad face.

"Look, uh . . ."

"Teresa," she said.

"Yeah, Teresa." He chuckled nervously. "I'm kinda new in
these parts. I could call you a cab. But I live nearby and I
really think we ought to get you outta here in case that ape
tries to take things out on you. Climb on back of my bike. I
can take you home."

The woman shook her head. "Take me to your place."

The young woman climbed aboard the Mean Machine.
Patch headed toward the freeway for the short ride back.
The speed of the bike blew Teresa's dress up her leg. *This girl
has been on a bike before.* She gripped Patch tighter and
leaned in as he curved off the Carefree exit and stopped at
the light on the highway. At the stoplight, Patch looked
down at Teresa's shapely legs in sheer nylon stockings. They
were wrapped tightly around him on the bike. He turned
around to gaze at her face, but she buried it into the back of
his leather jacket.

Patch signaled right and proceeded down the Carefree
Highway. Teresa settled in closer toward his body and
shifted her weight on the bike. She moved her hand from

around his chest and slowly down to his crotch. He slowed the bike down a little and traced his left hand up her leg, gradually up to her ass on the seat.

"Hold on," he instructed her. "It's only a few more miles to my place." He felt her warm breath on his neck.

Just then, in the rearview mirror, he noticed a pair of high-beam headlights coming from the freeway exit onto the Carefree. It was a pickup truck weaving across both lanes, gaining velocity until the distance between it and the Mean Machine shortened to a few car lengths. A horn blew.

Patch summoned extra torque from the Road King and shouted back, "Looks like we've got company."

The truck roared closer alongside the speeding bike, trying twice to force the Mean Machine into the desert-side ditch. The pickup's front bumper grazed Teresa's leg. Once again, the Mean Machine accelerated and sped farther down the Carefree Highway.

Patch swerved a sharp left turn off the highway and raced the last quarter mile up the dirt road to his doorstep. The pickup stayed in close pursuit as Patch and Teresa stopped and jumped off the bike in front of his house. Patch handed the shaking woman his door key and pointed to the front door.

"Go inside! Lock the doors, turn out the lights, and stay in the back room. Go!"

Patch stood and watched as the pickup skidded to a stop on the gravel driveway. Enrique was ready for the next round. Patch clenched his fists. *Let's go, motherfucker.* The driver jumped out of the truck's cab and charged toward Patch like a snorting bull.

It was Patch's turn to swing and miss. Enrique retaliated

by landing a rock-solid hard right into his stomach. The punch robbed Patch of his breath and down he went. Enrique stood over him and delivered a punishing series of hard kicks to his head and back. Patch winced and tried to curl up into a ball to absorb the assault, but soon his body went limp as he slipped out of consciousness. Then the kicking stopped.

The angry man squatted down and grabbed Patch by a handful of his hair. He yelled into his bloodied face, "I'll finish you off later, dickless."

Enrique stood up and dealt Patch another full-steam kick to the ribs. Then the young Latin stepped over his motionless body and walked toward the front door. The man beat on the door and yelled out.

"Teresa! It's me, Enrique."

The house remained dark and quiet.

"Teresa! You bitch. Don't make me break down this—"

At that instant Enrique felt a razor slice across his buttocks. Patch grabbed the man from behind and spun him around. Sharpfinger carved another path across the man's torso and belly. Stunned, the man dropped to his knees, then onto the ground, face first. He made a choking, gurgling sound.

Patch stood over Enrique, clutching Sharpfinger, and watched as his blood soaked into the ground. It resembled a pool of heavy motor oil. Patch bent down and flipped the man onto his back. He was still breathing. Patch went through his sport-coat pockets until he found a wallet and cell phone. Then he remembered he had his own. He reached into his jacket pocket and found his new phone. He turned it on, and the in-service signs flashed on the small green screen. Patch dialed a number and held the phone to his ear.

"Hello, Groover? It's Patch. Sorry to wake ya. Listen. I need you and a couple of the guys to come over to my place.

"I had a little dustup here with one of the locals. He took things a little too personal . . . Yeah, and bring a truck to empty the garbage."

Patch hung up and dragged the groaning man to the side of his house, out of view from the road.

Patch walked up to the front porch, found the spare key in his jeans pocket, opened the front door, and walked into the dark house. Teresa was hiding in the laundry room in the back of the house.

He flicked on the light. "Are you okay?" She was crouched on the floor.

Teresa looked up at Patch's split lip and the blood on his cheek and chin. "Did he hurt you?"

"Naw," he said as he dabbed his sore lip with his finger. "Nuthin' I couldn't handle." She wouldn't know the half of it. He'd be a mass of purple bruises by sunup.

"I was so scared," she cried, standing up. "I heard yelling and banging on the door."

"Enrique. Is that his name?"

Teresa nodded. "The bastard."

"He's gone now. Your old man ran off," Patch said. "Left his truck outside. How long have you known this guy?"

"Not too long. Only a couple of months really, and he's not my old man. He's a real bum. I don't know why I end up with guys like him."

Patch heard the engine of another vehicle drive up to the front of the house. He didn't check to see who it was. Then he heard footsteps and scurrying out front, then the sound of something heavy, no doubt Enrique, being dragged across the gravel. Patch hugged Teresa protectively and muffled the sounds of activity outside.

"It's okay, just the trashmen. Relax."

A few minutes later, two engines started up. Both trucks drove off. Then Patch and Teresa walked into the kitchen. Patch looked out the window. Enrique's pickup was gone. Only the bike remained out front. The stray black cat meandered across the front yard. Patch motioned for Teresa to come to the window.

"See?" He smiled. "What's-his-name must have run back, started up his truck, and split. He's gone, baby, so don't worry about him."

Teresa gave Patch an appreciative, relieved hug. "My God, you saved me and I don't even know your name. How can I ever thank you?"

"Let's keep this to ourselves. It never happened, okay?"

Teresa nodded and smiled. "Okay." Patch gave her a light tap on her bottom.

"Oh, and by the way," he said.

"What?"

"I think Enrique learned his lesson. He won't be threatening women anymore."

Ahab's Visit

One bloodshot eye popped open as Patch, disoriented and a bit groggy, heard heavy footsteps on the gravel outside. Teresa lay still on the mattress beside him. *It sure as hell wasn't Enrique. And whoever it was, they weren't sneaking around. Shit, what time was it?* Almost without thinking, Patch reached for Sharpfinger, next to his watch on the makeshift cardboard box nightstand by the mattress.

It was way too bright to be morning. Who knew he was here? The feds? Coming round to photograph the place?

Mellow out, man. Patch forced himself to relax. *It's probably the phone guy.*

Patch felt around until he found his watch. *Noon. What?* He rarely slept that long nowadays. *Who the hell is outside?*

Patch picked up his boxer shorts off the floor and slipped them on. The heavy footsteps continued up to his front door.

Teresa lifted her head off the pillow and looked around the room. Patch put his forefinger to his lips.

"Shhhh. Go back to sleep."

Dink, clunk. Pretty lame doorbell.

With Sharpfinger clenched in his right hand, Patch swung the door wide open. He was taken aback by what he saw. A huge man easily filled the entire doorframe. He had long, stringy, slicked-back dark black hair and wore a walrus mustache and greasy jeans. He was a little paunchy in his striped black-and-orange long-sleeve rugby shirt, frayed at the cuffs. The shirt poked through a leather vest, big and baggy as a tent. He wore black engineer boots with silver buckles, not exactly appropriate desert wear. Most of the ring finger was missing off his left hand. Garish sterling-silver rings cast with skulls and monsters decorated most of the remaining digits.

33 «

"Ahab. Jesus Christ. How the hell did you find me?"

Ahab, the president of the Oakland chapter of the Infidelz, had come into the world as Montgomery Charles Haywood the same year as Patch, forty-one years ago. He came from working-class stock. His mother was Irish. His father was from Spain. Or vice versa. Patch couldn't quite remember.

Ahab was a strange mix indeed. He was a hulking, lumbering fellow. He sometimes rode a custom Panhead he built from scratch, a beautiful bike. But he hated to ride. Even when he was a younger man, stealing bikes and chopping Harleys in his garage fueled his adrenaline more than actually riding them. Now he preferred a spacious pickup truck to a two-wheeler. But first and foremost, Ahab rode for the club, and the club dictated that he had to own and ride a Harley-Davidson, so he did.

Ahab was a mass of contradictions. He was well read but flunked out of high school. He was a crack shot with a rifle but, as a younger man, had managed to stay out of the army at a time in the seventies when all the guys in his neighborhood were joining up. Ahab *loved* jazz and hated rock and roll, and even pulled a deejay shift one night a week at one of the nearby public-radio stations. He had a head for West Coast jazz of the 1950s. That was his specialty. He loved the Lighthouse All-Stars. He was drawn to the music of West Coast smack addicts like saxophonist Art Pepper and trumpet player Chet Baker—especially Art, who did straight time in San Quentin rather than rat out some burglary partners and fellow dope fiends. And he hated Gerry Mulligan, the legendary baritone sax player, because the guy was a junkie snitch. Leave it to Ahab to have musical taste that was influenced by penitentiary bullshit.

Patch couldn't stand jazz. Compared with country and southern rock, jazz was just random noise. He couldn't hear the melody.

Patch set Sharpfinger on a box next to the door. "How'd ya find me?" he asked.

Ahab replied with a snort, like it was beneath him to dignify that with an answer. Who the fuck did Patch think found and rented the house for him? And arranged to have his shit packed and moved? A brother always looks out for a fellow member. Ahab never discussed Patch's transfer directly. It was a subject both men tiptoed around.

"Brother! Don't I get a sloppy kiss or at least a hug?"

"C'mon in. What are you doin' here?"

Patch, not exactly a small guy, was practically engulfed by Ahab's embrace.

"So, bro, are you ready to come back yet or what?" Ahab asked. But when he saw a grimace cross Patch's face, he added quickly, "How's things in Sun City?"

Patch rubbed his sore lip. "I'll spare you the details. How'd you get here?" he asked.

"Rode. I parked my bike down the road. I wasn't sure which house was yours. I left in the middle of the night and took the long way here. Four hundred fifty miles to Berdoo, three hundred fifty more to Phoenix."

Outside of the early morning pickup from Groover, Patch hadn't officially checked in with his new chapter. He wanted a few days alone to settle in.

Patch walked into the bedroom and put on his grimy black Frisco jeans and his cleanest dirty T-shirt, then reached for his boots. Teresa had gone back to sleep.

"Coffee or something?" he asked Ahab.

With that, Ahab's face suddenly turned serious. That's when Patch realized something must have gone down for Ahab to ride alone all the way from Oakland, especially in hundred-plus-degree heat.

"Marco" was the only word that came out from behind Ahab's walrus mustache.

"Marco? What about Marco? My boy fucking up already? He hasn't had his patch, what, a month maybe?"

Ahab ran his left hand, the one minus the ring finger, through his greasy, windblown hair.

"Man, I wish he was still here to be fucking up."

"Whattaya mean?"

Then Ahab turned his face away. It was a rare display of emotion from the man.

"Patch, he's fucking gone. He was alone when it happened. Shot down like a dog in the fucking parking lot at Trader's the night before last. I couldn't get in touch with you. I tried calling Groover. But at the last minute, I said, 'Fuck it,' and hopped on my bike. I wanted to discuss this man to man."

"Wait a minute." Patch paused. "Marco's dead? Bullshit."

"I wish I was bullshitting you, bro, but no, man. He's gone."

Marco was a good kid. He couldn't have been more than twenty-five. Patch had helped sponsor him, stood for him, stood *by* him. He was like a little brother and a drinking buddy all rolled into one. His girlfriend had a couple of kids, nice kids, smart ones. Patch admired Marco, who worked in the electrical union apprentice program. As a hang-around, he was a standout.

Hang-arounds were a necessary part of any thriving MC, a way to give guys the chance to "hang around" and ride with a club before they decided to try for membership. It was also an opportunity for the club to size up would-be members before they were officially nominated as prospects, in case an individual didn't fit in with the rest.

Hang-arounds either ended up as prospects or were beaten up or chased away.

Marco had prospected for only seven months and took the fast track toward membership by making himself useful around the club. He rewired the entire Oakland clubhouse. He crashed there off and on, did repairs, and fixed the place up. Despite his intimidating stature, he wasn't the hothead type. He rarely threw the first punch unless provoked. He was a helluva fighter, but only fought as a last resort. Then look out. The guy could kick ass. Now they found him shot to death at a biker bar?

"All this happened at Trader's?" Patch asked.

"Yeah, right."

"Trader's? That rat hole? What happened? What was he doing there alone? Nobody fucking listens. How many times have we all discussed this? When you're flying colors in a place like that, don't ride alone. Infidelz should always travel in threes at the *very* least."

Ahab's face tightened. He wished like hell he had an explanation. Patch was the type of guy who asked the hard questions out of the box, demanded answers, and Ahab hated it when he had nothing to say in return.

"All we know is that he got shot down, bro. There was a fight going down. A coupla shots were fired in the bar. The Soul Sacs got beat down pretty bad, too."

"Soul Sacs? Those crazy fuckers—" Patch stopped there, not wanting to finish the sentence. Ahab had a lot of pals in that club, but Patch had grown up with them on the streets of Oakland. No one knew them better.

Soul Sacrifice was a wacky mixed MC composed of blacks, Latinos, and a few white riders. They were known for their bike-show-quality Harleys, cherried out with an orgy of paint. Soul Sacrifice was a club all about paint. Snappy candy-apple red, cobalt blue, canary yellow, or kelly green gas tanks and chromed-out front ends. Their bikes carried as much blinding chrome as each rider could afford.

Patch had grown up with their leader, Rollie George, swapping bike parts, selling weed, and running from the cops. Rollie had been the Soul Sacs' president since the turn of the 1970s. His dark skin sported several square inches of faded club tattoos, some dating back to the Black Panther / Black Power movement. Celebrating thirty-plus years in Oakland, Soul Sacrifice was an all-male "1%er" club who often invited their friends, old ladies, and female social club main squeezes to ride along on runs.

"As far as we know," Ahab continued, "there had been a meltdown between the Soul Sacs and a couple of other clubs, a bunch of indies and ghost riders. Maybe the 2Wheelers and the Gun Runners."

"The 2Wheelers and the Gun Runners?" Patch grimaced. "We have no problems with them. We had things worked out. Peace in Oakland. The cops off our backs. No offense, Ahab, but whattaya want me to do about it? I'm here now, seven hundred miles away."

Before his transfer, Patch labored long and hard to strike a peace accord so that almost everybody got along. Bike clubs had enough trouble dodging the cops, the FBI, or worse yet, a grand jury investigation. The worst fate for any MC was to have to spend time and money off their bikes, fighting the suits downtown over something like a winner-take-all RICO prosecution.

All the clubs, whether it was the Wheelers, the Gunners, or "the Delz," risked the occasional clubhouse raid or stray indictment of an individual member who might be busted selling pills, powder, or guns. But it would be the club's name that got splashed across the headlines.

Patch felt it was important for all the clubs to unite against the police rather than fight one another. There were instances of extreme pride. Every club, while they were willing to make concessions, still looked for a leg up, something that would give their crew a hidden advantage. Peaceful coexistence was a puzzle. And after a lot of wheeling and dealing, Patch felt he'd left town with most of the pieces in place.

"You were the glue, bro," said Ahab. "You kept things together. All those guys, all those clubs, they trusted you. They still do."

"Yeah, but those days are over. I'm here now and this is where I stay."

Patch cut to the chase. He posed a touchy question to Ahab as diplomatically as he could, and risked a punch in the chops. Ahab wasn't one to be ridden.

"Listen," he asked, "do we still dominate or what? Do the Oakland Infidelz still have the juice to control the show in Northern California?"

"Hell, yeah," Ahab said.

"Well, if anybody is going to be shooting at motherfuckers, it should be *us* shooting *them*. Take charge, Ahab, for chrissakes," said Patch.

Ahab shrugged. "But that's what fucking gets me. A few shots fired in the bar, but outside Marco's got half a dozen holes in him? Collateral damage or a hit? An accident, or was Marco a target? Do we make peace or go to war? We have to figure this shit out."

"Not *we*, Ahab. *You.* You and the chapter members need to sort this shit out."

Patch looked out the back window and saw time-sculptured mesas that stretched out all the way to the north.

Who knew whether his being in Oakland would have changed anything. Patch did feel an obligation to the younger members like Marco whom he helped bring into the club. Had he ridden along that night, would Marco still be alive? Now there was a woman left behind with two kids to feed.

"I just got here and here is where I stay."

Patch watched Ahab stare out his front window. Ahab was a big man with a big heart. It was hard saying no to him. He was most effective when his opponent was within punching range, when circumstances were black or white. Add a shroud of mystery or a layer of uncertainty and he might get tripped up.

Trader's was a crisis that Ahab and the boys up north would have to work out on their own. Patch would resist the urge to run back and try to fix things. He would hold his mud and stay put in the desert.

"So where does Angelo stand on all this? What's his take?" Patch asked.

"We haven't talked about it," said Ahab.

"Well, talk about it! Angelo's a smart guy. Strong. Loyal. He's the perfect guy to help you sort through this mess."

"Angelo's cool, but I don't need someone who's gonna light up everyone who was at the bar that night. You're the guy who asks the right questions. You know everybody.

People talk to you. They trust you. No one's gonna open up to Angelo, especially after he kicks their ass. I need you to come back."

Just then Teresa walked into the room. She was wearing one of Patch's dirty T-shirts as a nightgown. Ahab looked at her, then at Patch, and shook his head.

"Look, bro. I rode all the way down here. But I'm not gonna beg. I'm stoppin' over to see Groover and the guys. Then I'm outta here. You know how to reach me."

5

Tora Bora Scora

Two bulky gringos shared a cramped booth in a Mexican coffee shop on the fringes of a mixed neighborhood in East Oakland. The special was a cholesterol-soaked *huevos rancheros* combo. One plateful and you were set till dinnertime.

The topic of conversation between the two drifted toward drugs. It was something both were street-smart about—whether it involved casual use or dealing on the side.

"If you ask me, blow has blown it," cracked Angelo Timmons of the Infidelz, amused at his own play on words. "The cocaine days peaked during the late nineties. People are looking to come down and chill."

"That's why weed is makin' a big comeback," said SeeSaw, Angelo's buddy. Angelo called him SeeSaw because of his powder-induced mood swings. Sometimes he was up and flyin' like a babbling evangelist preacher on meth; other times he was a total downer, slow, and a drag to be around. SeeSaw could be a sneaky son of a bitch, the kind of guy who would key somebody's brand-new Mustang GT at night just for laughs.

"If it was me, I'd risk it and go all the way. Sell smack," advised SeeSaw. "It's easier and faster to move. Especially if you're talkin' 'bout just one or two deals."

"I got connections with plenty of pot farmers up in Garberville and Humboldt," said Angelo. "But you're right. I need to score something big and fast."

Angelo paused, and then scratched the back of his neck hard. His voice fell to a whisper in the crowded, noisy coffee shop. He drew his face closer, eyeballing SeeSaw from across the booth.

"The reason I called you was to see if you had a handle on anybody who could supply me with a couple of quick shipments of heroin. Black tar. Golden brown. China white. I don't really care what kind or grade. I've scraped together as much dough as I can. I'm makin' my move. I've gone out on the street and nabbed a little over twelve grand. But I don't want anyone to find out what I'm doin', understand?"

Angelo gave SeeSaw a hard stare.

"I need a lot more fuckin' money, man," he explained. "I got a kid in high school who's gonna go to college or someplace. And I wanna get him a car, too. We're just scraping by. I got shit to show for. All I got is my bike. I need to get rollin' quick. I gotta put some points on the board, financially speakin'. All my friends are tired of me hittin' 'em up for dough, and I don't blame 'em."

Angelo flicked the ash of his cigarette carelessly into a saucer next to a half-eaten biscuit. The Hispanic owner of the café never bothered Infidelz about smoking on the premises. He'd rather risk the fine than piss the club off.

"I can move the big stuff fast and quick. I'll go through prison contacts I picked up inside," said Angelo. "Trust me, man. Not one spoonful will hit the streets."

He took a slow draw on his cigarette.

"My plan is to get in a couple shipments—one small, another one big. Then *boom!* Get the fuck out. That way, nobody in the club gets bent out of shape. Ahab doesn't want any more members dealing horse, so I want to avoid walking into that shit storm."

SeeSaw stroked his whiskered chin. He knew Angelo had a marker on him, and he was clearly cashing it in. Many times SeeSaw needed the presence of Angelo's Infidelz patch to help him shake up a few deadbeats in the dealing game.

"Let me ask around," he mumbled as he did an instinctual, speedy, three-sixty look-see around the crowded eatery. "I have contacts. Some Mexican *muchachos* I know. Could you hang with that, brother?"

Suddenly SeeSaw waved his hand in Angelo's face. "No,

wait. Cancel that thought, bro. Rewind. I think I got a line on something sweeter. I heard about this absolute killer shit from Tora Bora."

"Tora Bora?" Angelo asked. "You mean Tahiti?"

"No, you twat, that's Bora-Bora. I'm talking about Afghanistan. The war zone. The Euros have been getting their hard shit from there since forever, man."

Angelo was confused. "You mean I'd be moving H for the Taliban?"

"No, asshole! Some Amsterdam guys I know have been using Nepal and Afghanistan connections long before all this terrorist bullshit."

SeeSaw crossed his arms and smiled, satisfied at himself and his revelation, not to mention his geographic prowess. "Angelo, I think I've got just who you need."

Angelo made a sucking sound through his teeth. "Like I told ya, I only want in and out for a couple of boosts."

45 «

"I'll be in touch." SeeSaw reached over and swooped up the check, left the booth, and walked over toward the cashier. Angelo stared back into his cup of black coffee. His heart rushed at the thought of going through with it. Pushing hard dope. The faster it all went down and the fewer people who knew about it, the better. That included the club.

Angelo was sick and tired of being strapped for cash. When they closed the one remaining chrome plant in Oakland the year before, that was it. One more layoff and he'd choke. It had been a while since he'd last heard the eagle scream. His wife had run off and left nothing but a note over a year ago. Angelo was stuck with the part of Mr. Mom, looking after their teenage son. Hollister, age fifteen, got his name from the central California town where the infamous motorcycle riots went down, which inspired the Brando movie *The Wild One*. But unlike his old man, Hollister was hardly a "wild one," although he did love hanging with Ahab and Patch and the other members at the Infidelz barbecues. They were like tough uncles to him.

Hollister and Angelo rode motorcycles and dirt bikes together. Angelo kept a Sportster in the back of the garage at home for the kid. He was a pretty decent boy considering the touchy home life and the screaming domestics he endured. One thing was definite. Hollister unquestionably had more brains and common sense than both his parents combined.

Outside of cutting school a couple times, the kid wasn't much trouble. Hollister's wants were fairly modest compared with those of some adolescents. He rarely asked for anything, and got very little in return. But he still needed pocket cash, school clothes, and video games like any other kid his age. Nowadays, Angelo could barely buy a round of beer, much less tend to the personal needs of a son.

Angelo sat in the coffee-shop booth and finished off his smoke and his java as he watched SeeSaw drive off in his banged-up Toyota. As he left the coffee shop, he popped a hit of speed, started up his bike, and putted back home.

LATER THAT NIGHT AT ANGELO'S CRIB, THE PHONE RANG. Hollister screamed downstairs to his father from his bedroom, against the blaring, musical backdrop of a Seattle dirge chick band. Personally, Angelo dug sweet Curtis Mayfield, Lady Soul, and pre-Altamont Rolling Stones. His kid's music was positively grating.

"Daaaddddd," yelled Hollister for the second time.

Angelo lay spaced-out and bleary-eyed on the couch watching *Friends*. Twenty minutes before, he had popped a couple Vicodins to counteract the speed he had ingested at the diner.

"Pick up the phone, Dad. It's for you."

Angelo snatched the receiver downstairs and heard Hollister's cacophonous grunge leak into the phone line. *The bitch in the band sings like she's murdering a cat,* he thought. He held his hand over the mouthpiece and yelled back upstairs.

"Hollister! Hang up your fuckin' phone. I got it."

Angelo heard a loud click and the shriek of the music disappeared, replaced by SeeSaw's stoned-out drawl.

"Angelo, I'm on my cell phone. Where can we meet to talk in person?"

"How 'bout in front of the clubhouse? I'll ride down right now. See ya there." An invigorated Angelo slammed down the phone. He leaped up off the couch and grabbed his patch and lid. He bolted up the stairs and barged into Hollister's room.

"I'm outta here for a few hours. Finish your fucking homework, then you can watch TV."

Fifteen minutes later, he wheeled his bike off East Fourteenth Street and into the back of the Infidelz clubhouse, parking it right next to the carved-up picnic tables. He padlocked the metal chain-link gate when SeeSaw flicked the headlights of his weather-beaten Toyota. Angelo lit another cigarette and jumped into SeeSaw's cage. He tried to roll down the window so he could stick his arm out with the lit butt. It went down less than halfway, trapping the sickly smell of tobacco inside the small, stuffy Japanese auto.

"You gotta fix this window one of these days, or I gotta quit smokin'."

"Let's drive," SeeSaw replied as he shifted the funky Toyota into first gear and joined the procession on East Fourteenth. Then he took a quick right at the next light and headed toward the Oakland airport via the freeway on-ramp.

"Well, Angelo," drawled SeeSaw. "My Tora Bora connection is on. I can get you great Afghan stuff for Mexican prices. We're talking twenty-two Gs a kilo. The good news is they can swing a half key for twelve."

"Bingo," Angelo said. "Right on the money."

"Coolio. I spoke with the guy myself a couple hours ago. Face-to-face. The motherfucker looked like he was from Lebanon or somewhere. Dark hair. Accent. Arab looking."

Angelo fumbled his cigarette and fidgeted in his seat. "One of them Bin Laden guys? So, what's his fuckin' name? Mohammed?"

SeeSaw wasn't as dumb as he looked or talked. "No, meat. But you're close. The name is Ali. He says he's Nepalese. Lebanese. Maybe he's Pakistani. I dunno, whatever. Anyway, we're talking bona fide horse. Genuine Afghanistan shit."

"When do I meet him?"

"Tomorrow night. He's okay with your price. You're in business, pal. I only hope you know what the fuck you're doing here."

SeeSaw drove past the Oakland Coliseum, where the Athletics and the Raiders pounded it out. Luckily, there was no ball-game traffic, so SeeSaw merged off the next exit, heading west toward the airport.

Great! This whole thing is actually going to happen, Angelo thought to himself. SeeSaw didn't interrupt his thoughts. He respected the dangling silence as Angelo stared intensely out the window. One foot jiggled noticeably.

"I even had him throw in a couple of pieces," SeeSaw continued. "I also had to tell him you were involved in the club."

Angelo's face wrinkled as he shot back a stern glance.

"What the fuck! Why? How specific were you about it?"

"Pretty fucking specific. I mentioned Infidelz by name. Had to."

"I could run into some aggravation here."

"You ain't cookin' it, you ain't shootin' it. You're selling it, dummy. What do they care?"

"Yeah, but still. I don't want Infidelz getting sucked into anything. I'll end up getting kicked out of the club."

"Listen, I brought it up to the guy to show him I had a serious player on the other end."

Angelo exhaled a lengthy sigh. He was in this caper for the quick money. He composed himself. It was showtime.

"Okay, okay. When and where do I meet this guy?"

"Tomorrow night. I'll call you tomorrow with the location. If this guy knows you're Infidelz, he's a fuck of a lot less liable to screw you or burn you, ya know? Think about it on that level."

Angelo sucked a final drag and blew the smoke out hard. He flicked the butt out the window with his middle finger. Angelo gave SeeSaw a nod. He'd done his job. The shit was on. SeeSaw turned the car around and headed back to the clubhouse. Angelo rolled up the window and pulled out his

49 **«**

wallet. Looking for a certain slip of paper, he examined several until he found the right name and number. His prison dope contact. As they approached the clubhouse, he motioned for SeeSaw to pull over.

"Let me off right here." He pointed at El Bombardo, a Mexican burrito place. It was only a few blocks away from the clubhouse, where he'd stashed his bike.

Angelo opened the door and turned to SeeSaw before jumping out.

"Thanks, dude. When it all comes down, I'll drop you a few C-notes on the back end. Okay?"

"Peace, bro."

Angelo bypassed his cellular and threw a couple quarters into the pay phone by the corner liquor store. He phoned his prison connection in Solano County to alert him that things were on the move. His throat went dry at the realization.

Back at home, Angelo lay awake on the couch for the rest of the night. He lit up a joint to calm his nerves. But this time the rolling high of the herb only made his senses keener and his thought processes more active, until his heart pounded and his head roared.

Angelo got up and rooted through the kitchen junk drawer until he found a folded-up piece of aluminum foil. He unfurled the scrunched-up foil and counted out the pills inside. Then he picked out a couple Valium tablets and popped them into his mouth. Downers. *Big day tomorrow, this should knock a horse to sleep, no doubt,* he figured. Then he reached over and found a small juice glass sitting among the teetering stack of dirty dishes in the sink. He rinsed it out and poured in a shot of Old Crow. The whiskey slammed the back of his gullet. Angelo poured another shot of amber fluid and drank the contents down. Then another. Then another after that.

The chemicals and liquor inside his body began to take effect. His vision dimmed and his mind spun as he dropped his wasted, tired rack of bones back down on the living-room couch. He dozed off almost as soon as he propped up his boots on the old wooden coffee table.

6

Pajero

The next morning Angelo stirred awake to what sounded like a galloping herd of bison. It wasn't a TMC western on the cable; it was Hollister stomping down the stairs ready for school. Angelo had crashed out all night on the living-room couch again.

"Kiddo," he murmured as he sat up and fumbled for a wrinkled fiver in his front pocket. The words nearly stuck to his tongue. "Lunch money?" he croaked.

"Thanks, Dad," said Hollister cheerfully as he snapped up the bill, grabbed his yellow book bag, and slung it over one shoulder. The five bucks would do for later. Hollister's peers at school considered eating cafeteria food decidedly unhip. So he carried a small brown-paper-bag lunch he'd whipped up for himself the night before. School wasn't prison—well, not quite—but only losers and jailbirds ate their food off a tin tray.

"Holly, I'm too, uh, tired, to give you a ride. My bike is running a little rich. Take the bus, okay?" Angelo hoped Hollister bought his bullshit. He needed time alone to psych himself up and plan the dope buy in his head.

That afternoon the phone rang. Angelo ran from out in the garage and picked up the horn, puffing and panting. Last night's indulgence cast a hazy fog over his brain.

"Hello?"

"Angelo, it's me." SeeSaw. "Tonight. Twelve forty-five, in front of the Fruitvale BART station. Stay in your car, but park away from the front, a little past the streetlight, like you're waiting for someone on the last train. Don't park in the back of the lot. The security guys drive around there looking for young punks who do car break-ins.

"You'll meet a dark-haired guy who calls himself Ali. Don't dick with the price. Twelve grand. Let me know how everything shakes. Later."

12:40 A.M. THE BAY AREA RAPID TRANSIT—BART—COMMUTER train made a lonesome whistling sound through the balmy summer air. It was unusually warm as a high-pressure system offshore kept the fog bank from rolling into the bay. Angelo pulled his 1987 Ford Tempo sedan into the parking lot off Fruitvale Avenue. Following SeeSaw's instructions, he picked a spot close to the northern end of the lot, but away from the newspaper machines and the well-lit kiosks that sold train tickets and posted arrival and departure times. A handful of dour-faced riders bounded off the train and trudged down the stairs, probably home after working overtime in San Francisco or starting a graveyard shift in the East Bay. He sat in his funky Ford and waited for his connection.

Angelo pulled his baseball cap down. He had slid a small rusty revolver inside his boot for easy reach, just in case. To keep his courage and his energy up, he had popped another hit of speed about a half hour before.

He decided not to wear his patch for the drop. That would be damned stupid, especially sitting inside an '87 Tempo. Besides, he figured he didn't need to prove to this guy what the hell he was. Whether or not they believed he was in the club wasn't his fucking problem. That was See-Saw's rap. He didn't care either way.

Angelo spotted a dark-haired man walking past the kiosk in the direction of his car. He tightened up in anticipation. But the fellow strolled right past his vehicle. Careful not to appear overanxious, he toyed with the radio at a low volume to tame his racing mind. As he fingered the dial, a curly-haired figure came into his peripheral view and tapped twice on the back passenger window of the car. Angelo reached over and unlocked the front passenger side. The man opened the door and climbed inside. He nonchalantly carried with him a brown leather attaché case.

"Does this seat go back any further?" the man asked with a Middle Eastern accent as he settled in and searched for the seat adjuster down on the floor. He seemed much more agreeable and comfortable than Angelo had anticipated.

"Ali, right?" he asked.

The man nodded.

Initially Angelo wanted to put on a tough bike-rider front, but what would be the point? Instead he flicked a switch on his door handle that locked all four doors of the car.

"Yes. That is me. Here I am," said Ali. He turned the attaché around on his lap so its hinges faced the dashboard. He popped open the attaché about ten inches so Angelo could see two taped-up clear bags of white powder and two pistols in the yin-yang position, neatly arranged inside the case. *Looks like half a key all right.*

"Have the money, my friend?" Ali asked.

"Yeah, I do. But first thing's first," Angelo said. Ali's eyes tensed up and narrowed as he apprehensively stared back at Angelo. "Gotta check out this skag. I'm gonna do this thing real careful, partner. We don't know each other. That's the way it should stay."

Angelo slid out his Buck Strider from the side pocket of his leathers, unfolded it, and clicked the four-inch Tanto blade into place. He reached over and deftly poked it into one of the bags and then snorted the powder off the knife's point. He felt a slight opiate tingle in his nostril. It felt like cheap Mexican horse to him. He wiped the white residue from the knife onto his pants.

"Do you want to check the guns, too?"

"No. I'll trust you on those." Angelo could give a shit about the weapons.

"You belong to motorcycle gang. Infidelz? Where I come from, infidels very bad."

"Yeah, yeah. But here in America, pal, Infidelz good. And proud of it." Angelo was feeling cocky. He could hang with this dope thing.

Ali laughed, showing a set of very crooked and decayed teeth. "Yeah, infidels. Very good, proud of it. This stuff, it's for your infidels, no?"

"Sure, whatever you say, Osama."

Angelo handed Ali an unsealed envelope from under the dashboard view. Ali took the slim bundle of cash and peeked inside. The denominations added up with a quick flick through the bills. Ali seemed good at math. He smiled as he looked back over at Angelo.

"And I will trust you, too, my new partner." He stuffed the bills into his side jacket pocket and zipped it shut. Ali scratched his head and fumbled for the door latch.

"Deal's done. I go now."

As Angelo flipped the unlock switch in the car, another man in a bomber jacket, who had snuck up from behind, slid into the backseat on the driver's side of the car.

Before Angelo could reach his emergency piece, he felt the cold steel of a gun barrel pressed to the back of his neck. Ali drew his own weapon and aimed it squarely at Angelo's temple. It was either a burn or a bust.

"Don't. Or you die."

Ali's Middle Eastern accent had vanished.

"DEA, motherfucker. Now grab the steering wheel real tight with both hands so we can see them. Try anything and you're a dead man. I swear."

"Ali's" voice trembled as he screeched his command.

There was nobody to witness the scene in the parking lot. The entire place was deserted, even though the lot was half filled with cars. Blood rushed into Angelo's head; he thought he was going to have a brain aneurysm. All of his best-laid plan Bs were useless. He was stuck in the damned family car, both hands on the wheel, with two cops waving heat. There was nothing he could do but sit tight. The DEA guys phoned for a backup squad car.

"Te agars pajero." "Ali," the front seat cop winked.

Fuck, Angelo cursed to himself. *That's barrio talk, for 'jerkoff.' He ain't no Arab. The bastard's a goddamned undercover cop.*

7

On the Hook

Angelo sat alone at a stainless-steel inter-rogation table downstairs in the Alameda County jail facilities. Both wrists were hand-cuffed to the arms of his chair. It had been a couple hours since the DEA agents left him alone after Round One of rigorous question-ing. Where did he get the money? Who was he buying the dope for? What about the about the Vicodin and speed they found in his jacket pocket? Where did he get that?

Angelo had questions of his own but kept them to himself. Why did the DEA drop him off at county and not the feds' own cop shop? Had he walked into some kind of joint-task-force sting operation?

Both hands were already swollen from his fidgeting, and the sharp edges of the steel manacles were carving the hair off his wrists. He figured he'd get booked soon and moved into the main holding cell upstairs, where he could phone Ahab with the bad news. Ahab would then telephone Dapper Dave, the club's bail bondsman, and Angelo would be out by dawn.

The two DEA agents entered the room for Round Two. "Ali" was the shorter of the two men, athletically built and clean-shaven. He wore a loose black suit, a white shirt unbuttoned far enough to reveal a tank top underneath. A gold chain dangled around his neck. In contrast, his silent partner blended into the wall. He was dark-haired, with a dark pockmarked complexion. "Ali" did all of the talking.

"Hey, jerkoff, we've got something we want you to hear, and it ain't the latest Backstreet Boys. Check it out."

"Ali" slammed a Walkman cassette player onto the metal tabletop and hit the play button. Angelo heard "Ali's" lousy Middle Eastern impersonation, then his own voice.

"This stuff. It's for your Infidelz, no?"

"Sure, whatever you say, Osama."

"There you have it, fuckhead," said "Ali." "You on tape linking a drug and weapons deal to the Infidelz. Not only are you going down, *pajero,* you're taking the whole gang down with you. With all the other shit we have on you clowns, I smell RICO, baby."

A cheap ploy, slimy evidence, but fuck, he did say it. For some reason, Angelo thought of Patch.

God, if Patch or Ahab heard this shit, they'd hit the ceiling.

"Ali" grabbed the recorder and stuffed it into his suit-jacket pocket. Then he and his pockmarked partner headed for the door. "Ali" smiled at Angelo as he slammed the door, which gave the rider a chill. Round Two was a short one, and Angelo had clearly lost it.

Angelo was more disgusted with himself than with the DEA. He stared at the two-way mirrored wall and pictured a couple more scheming cops standing behind it. What else could he tell them? As far as he was concerned, the money was his, the drugs were theirs; the bust was simply entrapment. But he knew the cops and judges weren't persuaded by that, so he declined an attorney and just shut up.

Even though the DEA had supplied the dope, they had him by the nuts and could squeeze hard. "Ali" grilled Angelo over and over. He was in deep shit and was staring at multiple felonies, purchasing narcotics and weapons with intent to sell, plus the possession beef. With his priors, which included a couple of burglaries and one interstate hijacking rap, Angelo was fresh out of strikes. He could be inside for life.

The illegal Vicodin and meth tablets they'd found on him was minor compared with the heroin buy. Although he wouldn't admit it out loud, Angelo couldn't imagine walking on probation after a bust like this. He was looking at doing some hard time back in the joint. *Fuck.*

Did SeeSaw set him up or did he just fuck up? Angelo

would put his chips on the latter. Sometimes SeeSaw had no sense. A few of the club guys had warned Angelo about running with him. First, he wasn't a bike rider. Second, the guy was a flake. But right now, SeeSaw's culpability was the least of Angelo's headaches.

Angelo's body twitched and ached as the speed high wore off and left behind another throbbing headache. The boredom and the starkness inside the interrogation room overwhelmed him. Not ventilated, the room with the bare puke-green walls was roasting him alive. He wished he were on his bike heading home, the cool fresh wind blowing in his face. He shifted around in his chair and swore at himself for the fix he was in.

JUST AS ANGELO NEARED THE BREAKING POINT OF TEDIUM, a new interrogator walked in with a chilled can of Coke and a fresh pack of Marlboros. He sat down across from Angelo, popped open the soft drink, and pushed it toward the prisoner. Then he opened the cigarette pack, took two smokes out, lit one for himself, and then handed the other cig to Angelo, who fumbled it into his mouth, his hands still cuffed to the chair. The man slipped off his suit coat and folded it neatly over the chair.

FBI agent J. W. McIntosh flicked open his lighter again and lit Angelo's cigarette. A cloud of smoke framed the suspect's weary mug.

"Here. Keep the whole pack," said J.W., "I'm trying to quit anyway." He set the pack of cigarettes down on the table in front of the prisoner.

John Wilkes McIntosh, J.W. to his colleagues, was an FBI lifer. Lifer as in no life. He was a new transfer from the central valley of California, where he had also worked with the DEA and ATF, hunting down Mexican drug dealers and their roving, portable meth labs. It was an area where Mexican illegals cooked in run-down shacks outside of tiny farm towns like Wasco, Mendota, and Kettleman City.

Aged forty-two and only five-eight, J.W. fostered a Napoleon complex. New to the more cosmopolitan Bay Area, he had no close friends in or outside the Bureau. The other agents perceived him as a loose cannon. The scuttlebutt around the Bureau was that J.W. made waves. Throughout his career most agents kept their distance. Although J.W. had succeeded in breaking several difficult cases, he had a couple civil rights violations pending with the OPR, the Office of Professional Responsibility.

J.W. wasn't promotion material in the eyes of the Beltway brownnosers in D.C. As a result, he mostly worked alone. He kept close tabs on what the gang-squad feds were up to these days. Los Angeles street gangs. San Francisco and Oakland Asian youth mobs. Vietnamese and Chinese FOBs (fresh-off-the-boats). As far as J.W. was concerned, bike riders fell easily into the category of gangs, too. Anything that suggested brotherhood and crime intrigued him because he was a loner. He'd never married. Even he knew what a disaster that would be. J.W. kept his private life, what little there was, on the down-low.

Over the past few years, J.W. felt the FBI and his superiors had been showing more interest in the politics in Washington than in sticking to the bottom line of arresting bad guys and making their indictments stick. The only Bureau contemporaries he truly trusted were ex-military. They were becoming fewer and fewer. Now the FBI was made up mostly of fresh-faced, lily-white law-and-order boys with law degrees, businessman-special haircuts, and silk socks. They wore red power ties and went to acting school so they could look smooth on camera or appear trustworthy in front of judges and grand juries. Success to these guys meant a future appointment inside the Bureau clique, a run for Congress after retirement, or scoring a security consultancy for a downtown high-rise building.

With fifteen years of professional baggage weighing him down, J.W. sat slumped across the table from Angelo Timmons, a dog-tired, meth-addled bike rider.

J.W. spread the arrest report out on the table. He eyed a couple of loose pages and looked up at Angelo.

"Angelo Timmons." He paused. "You got anything to say?"

63 «

Angelo stared straight ahead and said nothing. Clammed up. Not a single word.

"You wanna phone your lawyer? After looking over this stuff, along with your rap sheet, you're gonna need an attorney."

Angelo stared back at him coldly, then looked back down at the table.

"You married, Angelo?"

Angelo shook his head. No.

"Got a job, Angelo?"

Angelo shook his head again.

"Family? Any kids?"

Angelo looked back up at the agent with a cold, mean

stare. The bike rider's green, beady eyes cast a laserlike gaze.

J.W. continued.

"Let's see. No wife. No job. But you do have kids. Girls? Boys?"

That triggered Angelo to break his silence. "I have a son . . ." His voice trailed off.

J.W. got to the point.

"You ride with the Infidelz?"

Angelo just stared back down at the table.

"I'll take that as a yes, Angelo."

The two locked eyes for five seconds, then J.W. spoke up.

"Look, Angelo. It's fucking three in the morning. I'm not going to bullshit around with you much longer. I got called in here tonight . . . well, never mind about that. Angelo, you know you're looking at hard prison time again, especially with this narcotics beef. Yeah, Angelo, I'll admit it's a chickenshit thing those DEA guys stuck you on. But they *can* make it stick. And they will. They've got their quotas and caseloads. You and I both know you fucked up royally. They got you, Angelo, and you're slippin' fast. You'll be convicted in sixty days and it won't even make page twelve. In the eyes of the prosecutors here, you're just another druggie scumbag threatening the lives and well-being of America's precious youth by selling dangerous narcotics. You might as well have been selling that heroin shit in the schoolyard."

Angelo kept his head down.

"The worst thing about it is that they won't let you plead out. The judge is not going to be lenient. Oh, no. And your motorcycle friends aren't gonna be able to save your ass, either. You'll just be another downed member of the Big Pen Crew for the Infidelz MC, Angelo."

Big Pen Crew. J.W. was showing off his "insider" knowledge of "biker gangs." The BPC was a roster of incarcerated members of the club.

J.W. rose from his seat and walked around the table to where Angelo sat, handcuffed. Angelo looked straight ahead and refused to make further eye contact with the FBI agent. J.W. leaned over and whispered into Angelo's ear.

"But you know what's the very worst thing that's gonna happen to you, Angelo Timmons? Your son's gonna be the big loser here, pal. He's gonna pay for all your fucked-up ways.

"Where's the kid's mother? Probably out getting loaded somewhere, and you don't have a clue where she is. I know your situation. I've seen it so many times before. You're an absolute fuckup. Your old lady took off and doesn't give a damn. Your son has nobody but you, and you know what? When you get locked up, he's going to become a ward of the state. Your only son, Angelo, is going to move from foster home to foster home or worse, maybe even hustling the streets, while you rot away in prison.

"Is that what you want for him?"

Angelo pounded his forehead on the table. He gulped a couple of quick breaths and tried to compose himself.

J.W. stood over Angelo, who saw his reflection in the mirror. J.W. shook his head and put a hand on his shoulder.

"Look, Angie. I've taken out a lot of trash like you, and the guys upstairs love me for it. But deep inside, it creeps me out, too. What if I told you I could make this all go away? What if I told you, Angelo, you could walk out of here tonight and not have this shit hanging over your head?

"You've got to choose right here and now to save your ass." J.W. paused. "And your son's, too."

J.W. backed away to let it all sink in. He strode silently back around the table and sat down.

"I can go upstairs right now and talk to those two DEA losers."

He held up the stack of arrest papers, then let them drop and scatter across the table.

"This shit could end up at the bottom of a forgotten pile somewhere. I can have the U.S. marshals rescue you from all this bullshit. Witness protection, a new life. Hell, I can probably even get you your twelve grand back.

"But it involves you giving *me* something I need, Angelo. You ride for the Infidelz. You know what we're talking about here. You need to choose your *real* family over your biker pals. And don't forget, they have you on tape implicating the Infidelz as buying heroin. Angelo, it looks to me like your ass is caught right between those DEA hard-ons and your biker accomplices."

J.W. walked back over toward Angelo, whose heart was pounding frantically. He felt dizzy. Cuffed to the chair, he wanted to puke, but couldn't stomach the thought of sitting in his own vomit, so he controlled himself.

"You need to make the choice," J.W. intoned, moving in closer. "Let me get you out from under this predicament. Otherwise, come morning, I'm going to phone Child Protective Services. You have two minutes to decide."

Angelo stared at the soft drink the agent had set next to him. He was parched. Just like the salty sweat on his brow, heavy droplets had formed on top of the can. Angelo nodded toward the pack of smokes. He had smoked the first one down to the filter. J.W. pulled another one out of the pack, stuck it in Angelo's snout, and lit it. Angelo inhaled the smoke as the cigarette dangled to the corner of his mouth. Then he spoke.

"Okay, lawman, let's make a deal."

In the Bag

Son of a bitch," Patch yelled out impatiently. "C'mon, people. Let's move it." His gloved right hand twisted the throttle.

Patch gunned the Mean Machine on the sun-drenched, two-lane rural highway. Seeing no oncoming traffic, he quickly passed a caravan of slow-moving cars, then guided the Road King back into his own lane. Just ahead, the broken white center line turned into a solid double yellow as the roadway curved. Tall cacti whizzed by in a blur on his right side.

Patch was goin' for it. The Mean Machine had broken free of the glut of cars and trucks that had been blocking him. It was a warm beautiful day. He maintained his speed, digging into a few mild curves, until he passed an Arizona state trooper parked on the roadside.

Patch abruptly slowed and checked his rearview mirror another half mile down the way.

"Shit." He pounded on his thigh. "I *fucking* knew it."

Patch watched as the police car, its lights flashing, cruised closer toward his bike. He let off on the gas and slowed down as he downshifted. He maneuvered his way to the shoulder on the side of the road.

Patch turned off the Mean Machine, staying put on his bike as he reached for his wallet. The patrol-car door opened and slammed shut. He heard the gravelly crunch of boots approaching him from behind. The cop, wearing mirrored shades, looked over at his latest stop.

"So, partner, where's the fire?"

Patch stared down at his gas tank and shook his head. "Aw, c'mon."

"How fast you reckon you were ridin'?"

Patch saw a nameplate over the policeman's left pocket. *F. Bushnell.*

"I'd say I was riding no faster than those broads who speed around here in their silver SUVs."

"Oh, really? I could cite you for speeding. Plus those handlebars seem a little high." The officer stepped back and eyed Patch's Infidelz colors, then the California plates on his bike.

69 «

"You ain't from around here, are you?"

"Well, actually, I am now."

"How's that?"

Patch waved his California driver's license. "Here's my ID, Bushnell. Let's get this over with," he said, looking up at the sky. "The sun's gettin' hot just sittin' here."

Bushnell studied the license. "Everett John Kinkade. What brings you to Arizona, Everett?"

"My friends call me Patch. You can call me John."

The patrolman glanced back down at the California address.

"That was a joke, Officer."

"Wait a minute. Patch Kinkade. The Infidelz motorcycle gang." He nodded his head knowingly and backed away a step, his hand drifting toward his holstered pistol. "Patch Kinkade. I know who you are. Mr. Kinkade, please step away from the motorcycle."

"Oh, shit."

Patch swung his leg over and faced Bushnell with his hands on his hips.

"What brings you to Arizona?" Bushnell repeated.

"I live here."

"Yeah, but this is a California driver's license."

"I've only been here a few days."

"You just moved here. Is that what you're telling me, Kinkade?"

"Yeah, I live here now. That's what I'm tryin' to tell you."

The cop cleared his throat. "Are you armed?"

"Only this." Patch tapped twice on Sharpfinger on his right hip.

"Reach down carefully, pull out the knife, and slowly

place it on the seat of your bike. Then step away from the motorcycle. Go on. Do it. Right now."

"What for?"

"Do exactly as I say. Right now."

Patch cautiously withdrew Sharpfinger and, in an exaggerated gesture, rested it on the Harley's seat.

"Now step away, Kinkade."

Patch's anger rose. "Crissakes. Is this really necessary? Just give me the damned ticket. You can't—"

"Listen, Kinkade. I'm calling the shots here. Now, you either cooperate or I'll call for backup and haul your ass to jail for suspicion of—"

"Suspicion of what? Carrying a knife that I'm legally entitled to own?"

"Listen, Kinkade. Don't make waves. I wanna see what's in those saddlebags."

The cop took his hand off the gun and walked over to the Mean Machine. He opened the first bag, emptied out its contents, and then did the same with the second. He examined each inconsequential item he found. A hairbrush. Maps. A plastic bottle of sunblock. An emergency road kit. Other personal stuff.

71 «

This sucks, Patch thought as the cop inspected his gear. "What's next? You gonna frisk me now?" he remarked. "Hell, I feel like I'm back on parole."

"Do you have any other weapons on you?"

"Look, you know the answer. I'm a convicted felon. I can't carry guns. But this knife is legal. You know it. I know it."

Bushnell pulled out a small pad from his breast pocket.

"Mr. Kinkade, what is your current address? Where are you staying?"

"I'm out off the Carefree Highway." Patch dictated his address as Bushnell scrawled down the info in his pad.

"Stay right here," the officer commanded. "I'll be back in a few minutes." He walked back to his car and radioed headquarters. Patch stood next to his bike and baked in the hot sun for another fifteen minutes.

The cop walked back. "Just put your stuff back in the bags. And the knife, too. I don't want you wearing that weapon."

"You know, you are outta line."

"Call a cop, Kinkade. You're in my state now. You do as I fuckin' tell ya."

Patch decided to ride the guy. How far could he push him?

"Let's drop the gloves, then," he muttered.

"What did you say?"

"You heard me," Patch snapped. "Let's go. Right here, right now."

Patch reached over, grabbed Sharpfinger off the bike seat, and slipped it back into the sheath.

"I told you to put that knife in the bag."

Patch stepped closer to the policeman. "Then take it away from me. Go ahead. Let's see you try."

The officer glanced both ways down the desolate road. Desert as far as the eye could see. There wasn't a cloud in the clear blue sky. Not one car passed them.

"Tell you what, hard guy. I'm gonna let the ticket slide." The cop handed Patch back his license. "But I know who you are, and the gang squad now knows where you live. If I were you, I wouldn't fuck around in these parts."

Then he strode back to his patrol car.

Patch replaced his gear, buckled up the left saddlebag, and watched the cop car swerve onto the highway and speed off. As the car drove out of sight, he reached down into a hidden side zip compartment of the right saddlebag and extracted a couple ounces of pot in a rolled-up sandwich baggie. He unrolled and turned the baggie upside down, dumping its contents on the ground. A dry, gusty breeze blew the particles away, scattering the stash in the wind. Leftover Northern California weed. Good stuff, too.

Arizona's marijuana laws were among the strictest in the States. Possession still constituted a felony. Patch laughed nervously, then hopped back on his bike. Close call. If Bushnell had half a brain, a ticky-tack pot bust might have landed Patch back in the joint and earned the trooper a big "atta boy" from the big shots upstairs.

Patch's strategy had worked like a charm. *Don't back down. Even when you've got something to hide, like a little weed in the bag, it's best to take a hard-line attitude.* It was the way he dealt with cops. And it had worked again.

73 **

9

Casino Unreal:
The Santa Paula Shootings

Two beers for two steers," said one energetic and thirsty bike rider to the poker-faced bartender, who leaned next to his cash register like a frozen fixture. The two bike riders were in Oakland for the next day's big Tribal Casino Poker Run. They wore red-and-blue 2Wheeler patches. In the far corner of the Porch Light Saloon, a loud group of black men hovered over a round of pool. The bar crowd was unusually sparse for a Friday night.

The glittering prize of the evening was the two slim and attractive girls sitting at the end of the dimly lit bar. One of the women, a long-legged blonde, wore a clingy, lime green minidress. She was rapaciously downing tequila shooters while her companion, red-haired and demure, nursed a double G&T.

The bartender slid two frosted glass mugs of American brew over to the riders. Handsome Hank, looking over at his longtime 2Wheeler comrade Reload, called for a toast. They clanged their glasses together extra hard. Reload held fast to all that was left of his libation, the handle of his mug, as shards of broken glass and spilled beer showered the two laughing riders. The bartender walked over with a towel and shook his head. Then he broke out into a smile as the girls seated at the end of the bar giggled.

"So, ladies," said Hank, toweling himself off and motioning to the young girls. "How about you two joining me and my brother here for"—he grinned after looking over at Reload—"a couple of cold ones?"

Blondie stood up, downed her shot, and walked over, followed more cautiously by her redheaded friend. Hank stood up and offered a chair that put Blondie closest to him, leaving the redheaded beauty next to Reload.

The conversation turned to the riders' motorcycles, parked conspicuously within view outside the barroom door. The blonde was curious.

"I've never had sex on a bike," said Blondie. "Is it better if you're moving or still?"

Hank pondered the question; he'd had it both ways. "You can get a whole lotta motion goin' in a stationary position."

Hank figured he was just one or two tequila shots shy of taking Blondie out for a "ride." He caught the eye of the bartender and nodded.

"Bartender," proclaimed Hank, banging his fist playfully on the bar, "two more beers and tequila and gin for the ladies. And keep 'em coming."

It was just past one o'clock in the morning and Hank was ready to make his move. But the redhead remained comparatively sober while her blond friend swayed sensually and with drunken abandon to the lure of cheap tequila and classic Bob Seger tunes. As the redhead eyeballed the door, Reload was in danger of losing her altogether and leaving the bar with the same hard-on he came in with. Handsome Hank, on the other hand, seemed headed in a luckier direction.

The teetering blonde stood up, grabbed Hank by his ponytail, and led him out the door. She walked in her heels as if she were high on stilts, but made it outside to the cycles and pointed to the two mechanical specimens parked on the sidewalk under a dim street lamp.

"Which one's yours? I'm gonna take a wild guess. The one with the red tank," she said, eyeing the bike's shiny paint job, its gleaming chrome, and its sleek black leather seat. Hank could see the wheels turning in her head.

"Right you are," he said, proud of the airbrush artistry on his '89 Harley Low Rider, a bike he had rebuilt many times with his own two hands.

"Why don't you wheel that baby round the back and I'll show you what we can do on this thing together. Meet you back there," purred Blondie as she pointed to the back of the building.

This was the best offer Hank had heard all week, so he fired up the bike and surged it the hundred feet behind the tavern, where the two were alone. He put the kickstand down, got off the bike, and stepped aside.

"Your chariot awaits, my dear, motor runnin'."

Blondie made her move and slipped off a pair of aqua panties and threw them Hank's way. He caught them and stuffed them into the back pocket of his leathers as she mounted and straddled the bike, hiked up her dress, leaned over, and stationed her arms firmly across his handlebars.

It had the look and feel of an *Easyriders* pictorial. Blondie pulled her dress top down past her shoulders, exposing a righteous pair of nipple-erect thirty-four-inch titties. Her breasts dangled sensually over the shiny red tank; her magnificent, tight ass swayed temptingly over the front part of the long, black leather seat. Good thing she was a tall girl. Her long legs easily cleared the Low Rider, and her spike-heeled feet remained firmly planted on the ground. She must have studied dance, judging by the way she slowly shimmied her tail from side to side and gyrated her hips.

Without any prompting, Hank eagerly mounted the bike right behind her, one of the very few times he didn't mind situating himself as a passenger on the back of his own ride. Hank pulled his leathers down and caressed her bottom. It was like a dream, porcelain colored, round, and firm. Then he grabbed his cock, unrolled a condom, and entered her from behind. Before he began thrusting, he leaned over and gunned the cycle. The statuesque beauty was arched over the idling Harley. Hank revved the accelerator again and again as he thrust, back and forth, up and down. As he gunned his motor, the vibration of the bike's powerful torque on the seat helped Blondie reach multiple, ecstatic orgasms. While she moaned and groaned, Hank huffed and puffed as fast as he could to keep up, working up a sweat while running his one free hand up and down her soft long leg and thigh. Hank and the bike both sputtered and roared as he came inside the girl. Immediately after the perform-ance, without uttering a word, Blondie slipped her long leg over the seat and off the bike and rearranged the short dress over her trim body. She gave Handsome Hank a long, tongue-filled kiss and walked back toward the front en-trance of the bar as if nothing uncommon had happened.

"Thanks for the ride," she called back over her shoulder, and then sashayed around the corner and disappeared.

"Don't mention it." Hank sighed deeply and sat a minute or two, drained and catching his breath. Then he ditched the used condom, hitched up his pants, and inched the bike back toward the bar's front door. Blondie was gone, a clear-cut case of sexual hit-and-run.

Hank looked around, hit the kill switch on his bike, and walked back into the bar zipping up his fly, a wide grin on his face. Reload was just where he had left him, but alone. Both girls had split. Reload was considering a final beer as Hank walked up and shook his partner by the shoulders.

"Time to hit it, pal. I'll race you to the Oakland estuary," he said.

"Where'd you go, bro?"

"Just for a quick spin. Details later," said Hank.

The two settled up their tab, left the bar, and started up their bikes. Hank high-fived Reload and threw him the aqua panties. The rumbling roar of their straight pipes faded into the distance as they raced toward the estuary.

Meanwhile, two strangers also left the bar. They climbed into their pickup truck and headed down the road in close pursuit.

THE 2WHEELERS MC STARTED OUT OF THE CENTRAL VALLEY of California's agricultural belt. "Wheeler" clubhouses were scattered around agri-towns like Salinas, Modesto, and Turlock. Their chapters were composed mostly of white bike riders with a few Latinos mixed in. The Wheelers were a suspicious, clannish bunch, a hotheaded posse of approximately twenty riders per charter. Statewide there were probably a hundred members. Their bikes, a mixture of new rides, rat bikes, and former basket cases, reflected modest flash, little ready cash, but a maximum of pride. Their three-piece patch featured a flaming motorcycle wheel with skulls and gears in red and blue. Individually, their best members won trophies at the Bakersfield drags for racing and trick riding. As a pack, they rode fast and punched hard.

79 **«**

THE TIPSY PAIR OF 2WHEELERS FIGURED THEY'D LOG IN A few more miles riding along the Oakland piers before heading back to their nearby motel rooms. The moon shone like a Vegas silver dollar, a gigantic orb reflected on the bay. But as the pair rode, the pickup truck passed the two Harleys. Neither rider acknowledged the passing vehicle alongside them, much less the Mossberg pump-action shotgun that protruded from the vehicle's rolled-down side window.

A thunderous discharge rose above the two meticulously tuned Harley motors. The first shotgun blast ripped through Hank's torso and spine, shooting him clean off his Low Rider. The buckshot-riddled corpse spun out onto the pavement as the motorcycle sped ahead riderless until a rail broke its forward momentum.

Reload's fate wasn't any kinder. The force of the next two shotgun shells tore his chest and shoulders into a thousand pieces of bone, blood, and muscle. Unlike Hank, who died instantly, Reload squeezed a dead man's grip on the throttle of his bike for another fifty yards. He died in the saddle and with his boots on after his head cracked open against a barrier of concrete and steel rail. Its mission accomplished, the dark vehicle sped off and disappeared into the Oakland night. Neither rider's body was discovered until sunup, when a jogger puked her guts out at the sight of their splattered remains.

THE ORGANIZERS OF THE TRIBAL POKER RUN HAD THEIR route well planned for an entire day's ride. Hundreds of riders attended from across the state. It was an ideal excuse to log in a hundred-plus miles, drink beer, hang out, meet women, dig some blues and rock and roll, and consume giant slabs of barbecued meat doused in hot and fiery sauces.

The poker run started at the biggest bike shop in Oakland, Morrie's Motors on Foothill, the event's organizer. The run had become so popular that dozens of motorcycle-related companies, manufacturing everything from custom bikes to after-market parts to helmets and gloves, anted up handsome sponsorship fees in order to be associated with it. Nobody was quite sure how much money changed hands, but a portion of the poker run's proceeds supposedly helped finance the continuing effort to repeal California's draconian helmet laws. The rest of the dough, after prizes and expenses, lined Morrie's already fat pockets.

Between nine and noon, riders threw down twenty-five bucks to sign in and get an entry form listing the sponsored stops. The final destination was Casino Santa Paula, a posh Indian gambling joint just off a steep freeway grade in a California town called Hercules.

A 140-mile course separated Morrie's and the casino. The stopovers, each a little over 30 miles apart, were all familiar, deluxe bike riders' bar hangs: the Red Boar Bar in Livermore; Five Easy Pieces in Niles; Crazy Mary's Saloon in Clayton; and the fourth stop toward Sacto, the Aftermath Bar 'n' Grill in Vacaville. From there it ended at the Santa Paula Casino.

At each stop, the riders drew a playing card. Selections from "the deck" were stamped and initialed onto an entry form. The results from all five stops, including the casino, constituted a five-card stud poker hand. Riders were encouraged to sample the food and spirits of each establishment while there. Whoever got the best poker hand took home the grand prize of two thousand bucks.

Just before sundown, the last riders completed the run and streamed into the Santa Paula parking lot for a massive outdoor barbecue. Hundreds of Harley riders were ready for the food, live music, and gambling, which included card playing, dice and roulette machines, and slots inside the casino. A tribute rock band called Stairway thrashed out a full set of note-for-note Led Zeppelin songs.

A strong contingent of forty 2Wheelers rode in to join the hundreds of revelers, but kept mainly to themselves. Across the lot, another thirty-plus Infidelz circulated through the crowd. This run was a mandatory Oakland Infidelz event, all members required to attend. Outside the casino entrance, Infidelz prez Ahab hung out in typically high spirits, flanked not only by his Oakland officers and 187 Crue bodyguards, but also by members and prospects from neighboring California Delz chapters. Nonaffiliated riders, American Motorcycle Association members, and the Christian Motorcycle Association helped to balance the rebel atmosphere outside.

When a 2Wheeler won the two-thousand-dollar Tribal Casino Poker Run pot, Ahab howled in mock disgust and slapped his buddy Angelo hard on the back.

"See what happens, boy, when you got Lady Luck on your side?"

Angelo pushed Ahab out of the way. "What the fuck," he snorted crossly.

"Hey, easy there, pal," warned Ahab. "What's your problem anyway?"

"I coulda used that two grand prize money," he complained. "My luck is nil on poker runs. I can't remember the last time I won anything in my whole goddamned life."

As night fell and the barbecue broke up, riders hit the freeway. The pack of Infidelz stayed behind to play the slots and dig into some seven-card stud. The 2Wheelers stuck around, too, and mostly gathered around the Mexican-style cantina situated on the far end of the casino.

A security camera's view of Casino Santa Paula detailed a

sea of embroidered patches. The 2Wheelers and their amigos fraternized on one side of the building while the Infidelz gambled up a storm on the other side. But as the night wore on, the MC colors, orange and black, blue and red, blended together, while citizens, waitresses, and the casino staff went out of their way to mix and be polite.

"Bring it on over here, darlin'. Don't be shy, sweetheart."

Chino Laughlin, the 2Wheelers prez, stuffed a twenty-dollar chip in the waitress's apron as she delivered his order of a dozen cans of Tecate, a bowl of sliced limes, a salt-shaker, and a giant combination platter of tacos and enchiladas. Then he reached over and grabbed the woman's ass and laughed loudly as she turned to make a hasty red-faced retreat back to the cantina kitchen.

CHINO HAD BECOME THE HEAD OF THE 2WHEELERS AFTER Augie Longfellow, their founding president of twenty-plus years, died from diabetic complications. Augie's funeral attracted a mile-long motorcycle procession that included almost every major MC in California. But now Chino ruled the Wheeler roost.

Compared to Augie, President Chino was more belligerent and high profile. He kept his stubby fingers in many dicey enterprises, including a Nevada cathouse and a few seedy Bay Area streetwalker motels.

Contrary to popular adage, Chino *could* bullshit a bullshitter, unless it was the IRS. He owed a mountain of back taxes, and there was a lien on every legal dollar he earned. While some members of the club worked honest blue-collar jobs, most 2Wheelers were like Chino and ran scams, pushed drugs, or sent their old ladies off to work, mostly as exotic dancers and strippers.

Three years before, Chino did fifteen months at the state men's prison facility in Southern California that bore his nickname. Upon his release, a zealous parole officer slapped a nonassociation clause on him. That meant he either steered clear of his chopper-riding brothers, or federal marshals could come knocking and bounce him right back in the joint for "associating" with his criminal friends. Miraculously, Chino kept active with the MC without getting violated. After he got off parole, the Wheelers elected him prez and threw an orgiastic party to celebrate his official return to the club. Chino brought in a virtual army of hotties ranging from college call girls to table-dancin' strippers racked with monster fakies. They serviced the partygoers generously, and the booze, smoke, nitrous, and flesh flowed like water.

THE INFIDELZ AND THE 2WHEELERS CONTINUED THEIR HARD partying at the Santa Paula casino. It was fairly typical, especially after a whole day of riding and a night of drinking, for bike riders to mix it up physically. These were rowdy guys for whom a little good-natured roughhousing was common.

So when Streeter, one of Ahab's 187 bodyguards, backhanded a 2Wheeler named Thor across the mouth at the bar for ogling his old lady, no one seemed too alarmed.

"Son of a bitch," Streeter cursed the 2Wheeler as he swatted the stunned Norwegian bike rider across his kisser. The oversized sterling-silver gargoyle ring on his finger caused half of Thor's face to swell up.

At the same time, Angelo and another 2Wheeler named Pepe, the guy who won the two-grand pot, righteously got into it at the cantina.

"The only way a dumb fuck like you could have won," growled Angelo, "is if they rigged the whole fucking thing."

Angelo was in the mood to fight. He reached around and punched Pepe soundly across the side of his head. Then the requisite shoving match ensued. Angelo and the lucky Wheeler threw a few roundhouse body punches.

Nobody took the fighting all that seriously, except for maybe the fighters. The rest egged them on.

"Stick it to him, Pepe," yelled Chino as he rooted for his guy and polished off another Mexican lager and lime.

Just then a Wheeler member named Cool Dave strutted through the noisy throng of gambling bike riders. A scowl showed on his face as he approached Chino's table.

"Bad news, boss. You were asking about Handsome Hank and Reload. Cops found them dead over by the Oakland estuary. They got shot off their fuckin' bikes."

Chino bolted forward incredulously in his chair.

"Who did it?" he asked.

"It's gotta be a local job," replied Cool Dave.

"Meaning?"

"Meaning, boss, I suspect the Infidelz. I wouldn't put it past 'em. Payback for their guy getting whacked at Trader's. That's my take. Two of our guys for one of theirs. That's their style. They lost Marco, so they killed Hank and Reload."

"Bullshit. Hank and Reload weren't even at Trader's that night."

"You think those pieces of shit care? They lost a guy, so they kill two to stay on top. Just like it's always been."

Chino jumped to his feet.

"This is fucked up. I'm gonna get to the bottom of this right now. Go round up our guys and meet me back here."

As Chino reacted hotly to the news of his two riders' deaths, word spread throughout the casino of Hank's and Reload's murder like a tinder-dry brushfire. As he gathered his forces, his rage and suspicions grew, which he half drunkenly directed toward the outnumbered Infidelz, obliviously playing their hands at poker and blackjack.

Chino wasn't the only one dumbfounded by the deaths of the two Wheelers. Brutus, Angelo, and Streeter approached Ahab and pulled him aside from the blackjack table.

"Yo, Prez," said Brutus. "Heard the news?"

"What news?" asked Ahab.

Streeter cut in. "2Wheelers just found out that two of their guys got whacked last night."

"Fuck," said Ahab. "Who got it?"

"Hank and Reload," said Angelo. "Late last night."

"Whoa, this shit is getting freaky," said Ahab. "First Marco, and now two of their guys."

"Chino's really pissed off," said Brutus. "He's gonna pin the blame on us, I bet."

"Let him try," replied Ahab. "Round up everybody on the double. Tell 'em to keep an eye out in case the Wheelers try somethin' stupid."

Ahab looked over and saw Chino and his mob striding toward him. It was the kind of scene that plays out in a prison yard. When rival groups converge, everyone else takes sides or hits the dirt. Three burly Infidelz stepped in and intercepted Chino's boys, one of them a kick boxer named Wrangler.

"Okay, hold it right there," said Wrangler to the Wheeler crew. "That's far enough."

"Get the fuck out of my way," bellowed Chino as he shook his fist in Ahab's direction. "We got business to talk about. Right now."

"What's up, Chino?" Wrangler yelled. "They cut you off at the bar or something?"

"Very funny, asshole. Two of my best guys are dead. Now get out of the way, you Infidelz cunt."

Wrangler delivered a swift karate kick into Chino's sternum. The kick knocked Chino on his ass. Wrangler's aggression summoned the first screaming wave of retaliating 2Wheelers. Punches were exchanged and Wrangler took down two more of Chino's lieutenants. The other Infidelz and Wheelers rushed headlong into the melee. The casino was immediately divided into three factions: pro-Infidelz, pro-2Wheelers, and the citizens caught helplessly in the cross fire.

The pushing and punching gave way to territorial warfare. Two gray-haired, patch-wearing old-timers went at it furiously like in their younger days, bare knuckles and bloody noses, thrashing around on the stained carpet floor in a pool of spilled drinks and broken glass. Flashlights, small hammers, and back-pocket wrenches turned into makeshift weapons. Blackjack tables were picked up and thrown over, barricading a few lucky citizens smart enough to hit the deck and hide. The Infidelz and 2Wheelers closed ranks again and tightened their positions. The Delz stationed men next to the exits ready to clobber any 1%ers running away from the battle.

Those carrying small but deadly knives were glad for it. One Infidelz member crouched between two banks of slot machines. When a 2Wheeler ran by, he jumped out and sliced him across the neck with a tactical folding knife. The Wheeler went down, clutching his bleeding throat. An Infidelz member was stabbed in the chest after a 2Wheeler drew the deadly hammer-gripped, double-bladed combat knife he kept housed in a hidden shoulder sheath. Another Delz brother jumped to his buddy's aid, applying direct pressure to the gushing wound and giving him emergency mouth-to-mouth.

The violence escalated. Gunfire rang throughout the casino. One 2Wheeler fired shots into a crowd of orange-and-black patches, some of whom dived behind the overturned blackjack tables and a bank of video poker machines. After firing six rounds, the 2Wheeler, without looking down at his gun, turned a full circle and surveyed the room closely as he speed-loaded the weapon.

Those who packed heat shot back as fast as they could reload. One of the Infidelz, wielding a semiautomatic Glock, fired two shots into another bike rider's ample belly. But it wasn't a 2Wheeler after all. The victim's only transgression was that he happened to be wearing a red-and-blue shirt. The stricken man doubled over in shock, then slumped onto a blackjack table and bled all over the strewn chips and playing cards.

A youthful, clean-shaven 2Wheeler prospect was hiding behind a post. One of his brothers spotted him, ran over, and slapped a Smith & Wesson .38 pistol into his palm.

"Here," the Wheeler shouted in the frightened prospect's face. "Now fucking use it!" The prospect dropped the gun and ran for the door.

More gunshots and knife-wielding lunges turned the casino into a street-fighting free-for-all. After only ninety-three seconds had passed, the battle was nearly over.

Ping, ping.

Two shots zoomed past Ahab's head. He dived behind a big wheel of fortune near the sports lounge.

At the entrance of the casino, the law arrived and fanned out across the main floor with shotguns and pistols drawn. They found a sickly, cough-inducing, gray cloudy haze of discharged gunpowder wafting through the entire Santa Paula casino. SWAT cops stormed the premises. Anybody who wore the slightest stitch of leather and denim was rounded up and thrown to the floor.

"Everybody drop your weapons," screeched a scratchy voice over a police bullhorn.

A couple of 2Wheeler patches lay empty and abandoned on the floor. Two bulletproof vests were also found dropped near the scene. A variety of ditched weapons littered the casino floor. Guns, knives, and ice picks were stashed in the planter boxes.

Those who dug in and braved the battle and hadn't bolted for the exits or hid in the toilets were now lying facedown, patches up, spread-eagled across the floor, waiting to be cuffed. Shotgun-toting lawmen prowled the casino lobby, nudging the bike riders with their barrels to lie still.

"Nobody fucking moves!" yelled one policeman.

When another cop accidentally discharged his weapon, a couple of frightened casino waitresses started to scream and sob uncontrollably.

Ahab, still hidden behind the wheel of fortune, pulled out

his cell and dialed as the cops intensified their occupation of the casino.

"Patch here. What's up, Ahab?"

"Yo, Patch. You won't fucking believe what's goin' on right this fucking minute."

"Where are you?"

"Fucking Casino Santa Paula," Ahab cursed.

"Speak up, Ahab. Can't hear you."

"The Santa Paula casino," screamed Ahab. "We just had a shoot-out inside the casino. Us and the 2Wheelers."

"Right now? Holy shit." In order to hear better, Patch pressed the phone close to his ear. The signal faded. "What happened?"

"Chino and the Wheelers got sore. A coupla his guys got clipped last night and they suspect us. So our guys threw punches. Then there were knives, then guns."

The conversation was interrupted by dead air.

"Ahab! Ahab, you there?"

"Yeah. I'm still here. I think we've lost a couple guys. It's fuckin' outta control."

"How you doing?"

"Patch, I better go. The cops have just . . . Man, I don't think we're gonna be able to get outta here without getting—"

The call died.

The unofficial body count stood at ten. An equal number of club members, four Infidelz and four 2Wheelers, lay among the dead. Stray bullets had also cut down two weekend gamblers. Over a dozen members of each club, stabbed or severely beaten, were carted away into waiting ambulances. Police cruisers and prisoner vans hauled away the uninjured suspects, one by one, after they were lifted up off the floor and onto their feet, handcuffed. Ambulances carrying the dead drove in a slow procession out of the parking lot and onto the nearby freeway entrance.

Several Infidelz and Wheelers were detained by police for questioning, including Ahab, Angelo, Wrangler, Streeter, and Chino. But everybody made bail shortly after midnight and were released. No arrests were made, pending an investigation and scrutiny of the security tapes.

"Santa Paula" became the latest slogan to enter the bikerider lexicon for many months to come, signifying a 1%er battle cry. After Santa Paula, self-described "motorcyclegang experts" predicted ongoing wars and bloody reprisals.

» C H A P T E R «

10

Back to
Bump City

Ahab's eyewitness telephone account to Patch from Casino Santa Paula broke up and dissolved in the digital ether. Patch folded his cell phone and set it down on the Iron Horse's bar, expecting Ahab to ring back again. It sounded like Ahab, Angelo, Brutus, Streeter, and the other guys were up to their necks in it.

After a few minutes—when the phone didn't ring again—Patch began to stew. He was miles away, what could he do? He might have to spend the rest of the night out of touch and trust that Ahab had the situation under control and would call back once he made bail.

One more tequila eased his anxiety. Patch leaned in and used his index finger to flag the lady bartender, the blond one, whose ass he'd been grooving on all night.

"One last shot," he said.

"For the road?"

"S'pose so."

"What's up?" she asked. "You seem, mmmm, distracted."

Patch scrunched his face and then shook his head.

The bartender shot back a concerned look.

"Bad news?"

Patch figured she'd eventually find out when everything hit the newspapers tomorrow. Still, he clammed up. Then he downed a parting shot of tequila in one gulp and slammed the glass loudly on the bartop. He laid a couple sawbucks on the bar and headed for home.

PATCH WAS SITTING ON THE PORCH IN THE HOT NIGHT AIR. He munched sunflower seeds, spitting the shells one after another into a clay flowerpot four feet away. He hadn't missed a shot. Even in the summer night's heat, he'd cooled considerably. The ride home helped. Then his cell rang. The caller ID readout revealed *Haywood*.

Patch answered immediately. It was Ahab.

"I'm out, bro."

"How 'bout the rest of the guys?"

"Everybody's out."

"What went down?"

"Hard to say what exactly happened. At first it was the usual bullshit, some of the guys horsing around, a little gambling, a little fightin'. Then things got out of control real fast."

"Normal, right?"

"Not like this, bro. Did you catch the news?"

"I was in the bar, they had Diamondback highlights on the tube. What happened?"

"Well, I'm tellin' ya, the shit was down. Gunfight at the OK Corral. One minute we're playing poker, the next we're dodging bullets. Four of us, four of them, got killed. We lost Dodge, Snake, Freddie, and Amos. That's five of our guys in the last week. Something's outta whack. I'm tellin' ya, you might want to come back here and see for yourself. Sniff around. Patch, you've got a way of getting to the root of things. People open up to you. The clubs respect you as a stand-up guy. You can move around among the other clubs. You've got the whole town wired."

"Fuck no. Like I told you, my days in Oakland are through. No offense, but the last thing that was holding me there was Eve. Now she hates the sight of me. My being there only reminds her that her kid brother, well—"

"Yeah, bro. I hear ya. But, man, we need ya. I need ya. The Wheelers, they've always been cool enough. Okay, maybe we needed to keep an extra eye on them, but shit, man, Chino's all right. We never shot any of their guys, at least not any that I know of. Main thing about this casino thing is that the cops are gonna come down hard now, especially the gang squad. They're gonna squeeze us. We don't need that comin' down on our, ah . . ." Ahab suddenly realized the possibility of the feds listening in on their conversation. "Our interests. Everybody's interests. Times are good right now. The last thing we need is for this shit to turn things upside down."

"Can't you clean this up without me?"

"Patch, don't you feel an obligation to the club, to Marco, God rest his soul, to any fucking one?"

"I told you my life in Oakland is finished. You know that better than anyone. Hell, I've given enough."

"All gave some, some gave all, bro."

Patch balled his hand into an angry fist. He would make a stand to keep his distance.

"No, Ahab. Fuck, no. I ain't ready. Clear up your own mess. I'm through with California. Why the hell do you think I came all the way down here? For my sinuses?"

"Fuck you, too, Patch. You ran away. Yeah, that's it. Rather than work things out with Eve and the club and the stuff in your head, you fuckin' ran for the border."

95 **«**

"This conversation is over, motherfucker." Patch hit the off button on the phone. His arms shook in anger while his heart pounded. Then he threw the phone onto the driveway. He opened the screen door and strode into the back bedroom. He eyed the beat-up mattress on the bare hardwood. *Oh no, not you again.* So far he was zero for three trying to score sleep on that thing. Tonight would not be any easier; in fact, it was worse.

LATE THE NEXT MORNING, PATCH PICKED UP THE TELEPHONE he had thrown on the driveway. He looked over at the Road

King. After he'd taken a sponge and a hose to it, the Mean Machine was clean and shiny, gleaming in the sunlight. No more road grime. Ready to ride.

It was a few minutes before the saddlebags were packed. A couple of T-shirts. Rain gear. Emergency road kit. Shaving and toiletries. Camo BDU pants. Gym shorts and New Balance cross trainers for workouts. The rest he wore on his person, including Sharpfinger. He'd need a lid, so he packed his beanie helmet. Patch quickly checked the cycle's brakes, fluid levels, battery, and tire pressure.

Bound for California again. Fucking Ahab. For better or worse, he's my brother. How can I say no?

Patch's focus before leaving on any long ride was always acute. While some of the Infidelz fidgeted and paced around before a run, asking a zillion questions—like who's got the maps, where's the first gas stop, is anybody carrying a spare cable?—Patch was the opposite. The comfort and security most people felt at home, he felt on his bike. His sense of relaxation was transportable. He anticipated the peace he'd feel in his belly at the hundred-mile point once he was out of the city and back onto the open highway. Patch figured a week in California would do it. A little maintenance. Mend a few fences. Things would lighten up.

Patch grabbed the morning newspaper off his neighbor's driveway. He unfolded the *Republic* and there it was, splashed on the front page. BIKER VIOLENCE ERUPTS. The article recounted the casino melee blow by blow. The story matched Ahab's account down to the smallest gory detail. Ten deaths and a few club casualties. Patch was strangely relieved. The boys certainly didn't lie down for anybody. They'd fought furiously and then some. He felt a mixture of pride and jealousy. He hadn't been there for the carnage.

While he was proud of how the guys responded, he was pissed off to see a peaceful era come to an end, considering all the work he had put into it. He'd been responsible for setting up meetings, separating the tough talk from the hard threats, taking into account pride and ego, including his own. But if the peace had to come to an end, and things got dicey again, then so be it. He could live with war, too.

The article in the *Republic* quoted the usual sources. Local police. Retired FBI. Never any of the Infidelz. They knew better than to talk to the press. Instead, the article quoted a couple riders from other clubs, including the Gun Runners.

When it came to the other clubs, Patch respected "the Gunners," as they were nicknamed by their California riding brothers. They were hard-assed and meaner than the 2Wheelers. The Gunners were tough and their presence in the north was spreading. The Delz had their run-ins with them, but things were honorable, given enough distance between the two clubs. While the Gunners' main turf was in SoCal, they'd ventured farther north, settling in San Jose and the South Bay, where they set down a couple of small chapters.

There were isolated incidents between the Gunners and the Delz, and the Delz and the Wheelers. A few punch-ups at the races or at bike shows, no big deal. When the Gunners fought, it was usually by committee. The Gunners flew colors of green and orange to the Infidelz's black and orange, which caused a little friction.

While the police openly condemned violence between

clubs, confrontation served law enforcement's interests by keeping the different MCs at odds with one another. Government infiltration of the clubs kept them agitated. Chaos was how law enforcement attempted to maintain control. Consequently, even the bitterest MC enemies might sit down together, confederation-style, in an effort to curtail mass arrests and infiltrations.

So while the Delz and Soul Sacs went back almost twenty years and were friendly, contact between the Oakland Infidelz, the 2Wheelers, and the Gun Runners still resulted in occasional skirmishes.

IN A FEW MORE MINUTES, PATCH WOULD BE ON HIS HARLEY, headed back to Oakland. He would patch things up with Ahab, maybe check up on Eve, and snoop around. It was just before noon; he'd grab a burger on the way out of town and then roll into the East Bay by midnight.

Before heading out, Patch cased the bedroom, looking for spare knives or anything else he may have forgotten to pack. Being a felon and not packing heat was no big deal, as long as some other brothers in the club were strapped. Besides, who needed the aggravation that carrying a gun brought in California? The way Patch figured, guns were okay, but knives were your true friends. They never jammed or let you down. The only maintenance required to keep a good carbon steel blade razor sharp was a little oil and a sharpening stone. Patch's choice of knives came down to this: Use a fat blade to go in for the kill, but use a slim one for pain, suffering, and intimidation. That's what was great about

Sharpfinger. Its uniquely shaped blade served both purposes.

On his way out the door, Patch caught his own reflection in the mirror. He wasn't sure he liked what he saw. He was aging. His face was weathered. Thanks to riding in the pack for so long, the hearing in his right ear was fading. He was in between homes, living in limbo. He was up for any challenge, but this time he feared it might take a bit more than diplomacy to reel things back into line up north. But conflict was what he lived for, and tension and conflict were boiling over again in mellow, laid-back California.

The exhaust from the Mean Machine sent swirls of gravel flying around the driveway. From its hiding place behind a mesquite shrub, the black stray cat watched Patch—the reluctant warrior—steer the bike and pull away.

At the first stoplight, Patch looked up at the sky. The dark clouds of an Arizona summer monsoon lurked on the horizon a half hour north. Flash floods would temporarily wash out parts of the Carefree Highway. Truth be told, he was leaving at precisely the right time. He looked down at the pavement and spoke without words to his motorcycle.

C'mon, brother. We got a shitload of miles to lay behind us. Then he let out a rebel yell.

"Let it roll!"

11

Nine Inch
Naylor

Patch pulled over at the last gas-up between Interstate 5 and Highway 580. He was just outside Livermore, a half hour east of Oakland. He dialed up his cell. *Damn, these gizmos are useful,* he thought as the call connected. A woman answered the phone after a dozen rings. Loud piano music played in the background.

"Jazz 88 studio line."

"Hello. Let me talk to the deejay."

"Ask who's calling?"

"Patch."

Patch waited for his call to transfer to the control booth. While on hold, he could hear the radio show.

"Patch. Brother, is that you? Can you hold?"

Without waiting for an answer, Ahab set the phone receiver down. He sidled up next to the microphone and delivered a break between music sets.

"You just heard pianist Michel Camilo on Jazz 88. A sad tune entitled 'Remembrance,' which I dedicate to five fallen friends of mine. Next up, on a much lighter note, a funky bop piece by trumpet player Lee Morgan. Morgan died in 1972 after he was shot by a pissed-off girlfriend, five days after Valentine's Day. Maybe he forgot to send her a card. Anyway, check out this song. 'Cornbread' on Jazz 88."

101 «

When the music kicked back in, Ahab grabbed the telephone. "Patch, you at home?"

"Ahab, listen . . ."

"Don't think about it, buddy. We'll get to the bottom of all this bullshit. We always do."

"I'm just outside of Oakland."

"Oakland? No shit?"

"That's right," said Patch. "I should be ridin' in within the next half hour or so."

"You got a place to bunk?" Ahab paused. "Shit. I'm on the air here for another four hours."

"No worries. I'll figure something out. Listen, nobody needs to know I'm around. I'll check back, but I don't know when. Okay?"

"Cool. Jesus, man, what can I say?"

Patch ignored Ahab's sentiment. "I gotta roll. Later."

THE GIANT DOTS ON A DIGITAL CLOCK LOCATED OFF THE freeway blinked 12:30 just as Patch pulled off Highway 580 and downshifted onto the Oakland MacArthur Boulevard exit. He had crossed so many state, county, and city lines over the past twelve hours, he felt like a fugitive.

Patch popped the clutch and decelerated to a more comfortable cruising speed. He navigated a sharp left turn from MacArthur onto High Street and headed toward an old warehouse district of the city. He felt fatigued and ve-locitized after hours of swift riding, darting in and out of fast lanes and avoiding hazardous tailgaters. He didn't have much farther to roll, so at the next stoplight, he idled his bike. He liked the rush of Oakland's natural air-conditioning, a mixture of light summer wind cooled down by coastal gusts off the bay. The gentle breeze evap-orated the sweat off his face.

Passing East Fourteenth Street, Patch waved at a wan-dering horde of pants-dragging teenage hip-hoppers who exchanged insults and gang finger signs with a coven of Latino hookers. Under the revitalizing night air of the city, he tooled the Oakland streets once again. But his deltoids ached with tension from the long ride. His ears rang from the constant bellow of the straight pipes all day and night. He felt his usually sharp attention slide into torpor.

He thought about phoning Eve, but a postmidnight call

might send the wrong message. Besides, he had an important stop to make.

WHEN HE FOUND THE CORRECT STREET AND ADDRESS,
Patch turned the bike widely, cut off the engine and head-
light, and rolled the Mean Machine back to the curb. He
dismounted and pulled a tiny flashlight out of his jacket
pocket. He approached the darkened compound situated on
the corner. When he walked into the vicinity of the gated
stronghold, a motion-detecting beam illuminated his footsteps.

"Shit," Patch muttered to himself. "It's like a maximum-
security lockup."

It wasn't a lockup, it was a home, a modern two-story
high-tech loft. Through the Cyclone fence he could see that
a couple of lights were on—signs of life inside. The fence
was topped with intertwining rolls of prison-style razor wire,
enclosing the parameter of the compound. At the main gate
Patch located a dimly lit row of push buttons. He pulled a
wrinkled slip of paper out of his pocket, which bore four
numbers scrawled in pencil.

He stuck the slim flashlight in his mouth and punched the
numbers on the keypad. He waited a few seconds, then
heard the whirring sound of a security camera aiming and ad-
justing its lens where he stood. An overmodulated, distorted
voice piped through the speaker mounted on the gate.

A loud buzz and static blared from the intercom. "State
your business," the voice commanded.

Patch cleared his throat and spat on the sidewalk. He said

nothing and turned his back toward the camera to show his colors.

There was a pause and a mechanical click. The gate automatically cracked open a few inches. Patch shoved it aside and stalked into the grounds of the complex. He unsnapped the strap of Sharpfinger, just in case. Then he ventured toward an enormous brushed metallic door.

Patch held his hand on the sheathed knife at his right hip as he heard footsteps approach from behind the door. Following the clatter of locks being released, the door opened wide, revealing a rich blue beam backlighting a silhouette of a thin, wiry young man dressed in leather pants and a tight body shirt.

"Tony, is that you?" asked Patch.

"Patch! Fuckin' hell. I can't believe you're standin' here."

Patch kept Sharpfinger in its sheath. A big grin shone on his face as he hugged Tony and gave him a few vigorous backslaps.

"Let me get my bike and push it in."

"Yeah, right. I'll leave the front gate open. You still have the same ride? The Mean Machine?"

"You got it, little pard." Patch paced off in the direction of his ride, parked out on the pitch-black street.

The young man shook his head. "Little pard," he echoed, snickering at the thought of being referred to as a little kid. He let the comment slide.

After moving his bike, Patch walked into the loft and gave the premises a careful inspection. He noticed a spiral staircase at both ends of the large rectangular structure. The ceilings must have been twenty feet high. He made a clicking sound with his tongue and listened to how live the room sounded. Tony's crib was massive. The rubber soles of his boots squeaked on the immaculate, shiny-finished walnut floor.

Atop each circular stairway on the second floor were sleeping quarters, beds mounted on walnut platforms matching the color of the floorboards below. It was a set of digs right out of *Architectural Digest*. Patch wasn't accustomed to such high-tech surroundings. The kitchen on the main floor had a long, knotty-pine butcher-block counter, a row of suspended long-handled pots and pans, and a jet-black industrial Viking range and oven. At the other side of the complex was a full-scale photography studio. Cameras, lenses, and flashing equipment were sprawled out across carpeted tabletops. Several quartz lighting trees on wheels surrounded the fashion set. Tony's custom darkroom was housed in a separate structure behind the loft.

"Damn, Tony. You've certainly done well for yourself. I'll tell ya, Big Jab would be proud."

105 **«**

Tony smiled warmly and only shrugged at the mention of his father, the 187 Crue member who blazed the seventies and eighties glory days with the Oakland Infidelz. He saw Patch's overnight bag on the floor and pointed at one of the empty beds upstairs.

"Throw your bag on that bed up there," Tony said. "You know you're welcome to stay as long as you want. I've been following all the shit that's been going down."

"Yeah, Tony. Looks like I gotta put my transfer on ice for a couple of weeks longer."

"Understood." Tony walked over to a small wall safe and quickly dialed a combination. He opened the door and pulled out a key ring that hung inside.

"Here you go. This is my last set, so guard them with your life," he said as he tossed the keys in Patch's direction. Patch snatched them and stuffed them into his pocket.

Tony was "Tony" to a select few, including Patch. Most of his friends called Tony Naylor "Nine Inch," after the band "Nine Inch Nails." The ladies called him Nine Inch for another reason.

Nine Inch was arty and edgy, a techie burnout with a taste for Goth chicks, photography, and graphic arts. The pierced and tattooed girls were as hard-boiled as they were young—purple-and-green bobbed haircuts on pallid, pasty white skin. Much to the delight of Ahab and his pals, Nine Inch brought the far-out, freaky-looking nineteen-year-olds he dated to a lot of the Delz' clubhouse parties.

Nine Inch loved his bikes to be as fast and free-spirited as his women. He rode a chromed-out Harley FXR by day. By night, he swung to the "extreme" and raced through the metro hunched over the latest model of some European racer. Patch couldn't visualize riding long distances on those things. They were torture racks on two wheels. The windscreen on those bikes was barely six inches high. Riders lay nearly on their bellies on such extreme machines. But they cornered sideways around speed courses and racetracks like no other motorcycle—low enough to the ground for a traditional Harley rider like Patch to risk scraping his bum knee on the track and stacking the damn thing.

Nine Inch had earned his nickname eight years earlier after hitting the legal drinking age. He had developed a keen eye for computer cybergraphics. But he dropped out of design college to build up his chops as a crack photographer.

Nine Inch assisted regularly on freelance commercial and magazine shoots. Then one day, during a NASCAR qualifying heat at Sears Point Raceway, his lens chronicled the death of a famous and beloved driver. When he was only nineteen years old, a major magazine published the full sequence of photographs. The images spread immediately across all the wire services and became legendary. Money and more assignments quickly followed.

Nine Inch immersed himself in still photography. He modernized his darkroom and freelanced aggressively. Ad agency honchos and art directors agreed: the kid had a natural, creative eye. Top agencies called in Nine Inch when they needed something ultrahip and outrageous on a tight deadline.

Nine Inch was more hyper than his late father. It was a wonder the two were related. Big Jab spoke gruffly and in simple bursts, slapped first, then asked questions. Nine Inch had the gift of gab times two. But he inherited Big Jab's love for cycles. Nine Inch grew up around 1%ers. Chromed choppers, foulmouthed biker chicks, and loud rock music were elements of his everyday life. Unlike his father, he didn't join the Infidelz. It had been a touchy point between father and son. Big Jab didn't sponsor him because he'd felt he lacked the toughness to ride with the crew.

107 «

Patch kicked his boots off and sprawled out on the oversize leather couch. Nine Inch, thrilled to have his undivided attention, stood over him and babbled enthusiastically.

"Patch, I know you got a lotta things on your mind, but we need to talk about something I've been working on."

As physically exhausted as Patch was, Little Pard was already wearing him a little thin. But as much as Nine Inch grated on his nerves, he was curious about the giant framed photo pieces that surrounded the loft compound.

"What kind of photography are you up to these days, Tony?"

"Mostly sex stuff. The photo ad agency gigs have died down a little over the past year or so, but I have more work than I need shooting straight erotic imagery. By *straight*, I mean 'hetero.' "

"Yeah, I figured."

"I'm doing a lot of shoots for Larry Flynt's people. *Cherie, Big Jugs, Barely Legal.* They fly the girls up here from L.A. My assistant picks them up at the Oakland airport, and we have 'em out on the last plane back to Burbank airport by ten. That is, unless they decide they want to stay and party. You know what I mean?"

"Foolin' around with the talent, eh? A bite off the same apple as the old man." Patch couldn't help bringing up Big Jab again.

Nine Inch ignored the reference. "I also work with a line of Japanese photo houses. They specialize in the real wacky Internet porn stuff. I do a little bit of that, too. I can go as far out as I want. But I do draw the line. No trannies, she-males, guys on guys, foot fetish, or weird stuff with objects. Know what I mean?"

Nine Inch burst out laughing at Patch's confused look.

"You lost me after she-males. What kind of objects? I must be *way* the hell out of touch."

"You are, dude," snorted Nine Inch. "Believe me, you are."

Patch looked down at his watch. It was just past two in the morning. "Look, Tony, we can talk all night, but . . ." He grunted as he rose up on his stocking feet, boots in hand. "I just put in over eight hundred miles on my bike. I am glad to see you and I appreciate you letting me crash here. As for my being here, let's keep it quiet."

"No problemo, Patch. Blankets and towels are next to the bed."

Patch laid his tired rack on the guest bed. It had a hard, solid mattress, but it was surprisingly comfortable after the long journey sitting upright on the rumbling Harley. The clean smell of the freshly laundered Egyptian cotton sheets was a far cry from the musty, lumpy mattress at his funky digs in the desert. It was like a luxury hotel. The closest he had come to that experience was the "St. Valentine's" suite he and Eve checked into at the Tangiers Hotel in Vegas when they'd decided, on a whim, to get hitched.

Patch had a temporary home base now established. Tomorrow he would start searching for clues. He didn't really know where to start. Trader's was probably a dead end. The trail was cold there. The casino was flooded with cops, security, and news media. No point stopping by there, either. Once again it came down to his usual method: hang out, play it cool, follow his nose, and just see what happens.

Lining Your Ducs
All in a Row

Patch awoke in the morning to the smell of freshly ground gourmet coffee. As he felt the sunlight hit his face, he jumped up stark naked. For a split second he had forgotten where he was. He had dreamed he was back in prison. Then he realized he was in Oakland. Lately, there were days when he'd have preferred prison.

One size fits all, he thought as he slipped on the white terrycloth robe Nine Inch had dutifully laid out for him. *How many babes have worn this robe?* Patch stroked the plush texture of the garment and felt a little silly putting it on. Eager for a cup of coffee, he navigated the spiral staircase down to the main floor. Nine Inch, sitting over at the leather couch, already had a mug waiting on the kitchen counter.

"I figured I'd let you sleep," said Nine Inch, his face buried in a stack of photo proof sheets that he examined with a Sharpie and magnifying viewer. "I'm ready to hang out. I don't have any shoots booked for a few days."

Nine Inch looked up from his work and saw Patch standing in the terrycloth robe with a cup of coffee in his hand. He burst out laughing. Patch sheepishly put down the mug and trudged back upstairs. He slipped on his black jeans and an old club T-shirt. He couldn't blame Nine Inch for laughing. Back downstairs, Nine Inch was puttering around the loft. His rubber-soled running shoes squeaked around the premises.

"Patch, c'mon down. I wanna show you something. Follow me."

Nine Inch kicked open a thick metal door that led outside to the paved back area of the compound. He motioned toward another small concrete structure, next to the one that was his darkroom. He fumbled through his key ring for the appropriate one and unlocked the dead bolt. They pushed the door open, revealing a row of immaculate, shiny yellow dirt bikes. But they weren't soulless scramblers or off-road beaters. They were "extreme"—Nine Inch's brand of cutting-edge chic. Each bike was uniformly painted bright yellow with a bloodred racing stripe across its high-

111 «

gloss front fender and gas tank. A closer inspection showed that the fleet of what first appeared to be rice burners wasn't built in the Land of the Rising Sun after all. They were Italian.

"Ducati Monster S4s," Nine Inch proclaimed as he waved his arms excitedly. "You gotta take one for a spin. These things are *thee* shit, dawg. They accelerate off the line to a hundred and fifty miles per hour. That's why they're called Monsters. I love 'em."

Nine Inch hopped on one of the S4s and made a roaring sound. An animated smile shone across his youthful face. His unkempt hair stood up in spikes.

It was Patch's turn to burst out laughing. Nine Inch looked like a child on Christmas morning. Patch had seen a few Ducati Monsters. He sat down on the seat of the bike next to Tony.

"Just the other day, on the way to Flagstaff, a swarm of rice rockets zoomed past me on Highway 17. I switched lanes to let the sons of bitches fly by. They were dressed in red-and-black racing leathers and had spotted my patch. Each guy gave me the clench-fisted salute as they revved past. The last rider, riding a candy-apple-red Suzuki Bandit 1200S, popped a three-quarter-mile wheelie. The motherfucker must have been pushing over a hundred when he did it.

"The guy was showing off. It made me feel ten years too old. Don't get me wrong. I dig the speed of these things. But there's nothing like the stability and power of a Road King, one of the remaining reasons I ride goddamned Harleys. And you know what the Infidelz say: 'Ride American or else.' "

Patch drummed his fingers on the Duc's five-gallon gas

tank. "Now be honest. Can you really picture Ahab riding one of these?"

Both men laughed. "Tony, what's the difference between these Ducs and the Jap bikes?"

"That's like asking what's the difference between samurai movies and spaghetti westerns?"

"Just answer the fucking question."

"The Ducs corner at high speeds better than the Hondas. What's the difference between your Road King and the Suzuki that guy rode? It's just the rumble you feel under your legs. In my opinion, Monsters are the extreme version of the Harley. The Ducati has a similar torque vibe. It has personality to go with its ridiculous speed off the line."

"Who rides these bikes? How come you have so many?"

Nine Inch looked down at his own reflection on the Duc's yellow and red mirror-finished gas tank. "They're not all mine. I wanna tell you about a new MC I just put together. We've been around for over five months. There are about twenty of us in the club."

113 **«**

Nine Inch jumped off the bike and picked up a leather jacket draped over a nearby chair. It also came from Italy; after all, he *was* riding Italian. Emblazoned on the back was a two-piece patch. One pictured a robed Japanese samurai holding a sword with a long, thin blade. The other read *Bushido Blades*.

"That's us," said Nine Inch excitedly as he waved the jacket like a flag. "We're the Bushido Blades. I got the name from a Sonny Chiba flick."

"The kung fu movie guy?" Patch asked. He wasn't a total square. The Infidelz used to go to the midnight movies during the 1970s when Sonny Chiba, Clint Eastwood, and

Bruce Lee headlined the marquee. *The Street Fighter. The Good, the Bad, and the Ugly. Enter the Dragon.* Club guys pumped up on speed, others tripping on tabs of Owsley windowpane, stood up from their seats and screamed blue murder as Ninja warriors mowed down their opponents and kicked one another in the nuts. It was art imitating *their* lives.

"Right-o. Sonny Chiba. The one and only," replied Nine Inch.

"But why ride Ducs? These aren't your full-time rides, are they?"

Nine Inch could see that Patch was getting warm in his analysis.

"No, Patch. We ride Harleys, all right. I traded up for my FXR. It wasn't easy to find. It's a pretty good bike, as far as cruising bikes go.

"You see, the Bushido Blades are really onto something, in terms of a business plan. International NAFTA-style commerce, if you get my drift."

"You guys use these bikes for smuggling?" guessed Patch. "I know the cops long ago gave up trying to chase these bad boys down."

"Check it out." Nine Inch put his coffee cup down and moved in closer, as if somebody across the room were listening in. "The guys in the Blades, ahem, myself included, are involved in a few interesting deals."

"Narco trade?"

"Not exactly. We don't wanna get involved with those ruthless South Americans, believe me. It's not worth getting my limbs chainsawed off."

"That's good," Patch observed.

"We ride these Monster babies down to Mexico. Well, not me as much as the other guys in the club. We have this deal where we supply all the top athletes and college phys-ed departments with legal 'juice' from Mexico."

"Steroids?"

"Exactly. There's a handful of Mexican drug houses that sell the stuff legally south of the border. They supply us to serve our 'clients' in the States. The guys and gals that buy the juice from us know exactly what they're in for."

Nine Inch rattled off a few names of athletes that even Patch knew. He wasn't impressed with overpaid athletes, no matter what world records they held.

"The colleges, the agents, the teams, managers, coaches, personal trainers, everybody, they all put the pressure on athletes to bulk up. It's a fact of life in the sports world."

"Sounds like you got quite a promising operation here, junior," Patch replied. "If the Infidelz tried monkeying with that stuff, the feds would shut us down. But, hey, if you can get away with it, why not? I'll say one thing, though. It's a cliché and you've heard it before. If you can't do the time, then don't do the crime."

"I know, but the bodybuilders, boxers, exhibition wrestlers, and big-shot athletes are gulping this stuff down like candy every day. Literally."

"Lately we've been using more bike-riding mules from Mexico to do the drop-offs," added Nine Inch.

"Yeah. Let some poor Mexican bastard take the fall instead of you. Hey, I won't judge you, like you never judged what Big Jab and I were up to. I just think the steroids thing is kinda weird. I know a few bodybuilder bike riders who use the stuff. I've never seen them shoot or ingest the shit. But

I do know something's odd when I'm working out nonstop and these guys I see every other day next to me are twice as bulked as I am."

"Give 'em my number," said Nine Inch. "We aim to please. Look, I guess the point of all this is that the Bushido Blades are players and we want to get real active in the NoCal bike world. I want you to help me explore the possibility of the Blades becoming a prospect MC for the Infidelz. That's my pitch. I'll leave it at that."

"Okay, Tony. I'll consider it and pass it on."

Nine Inch leaned in closer, face-to-face with Patch. His expression turned serious.

"Patch, if there's anything you need done while you're here, just say so. The Blades are Infidelz supporters through and through. We get things done. In fact, we'll be out in force tomorrow, riding the streets. You could join the pack. Then you'll see."

Patch was impressed by Nine Inch's enthusiasm. Support clubs were good to have, especially when a club needed extra muscle on a run or at an event. Patch considered them associates and friends. Although he wouldn't air club business to a nonmember like Nine Inch, he figured he might need help while he was in town. He could always use the eager services of a young supporter like Nine Inch and his Bushido Blades.

» CHAPTER «

13

Hot Pursuit

From three blocks away, Patch could see a long row of bikes parked in front of the Infidelz clubhouse on East Fourteenth. Thirty-three bikes, mostly late-model Harleys, sat in the dusky stillness. Business was good. The Infidelz had been prospering lately. Club membership was on the rise. In fact, all of the NoCal clubs in the area were healthy. That's what made a potential bike war such a drag.

As part of the MC peace alliance, Northern California had been split up in a unique arrangement unheard of in the bike-riding world, although pretty standard for mob guys and gangsters. The region was organized by enterprise and not geography. As opposed to carving the state into traditional turf areas, it was understood that the "majors," clubs like the Infidelz, 2Wheelers, and the Gun Runners, could pursue their own designated enterprises undisturbed, from Bakersfield to the Oregon border. It was hard for law enforcement to believe that a group of MCs could possibly be as organized as mob families. Usually, MCs fought vigorously among themselves for territory.

While it was considered surprising to the cops that the Infidelz, the top dogs, would permit such an arrangement, it was rumored among the local bike riders that the treaty was designed to curb escalating law enforcement crackdowns. The federally funded gang task forces were starting to hit hard. When Eagle and Lars, two Infidelz members, were busted on drug beefs, prosecutors considered charging them under federal Racketeer Influenced and Corrupt Organizations (RICO) statutes used to combat factions as diverse as gangbangers, mobsters, sometimes even right-wing religious groups. Being prosecuted by means of laws designed to deal with urban street gangs and Middle Eastern terrorists pissed off the bike clubs, who considered themselves a patriotic lot.

To keep track of each club's activities, you needed a scorecard. Individual members of the Infidelz dabbled in all kinds of schemes. For instance, there were sizable pot deals linked to the Delz and some Northern California pot farms sprinkled in and around Garberville, Mendocino, and Humboldt Counties. Branching out internationally, the club occasionally brought in modest hashish shipments from Katmandu and Calcutta through Seattle.

Sometimes the age of a club member influenced what he was up to. Older Infidelz who were not into dealing weed aligned themselves with East Bay labor unions, primarily as workers, bodyguards, and strike enforcers. At the other extreme, the youngest members were players in the Ecstasy drug trade, servicing local raves and happenings on and around the abandoned army-base buildings along the Alameda shipyards. If you were a hot deejay fixing to organize a rave for several thousand, you went through Infidelz members Skank and EX before even thinking about setting up shop. Even during the worst of times, economically and otherwise, the Infidelz remained on top of the game.

The other clubs were also industrious. The 2Wheelers were players in the sex trade, with a diverse set of operations that included strip clubs, massage parlors, escort services, and a couple of Nevada cathouses. Riders joked that if it got you hard, chances were the 2Wheelers had a hand on it. These were tricky businesses. To handle the talent and demand, you needed to be smart in order to stay on top. To help fuel the fire, the 2Wheelers peddled illicit Viagra. Members were able to buy off a few pharmacy managers from the large HMOs, which ensured a steady supply of stimuli to keep the clientele hard and horny.

Members of the Gun Runners stayed busy, too, but mostly on a darker and edgier side of the underground economy. The Gunners were deeply into the Southern California meth trade. Most clubs considered it too risky, especially the Delz and the Wheelers, because law enforcement over the years had come to expect a club's involvement in methamphetamine. All the great cookers of the eighties had been bike riders. Now it was a crowded field, occupied by immigrant groups like the Mexicans and Vietnamese. So the Gunners also dabbled in heroin. This pitted them against the Hispanic and black gangs in Los Angeles, so out of a need for self-preservation, they also took up gunrunning and automatic-weapons trading. The Gunners' meth, heroin, and gun trade moved north as they increased their number of charters.

As times were prosperous, Patch felt it was important to stop the infighting, violence, and murder before the cops did.

DONNING HIS BEANIE HELMET, PATCH REACHED THE CLUB-house gate on his motorcycle.

"Jesus Christ, Patch. You back in town?" It was two young prospects, Lester and Luke, at the Infidelz clubhouse gate. "It's like you never left."

"What's cooking, Lester? Why all the bikes? Havin' a party?"

"You might say. A little get-together."

Lester waved Patch into the Infidelz clubhouse driveway. The clubhouse had been modified into a brick fortress from its previous life as a nightclub years ago. The club had gotten a good deal on the building during the late seventies before

California real estate prices skyrocketed. It was located on the fringe of the barrio, and Mexican and black locals usually tiptoed past its daunting steel front doors. During parties, they flat-out crossed the street.

Patch stashed his bike behind the clubhouse and parked a few feet from the back door. He entered through the kitchen, then into the main meeting room just as things were breaking up.

"Patch!" one of his brothers called out. It was Ernie, a fellow twenty-year member. He was genuinely surprised to see Patch back so soon. Ahab must have kept quiet about his recent visit to Arizona and their phone conversation about the casino mess. Still, with all the funerals, pow-wows, and meetings, members from all over the country were coming and going. Oakland had once again become the hot spot.

The clubhouse was a rogues' gallery. The faces on the wall "at church" matched the row of bikes parked outside. Eight Ball and Brutus were there, two close buddies who rode an FXT and a Road Glide, respectively. Chick, an unkempt Italian from New York, rode the black-and-orange FXR3. 12-12 was a righteous member who got his name by always choosing to serve out his entire sentence rather than get out on parole. There was Streeter, Teardrop, Tats, Shank, Ripper, Stash, and of course Albert, a fearsome but fun-loving member. Sergio, whom Patch hadn't seen in several months, must have just gotten out of jail. Angelo was behind the bar, popping the caps off a row of long-neck Buds. Ahab, who had run the meeting, was still in a serious conversation with Grimes and a tough, aging 'Nam vet whom everyone called Full Metal. The three seemed tense, arguing about something and waving their arms. It was a wonder someone hadn't thrown a punch.

Patch sauntered up to the bar, where Angelo shepherded the flock of cold Buds. An Eminem CD played in the background.

"Tell me something good, Angelo."

"Man, what the hell are you doing here? How we gonna miss you, Patch, if you don't go away? Have a beer while I give you a squeeze."

Angelo stepped over from behind the bar and nearly knocked Patch over. Then the two men hugged. It was the Infidelz Vise Grip. Patch broke free first.

"I can tell you're stayin' strong, brother," Patch said to Angelo. "How you doin'?"

"I've been better, I've been worse. Been spending a little time in the gym, though."

Angelo flexed his right arm, showing off iron-solid biceps. "Fourteen and a half inches, brother. Measured them yesterday."

Just then a loud sequential burp of gunfire erupted from outside. "AK-47!" Full Metal screamed, recognizing the sound. He had his pistol out and cocked in a second. Then came the sound of breaking glass followed by the smell of smoke. A couple other guys hit the deck. Most followed Full Metal's lead and pulled out their pistols. Lester the prospect came running into the meeting room with Luke. Lester was bleeding. He'd been shot in the shoulder.

"Two crazy motherfuckers just stopped out front and shot Lester!" said Luke. "Before we could do anything, they shot the fuck out of our bikes, threw a Molotov cocktail, and took off. A couple of our bikes are on fire. They're headed west on East Fourteenth! One's wearing a red-and-blue patch. The other, I dunno."

Lester collapsed on the floor.

While the members tended to Lester, Patch darted out the back. He strapped on his helmet, hurdled the stairwell, and jumped on his bike. The gate was ajar. He looked down East Fourteenth. He glanced over at the line of bikes. Chick's Harley was blazing. Ahab and some of the others were dousing the burning bikes with fire extinguishers. Nobody besides Lester was hurt, but there were shattered headlights and mirrors, nicked tanks and fenders. Patch sped off, throttling and shifting furiously, in hot pursuit up East Fourteenth. As the Mean Machine sliced through the sparse traffic, he could see two Harleys turning onto High Street, heading inland up the Oakland Hills. One of the guys was indeed flying red-and-blue colors. *2Wheelers,* Patch deduced.

Pulling out his cell with one hand, he used his thumb to punch up Nine Inch. He heard a voice answer. Patch screamed into the phone as he bobbed and weaved with his throttle hand around two lanes of traffic.

"Tony!"

"Yeah, boss."

"Where are you?"

"Not far from your clubhouse. The Blades are with me. We're out riding. Why?"

"I'm chasing two riders up High Street into the hills. I'm betting they'll turn left on MacArthur, then onto Thirty-fifth, which leads up into the hills. Get your ass up here."

"Roger," said Nine Inch.

The two shooters did turn onto MacArthur as Patch

followed them for another couple of miles. He wondered if Nine Inch would make it. Then, appearing in his rearview mirror was the welcome sight of not one, but four canary-yellow-and-red-striped Ducati Monsters. They joined the chase wearing tinted full-faced helmets and leather racing outfits. *Damned if they don't resemble a swarm of bees.* As Patch veered up onto Thirty-fifth Avenue toward the Oakland Hills, two of the Blades effortlessly passed him in screaming pursuit. One was Nine Inch.

Goddamn, Patch thought as he kicked up his speed, *those sons of bitches really move.*

Nine hundred and sixteen cc's of Ducati power kicked in for the kill. Patch tried his best to keep up with the Ducs. What he lacked in speed, he made up for by knowing the lay of the land. He knew the streets like the back of his hand, having ridden them as a kid on minibikes and shitty little Yamahas. The shooters maintained a lead, and it looked like Patch's Mean Machine or the Ducati Monsters would have trouble catching up to them. The two shooters were headed uphill for the parklands, where the roads grew dark and winding. In that part of the Oakland Hills, paved city streets gave way to narrow country roads.

The roadways of the Oakland Hills were transformed into an enduro course. Patch and the Blades were in hot pursuit. As they narrowed the gap, the shooters' bikes raced deeper into the darkened parks region. The winding roads continued for another four or five miles. Patch got close enough to one rider to be certain he was wearing a 2Wheeler patch and riding a custom bike. His partner rode a superfast Sportster.

Preparing for a sharp right-hand swerve, Patch saw the

Sportster rider pull something, possibly a pistol, out of his jacket. Patch braced himself to dodge a bullet only to witness the Sportster guy shoot his 2Wheeler accomplice in the chest. The 2Wheeler bike went down, producing a fireworks display of sparks as it scraped sideways across the gravel before flipping over and crashing into a dirt embankment.

When the cycle came to rest, the 2Wheeler lay motionless. Roadkill. Nine Inch and his three Bushido Blades hit their brakes, skidded to a stop, jumped off their bikes, and ran back toward the fallen Wheeler. Patch, however, maintained his pursuit of the unmarked Sportster rider.

In a gasoline and adrenaline rush, Patch's Mean Machine surged ahead. He was dead even, side by side with the souped-up Sportster. Patch approached the rider on the right, his throttle side, in order to avoid being shot at. Inches away from the rider, he gave the Sportster a swift kick. The bike rider dropped his pistol and zigzagged in the road before expertly laying the bike down. Patch brought the Mean Machine to a stop. He leaped off his bike and ran toward the shooter, who had gotten up and was pulling off his helmet.

Patch tackled the rider, knocking him over, flailing and punching him on the dusty roadside. The two rolled around in the dirt, got back up, and exchanged blows. Patch needed to prevent the rider from reaching for the AK-47 slung over his shoulder and delivered a swift kick into the man's groin. The rider doubled over and groaned. Patch finished him with a Sharpfinger jab through the ribs. The man collapsed into a thick carpet of pine needles along the roadside.

Patch stood over his unmarked victim. He dragged the Sportster and the rider off the roadside. The man had long, straight dark hair and appeared to be in his midthirties.

Patch ripped his jacket and shirt open, looking for any sign of club tattoos, but found nothing. He rolled the body over. No wallet. He checked the Sportster's saddlebags. Nothing. The identity of the rider was a mystery.

Patch scratched his head. *Why would the guy on the Sportster shoot his partner?*

He ran down to where Nine Inch and the Blades were tending to the body of the 2Wheeler.

Miraculously there were no cops or park rangers patrolling the area. Nine Inch and his boys had gone to work on the downed 2Wheeler and his bike. They dragged the bike over to the ditch on the side of the road while one of the Blades kept watch. They carried the lifeless 2Wheeler farther off the side of the road, stashing him behind some high brush. Nine Inch produced a flashlight from his zippered jacket pocket and yanked the helmet off the corpse, inspecting the dead man. A bright beam lit an unfamiliar face.

"Anybody figure out who these guys are?" asked Patch.

"Nobody I recognize," Nine Inch replied.

Patch ripped off the 2Wheeler patch, folded it, and tucked it under his arm.

"We'll be needing this as evidence to show the club."

His next move was to call Ahab. The prez would dispose of the bikes and the bodies once Patch gave him the exact locations.

"Send a truck over here before the rangers show up and bust us all."

The fourth helmeted Blade, who was standing watch, wheeled the yellow Ducati over to Patch and Nine Inch. Tall and thin, the rider stopped the bike and pulled off a tinted full-faced helmet. The rider's face literally took Patch's breath away. He hadn't expected a beautiful, young Asian woman, who, in a low voice, asked the question on everybody's mind.

"Why are we chasing 2Wheelers through the back roads of the parklands?"

"After the casino shootings, I can't say I'm surprised," said Nine Inch. "Patch, say hello to one of the Blades, LiLac."

LiLac nodded. "Patch Kinkade. I've heard of you."

Patch was momentarily speechless. He discreetly nudged Nine Inch with his elbow, showing a perplexed look on his face.

"What and who the fuck is she?"

Nine Inch grinned back at him. "Not bad, eh? You likey?"

"Ah, yeah, but . . ."

The group waited twenty minutes until a large, blue late-model Chevy truck pulled up to the tangled wreck. They collected the 2Wheeler and his bike and covered him with a tarp. Farther up the road, the two burly club members jumped out and without conversation threw the other dead rider and the Sportster into the bed of the truck and tied down the tarp. They quickly drove off without a word. Neither Patch nor the Blades needed to know where they'd be stashing their cargo.

Patch walked over to LiLac's Ducati and grabbed the handlebars.

"One question. What would you have done if you had met up with one of those guys?" He smiled.

LiLac reached into her jacket and pulled out an oversize Browning semiautomatic pistol. She had no trouble wrapping her long fingers around the pistol grips and trigger.

"Probably would have fucked them up with this."

Patch's smile got bigger. Then he whipped out his phone. "Ahab."

"Patch, what the fuck?"

"No worries. I'm still up in the hills. The truck has come and gone."

"Whatta we got?"

"Strange. Two dead bike riders. One flying 2Wheeler colors, but get this: One rider shot and killed the other rider."

"No shit. Both dead? One guy shoots the other? I don't get it."

"Me neither. Had to take out the shooter. Too bad, but it was him or me."

"Two guys out? How'd you manage that?"

"With a little help from my friends. Anyway, I got something to show you."

"Well, steer clear of the clubhouse, bro. The place is swarming with cops. Got a place to lay low?"

"Yeah. I got just the place. We'll talk later."

BACK AT NINE INCH'S COMPOUND, PATCH, NINE INCH, AND LiLac talked over the night's events over a bottle of Jack Daniel's. The adrenaline of the chase was still flowing. So was the sour-mash whiskey. Eventually Nine Inch set his empty glass down and stood up.

"I'll leave you two to it. I've had enough for one day," he said. Then he stumbled upstairs toward his sleeping quarters on the opposite end of the loft.

Through the haze of the Jack, Patch leaned back on Nine

Inch's leather sofa, admiring the profile of LiLac's delicate face. She sat on the floor at the wooden coffee table, arms drunkenly propping herself up.

It was LiLac who broke the ice.

"How long have you and Nine Inch been friends?"

"You mean Tony? I knew his father. We rode together. Probably while you were pedaling your tricycle."

"I never owned a tricycle."

LiLac shrugged. Her complexion was a pale, neutral tan. The shoulder length of her hair complemented a small, turned-up nose. She curled strands of her black hair, which was streaked with tendrils of blond and scarlet, around her finger. Her face was flat but beautiful. Lilac's English was flawless, though she pronounced certain words oddly as her thin lips took on an oval shape when she talked.

Patch took another long swig off the bottle. "Never owned a trike? What kind of childhood did you have, and what kind of a name is LiLac?"

129 **«**

"I was a boat person. My real name is Hoa Kieu Dinh. *Hoa* means 'flower.' "

You are, indeed, a flower. "Where do you come from?"

"Around," she continued. "It's kind of a long story."

A pained expression crossed LiLac's face. Then she caught her sadness and smiled weakly. Clearly the past wasn't a fun place for her to go.

"We've got time," Patch insisted.

LiLac frowned, but proceeded.

"My father served as a lieutenant in the South Vietnamese Army. He was proud that he fought alongside the Americans. He loved them."

"Well, hurray for the red, white, and blue," Patch said.

LiLac hooked a few errant strands of hair behind her ear. She moved drunkenly next to Patch on the sofa.

"After the Americans left in seventy-three, my dad found himself in a Viet Cong 'reeducation camp.' My mom raised us, me and my sisters. After a year, my father got out. We escaped to Malaysia, where we lived in a refugee camp, then on the streets."

"How'd you get to the States?"

"A small Baptist church outside of Hayward sponsored our family so we could come to this country."

"When was that?"

"In 1980. I was four."

"Ouch. So how'd a little girl from 'Nam end up on a Harley?"

"Maybe it was you. I got interested in bikes when I was twelve. I used to watch the Infidelz on their bikes, racing in the streets."

"Where was this?"

"Hayward. The sound of motorcycles made quite an impression on me back then. I remember how everyone . . . the shopkeepers and the people in town were frightened of you guys. But I was never scared. Even as a little girl. You guys were fast and cool. Maybe one of those guys was you?"

Patch grinned at the possibility, but was having trouble picturing the beautiful young woman sitting next to him as a little girl watching his crew partying.

"Anyway," LiLac continued, "it didn't take long before I fell in love with America. *Top Gun*, KFC, Cheap Trick."

"You seem so . . . American."

"I was in between. Sometimes the Americans called me 'gook' or 'chink.' And the Vietnamese didn't like me because

I spoke English. I dated a few Vietnamese gang members, but I guess I preferred the Yankee motorcycle riders from when I was a little girl. They reminded me of the cowboys and outlaws I saw on TV."

"How'd you learn to ride?" Patch asked.

"My first bike was a little Italian Vespa when I was sixteen, which reminded me too much of the Vietnam I vaguely remembered as a girl. That's why I couldn't wait to wrap my legs around something bigger."

LiLac moved in closer to Patch.

"I started riding seriously after I bought my first Harley, a used one, when I turned eighteen. A boyfriend from school taught me to ride. It came easy to me."

Yes, Patch thought, *a girl with a story and a natural feel for riding.*

"What about you?" LiLac moved in even closer toward him on the sofa, brushing his hair back.

"Never mind about me."

"That's hardly fair. I showed you mine, now you show me yours. First, show me your hands."

LiLac caressed Patch's hands and squeezed them, then studied his palms.

"Uh-oh," she said, frowning. "You're not going to be around much longer." Her soft fingertips traced the lines on his callused right palm.

"Let's start with . . ." LiLac continued, "your family. Tell me about *your* family."

"My family? Shit. Not much to tell. I come from a long line of unsung heroes, doers as opposed to talkers, I guess."

"Your father?"

"My father was in the service, a flier in the Korean War.

Then he reenlisted. The CIA used to fly high-altitude U-2 spy planes over the Soviet Union during the Cold War in the 1950s. This was before they had satellites up in space. A bunch of guys flew over and took pictures, many more than the government admits.

"He got shot down over Russia or someplace. My mother got a lousy pension. That's it. We never found out what exactly happened. He just went missing. Years later, a friend of mine who rode for a Vietnam Vets club helped me with stuff like Freedom of Information requests and declassified Pentagon documents. It took years just to get the military to admit my father even existed. To me, he's always been a ghost."

"Did you even know your father?"

Patch laughed. "Know him? Hell, I was only a year old when he went missing, the youngest of three kids he left behind. A brother, a sister, and me. I was probably conceived just before he transferred to a base in Norway for his last tour of duty.

"We Kinkades are a wild bunch; let's leave it at that. My father, John Michael Kinkade, was a born soldier, a real cowboy. My mother always said I took after him, had the same kind of restlessness. I'm not exactly sure if that was a compliment."

"And your mother?"

Patch knocked back another hit of Jack. It was easier for him to talk about his father.

"She died back in the eighties, before I went into prison."

"Prison?"

"Yeah, well, that's another story for another night. Tell you what, let's just stick to the happy family, okay?"

Patch had put up a barrier, the kind that used to drive

Eve crazy. LiLac took it in stride and dropped the subject of prison. She studied the tattoos on his arms.

"A brother and sister?"

"Yeah. A brother and a sister, but they scattered. I bumped into my brother Rip in jail in Durango back in ninety-one. We were both 'drunk and disorderly.' And my sister? Your guess is as good as mine. She gave up on me a while back.

"Otherwise, my family is the club. Has been since the late seventies."

Patch paused a minute. He stroked LiLac's soft dark hair. She looked down at the half-empty bottle of Jack Daniel's.

"I hope I haven't seemed too nosy."

"Naw. That's the most I've told anybody about myself in a while. You're the first who's asked in a long time."

Patch reached around inside LiLac's leather jacket and pulled her toward him. He had to get a taste of this. She offered no resistance, so he pressed his lips onto hers. Then he put his hands on her smooth, black-leathered shoulders. The two kissed until she pulled her face away.

"So, lemme get this straight. You like to ride," Patch said.

"Every chance I get. I love the speed, the thrill. I love being on top of anything that's dangerous and out of control."

"Would you consider me dangerous and out of control?"

"You'll do," LiLac said.

133 «

WHEN PATCH AWOKE ON THE COUCH THE NEXT MORNING, he wore nothing but a scratchy wool blanket. His shirt and pants were within arm's reach on the wooden floor. Knives, keys, a phone, cash, and loose change were strewn carelessly across the table and floor. The bottle of Jack was empty and on its side. It took him another few seconds before he realized what else was missing.

LiLac.

14

Countdown
to Revenge

Two surveillance monitors over the Infidelz
clubhouse bar recorded the afternoon activity outside. The camera angles changed in
sequence every few seconds on the screens.
Members stationed outside and around the
clubhouse communicated with one another
via walkie-talkies. The guards, bearded and
wearing dark glasses, stared aloof past

the media camera crews and police surveillance personnel set up across the street, on roofs and on lookout points aloft.

"No comment."

"Move on."

"No fucking comment."

"Move on."

The Infidelz waved the press and other traffic ahead. Oakland PD squad cars, Alameda County sheriff mobiles, highway patrol, unmarked state police cruisers, and even park ranger vehicles motored past the Infidelz clubhouse.

The clubhouse meeting room was filled with members and officers from Oakland and the surrounding Northern California chapters, including Vallejo, Sacto, Napa, Sonoma, Richmond, and Monterey. Even San Francisco showed up with a full contingent. There were about seventy-five stocky bike riders crammed inside the wood-paneled room, all wearing their orange-and-black colors. On the walls were wooden plaques commemorating the twenty-year anniversaries of several members. Next to each was a corresponding police mug shot.

Members were there to learn the latest news and report back to their chapters on what action would be taken in response to what had gone down over the past few volatile days.

The main discussion points on the agenda centered on three key events: (1) the casino shootings of the 2Wheelers at Santa Paula; (2) Marco's death at Trader's; (3) the shooting and firebombing in front of the Delz' Oakland clubhouse.

Just before the meeting, Eight Ball and Brutus finished

their smokes outside the clubhouse door and joked with a couple of burly prospects.

"How you guys doin'?" asked Eight Ball, with cigarette smoke drawing out of his nose. "Smilin' pretty for the feds' cameras?"

One of the prospects laughed. "I saw both you guys on the eleven o'clock news the other night. It's Ahab. He's the one who made us get here so early. Somethin' about doublin' up on security. It's all these news guys and cops."

"Can't be too careful," said Brutus as he flicked his cigar ash into the curb and pointed across the street. "Jesus, look at all those TV guys over there with their Grecian Formula and hairspray."

"Let's go," said Eight Ball. "Prez wants to start on time. This meeting is gonna be downright Arab."

"Arab?" Brutus took the bait.

"Fucking in tents." Eight Ball laughed.

Brutus whacked Eight Ball across the back of his head with a gloved hand as the two headed inside. Eight Ball, who tipped the scales at 280 pounds, grabbed a can of diet cola from the fridge next to a wooden rack full of ax handles by the front door.

Inside the main hall, Ahab wielded his oversize gavel and pounded it authoritatively. "All right, you guys, sit your asses down. This meeting's officially come to order."

Patch leaned against the back wall. There were lots of "standees" at meetings like these. Guys were either too pissed off or hopped up over the current situation to remain seated and calm.

Uncertainty loomed large throughout the meeting. Too many questions and not enough answers. Who instigated the shootings at the clubhouse? What plans were being made to retaliate and against whom? What was the legal and bail situation of Infidelz members arrested after the casino shootings? What about the five dead members? And lastly, how did these incidents affect business and the cobbled-together peace accords?

Ahab read a short, prepared statement from a torn scrap of yellow notepaper he held in his four-and-a-half-fingered hand. He appealed for unity and camaraderie. Then he threw the meeting points open for discussion.

"I wanted to start this meeting on a note of solidarity. Everybody in this room wears the same patch on his back. Now the chair recognizes Wrangler."

Wrangler stood up and addressed the group.

"I've been an Oakland club member for almost twenty years," he said. "That's long enough for me to remember a few of the bloody wars we've had in this town. I'm talkin' about other clubs trying to take us down. It wasn't always safe out there. Sometimes you thought twice about bein' on your own, ridin' the streets flying colors or even sitting at the Doggie Diner with your back to the front door.

"The 2Wheelers fucked with us at Santa Paula. They shot up our clubhouse, too. It's simple: Let's go kill the guilty motherfuckers who whacked our guys and blasted our club-house. Let's get this thing over with right now."

Ahab then recognized Frisco Paul, a respected member of the San Francisco Infidelz club.

"Have we considered any official sit-down with Chino and the Wheelers?"

"Actually," Ahab replied, "we did get an offer from the president of the Gunner Runners, Lock N Load, to serve as a mediator in case we wanted to discuss keeping the peace. He could offer us neutral ground, so neither side would have to walk into the other's territory."

"Sounds like a good offer to me," Frisco Paul said.

Wrangler's face turned crimson. He stood up and pointed his finger at Paul and yelled.

"I can't fuckin' believe what I'm hearing! How long have you been a member of our club?"

"You know the answer to that. I just turned five years."

"Five years of peace and prosperity," spat Wrangler, "all courtesy of guys who have ridden with this club through thick and thin. All you guys in the room who have ridden with us for over ten years, put your hands up in the air."

Hands shot up in the room from more than half of the members in attendance.

"Okay," Wrangler continued. "Now, how many of you veterans with your hands up think we should move on these cocksuckin' 2Wheelers right now?"

Only a few hands went down.

"I rest my case," said Wrangler. "How decisively we crush these assholes reflects our standing in this town, this state, and the rest of the country."

A new officer from Sonoma named Mitch took the floor next.

"I wanna speak for the newer and younger members in this room. I'm not a ten-year rider with this club 'cause my charter is only a year old. But you older members better think twice before you buffalo us. If we're gonna commit to killing 2Wheelers, we sure as hell better have our intelligence together. I wanna know what we're getting into in terms of manpower."

A bunch of newer members grunted and nodded in agreement.

"Manpower, my ass," screamed Red, another Oakland veteran. "It wasn't your fucking clubhouse that got shot up. I say we act fast. Mitch, you pussy. Don't be coming off like such a yuppie punk."

Mitch stood up and squared off against old Red. "Who you callin' 'yuppie punk,' old man? I oughta . . ."

"You callin' me out, farm boy?" Red sneered. "Then let's get it on. I'll take you outside and kick your fuckin' country ass right in front of all those TV cameras."

Ahab stepped in between the two angry members. "Fuck you, Red. Didn't you hear my opening statement? Unity? Fuckin' unity!"

"You're both right," insisted Patch. Everyone turned to look at the former president. "We need to act fast *and* know what we're getting into. Patton said it best: 'I'd rather have a good plan now than a perfect plan in an hour.'

"If we don't even the score quickly, the people who fear and respect us may now doubt the club. Cops and politicians, both in and out of our corner, may question our guts."

Ahab broke in. "I should reiterate that the Gun Runners have come forward to mediate a sit-down between us and the Wheelers."

A round of boos filled the room.

"Hey, don't jump on me. I'm just giving you guys the latest."

The difference of opinion was what Patch loved and also hated about the Infidelz. So long as you had the balls and brawn to defend your point of view, you were free to think and express whatever the hell you wanted. Sometimes fist-fights broke out between conflicting members. To Patch, fighting during meetings was a good thing. It was the best way—the only way—real men settled their impassioned differences.

Patch thought a good fistfight kept everybody honest and aboveboard. If there were bad feelings, they surfaced immediately, no screwing around. And no grudges. The fine for fistfighting was a measly five bucks, the same as it had been since the club was formed back in 1976. A fiver was hardly a deterrent to throwing a few punches, and the guys liked it that way.

Red put his fists down and patted Mitch solidly on the back. "I'm just bein' straight up with you. We gotta resolve these issues fast. Let's get 'em out in the open right now. I think we gotta hit 'em hard and fast."

Angelo used his position as sergeant-at-arms to take the floor and deliver his view. But he was cranked up on pills, mad as a hornet, and almost incoherent.

"Fuck these guys," he shouted as he ground his fist into the palm of his hand. "Let's take them on. One at a time, or the whole fuckin' lot of 'em. Shit, man. Look at the muscle we got just in this room."

Angelo stopped in midthought and appeared dazed.

"Where was I? Oh yeah. Shit, man. It was the 2Wheelers who shot up our clubhouse and torched our bikes. That's crossing the line. Shit, man. During the 1988 wars, hell, nobody shot a gun outside a guy's clubhouse. And, uh, that's where we draw the line. I don't need no more convincing that the 2Wheelers need paybackin' because so many of their guys got, uh, fucked up at, uh, Santa Anita, uh, I mean, uh, Santa Paula, you know, that fuckin' casino. Shit, man."

Patch had rarely seen Angelo in such a blathering, drugged-out state, stuttering as he spoke. Most of the rage, he suspected, was chemically induced.

Eagle from Sweden stood up next. He reminded the room that in Scandinavia, MCs used tank guns and rocket launchers to make a statement. Although his point of view was respected, guys like Full Metal questioned the plan's practicality.

"Like, where we gonna score rocket launchers, Eagle? Import the fuckers from the Swedish clubs? Get serious. Besides, you and I are the only members here who know how to fuckin' shoot one of them babies."

Angelo spoke up again.

"I'm talkin' about bombs, man. We can build bombs. Yeah. I say we bomb all them motherfuckers. Remember that cop from the San Jose PD who fucked with us? After his front porch got bombed—*boom!*—we never heard peep one from him again. He cut and ran like some chickenshit."

Then his cell phone rang. A singsong musical line from Metallica's "Enter Sandman" tweeted from the device and interrupted his diatribe about bombs and instant payback.

Angelo glanced down at his phone's display. Suddenly his fire and brimstone was doused. He seemed much more interested in answering a damned phone call than he was in blowing the 2Wheelers to kingdom come. Angelo mumbled an inaudible apology, then took the call, walking out of the meeting room and into the kitchen. The cell phone looked tiny tucked inside his large mitt. Patch found Angelo's behavior strange. He checked his watch: 2:34 P.M.

The meeting's discussion boiled over. Ahab rolled his eyes, sitting in the corner trying to restore order with his giant mallet. But members and officers needed to say their piece.

Patch was part of the "act fast" group, but introducing full-scale bombings into the conflict was hardball stuff. He hoped there wasn't a live-wire bug planted anywhere or, worse, *on anyone*. All this ranting about artillery and bombing campaigns would get them hauled away and tried as terrorists, considering the government's aggressive stance on "homeland security" and their unrestrained enthusiasm for rounding up enemies of the state.

After a few minutes, Angelo reentered the room. He noticed Patch still holding up the back wall and stood next to him. The agenda shifted to Marco's death and how the investigation was proceeding.

Patch leaned over and whispered, "Angelo. You really got the room going."

"Yeah, well, those fucking bastards," he whispered, "I meant each and every one of my words. And I'm gonna do more than just talk about it."

"I hear ya."

The room grew heated again when two Richmond members, Pete and Sergio, disagreed over the implications of Marco's death.

"Marco shoulda had enough sense not to ride to Trader's on his own," said Richmond Pete.

"What the fuck are you sayin'?" replied Sergio. "That he deserved to get popped?"

"Use your fuckin' head," said Pete. "That's not what I said at all. The whole point of hangin' out is to circulate with the other members. That way it's safer, too. Marco was careless—"

"Careless?" Sergio responded. "What? You never walked into a joint on your own for a quick beer? I know what you're getting at. You're disgracing the memory of Marco. That's disrespect."

"Stop talking like an asshole," said Pete.

"Who's the asshole?" screamed Sergio. "You're talking shit like that about Marco from Oakland, who's fucking dead."

Pete reached over and smacked Sergio across the mouth. Members jumped out of their seats, anticipating a rumble. Sergio rallied and kicked Pete in the stomach, knocking him face first into a bunch of empty chairs. Pete jumped back up and tackled Sergio. The two got twisted into mutual head-locks like human pretzels. The crowd cheered the combatants and let them get on with it. As long as it was just bare fists, no knives or clubs or any rings on their fingers, fist-fights were okay.

"We gotta figure out a plan with this Marco thing," Patch said to Angelo. "Look at this. Weren't these two guys friends in prison together? Now they're takin' swings at each other. The troops are getting restless.

"Say, Angelo," he added as he pointed to the scuffle, "as sergeant-at-arms, aren't you supposed to be breaking up these things?"

"Guess so," drawled Angelo, "but I ain't gonna rush it. A little rumblin' keeps guys mean." Laughing, he shuffled toward the front of the room, where more reckless punches were being exchanged by Pete and Sergio, now both on the floor.

As Angelo passed him, Patch nudged him and swiped the cell phone from his leather jacket pocket. It took him back to his days as a pickpocket in prison when stuff was lifted from under the eyes of COs—correctional officers—and surreptitiously passed around the yard. While Angelo separated Pete and Sergio and collected the fines, Patch turned the cell phone off and tucked it into his front pocket.

The meeting went on for another forty minutes, then emptied out into the front of the clubhouse. There followed a chorus of Harley engines starting up. Considering the serious nature of the agenda, the meeting had ended abruptly. Despite all the discussion, no concrete decision had been voted on. Each rep would go back to his respective chapter while the Oakland chapter planned a course of action in the coming days. *Then* action would be taken. So much for being swift and decisive.

Outside, as Patch started up his Mean Machine, he saw Angelo leave the clubhouse, frantically checking his pockets. A puzzled look crossed his face. As he watched Angelo walk back into the clubhouse to hunt down his missing cellular, he gunned his engine, slipped it in gear, turned his bike eastward, and headed back toward Nine Inch's compound.

145 «

On the ride back, Patch wondered to himself why he had nicked Angelo's cell phone. He didn't really know the answer. He'd merely followed that little voice in his head that prompted him to "just do it." It was an impulse that he'd learned to obey, a voice that, so far, had yet to steer him wrong.

IT WAS AN EARLY NIGHT FOR NINE INCH, TOO. HE WAS ALready at home in the compound when Patch push-buttoned himself inside and unlocked the titanium dead bolts to enter the loft. He still couldn't get over this place. It had security like the state pen. Nine Inch sat at the butcher-block table in the kitchen wolfing down a designer TV dinner of Oriental vegetables and drinking a huge goblet of red wine. Patch walked over and turned down the stabbing volume of thrash metal blaring on the sound system. Catching Nine Inch's attention, he held up the silver cell phone he'd purloined at the meeting.

"Let me ask you something. If you pushed the right buttons, could you find out who called in and out on this thing?"

"Sure. With caller ID you can see a log of the last dozen or so phone calls that came in and went out—names, too, if they are programmed into the phone. Depends if the phone has a security lock, though. Why?"

"Okay, do that on this."

Patch tossed him the cell phone. Nine Inch looked down at the keypad and studied the buttons. It was a cheap model—Nine Inch snorted—one of those Sprint PCS twenty-dollar-rebate jobs from RadioShack. But it had Internet access and voice command, too. After a few beeps and squawks, he easily had the information in hand.

"Gimme that pad and pen." Nine Inch scribbled down a list of the most recent phone numbers. "Patch, I can probably figure out how to hook this thing up to my computer and make you a printout if you want."

"Maybe later. But for now, find me a call that came in today around two-thirty."

Nine Inch booped and beeped the phone, scrolling a series of numbers up and down the tiny screen until he found the correct time. There it was: 2:34.

The readout showed: *2:34pm 510-555-9178.*

"It just lists a phone number, no name. Want me to call it?"

"Yeah, go ahead."

Nine Inch pushed just one button and the number was instantly dialed and connected. He switched the cell to speakerphone so both of them could hear whoever answered the call.

After four rings, the call slipped into a voice-mail system. The recorded voice was a rushed monotone, its greeting delivered in a single run-on sentence.

"You've-reached-John-W.-McIntosh-East-Bay-outpost-leave-a-message. *BEEEEEP.*" Nine Inch hung up without leaving a message.

"Sounds harmless enough to me," Nine Inch said, handing the device back to Patch. "Whose phone is this?"

"Never mind" was Patch's curt reply.

Only a few seconds later, the cell phone rang in Patch's hand, which startled both men. It was the same Metallica ring that had interrupted the clubhouse meeting. Patch hit the answer button on speaker and gave Nine Inch the signal for silence.

"Hello?" There was a long pause.

"Hello?" screamed a voice coming over the phone. "Hey, you son of a bitch! Whoever the fuck this is, you got a stolen phone. I'm gonna find your ass and—"

The fury in Angelo's voice made Patch cut the call off. Nine Inch looked over at him with a quizzical face.

"That was Angelo. I could tell by the Texas drawl. What's up with him?"

Patch scratched his head. "I can understand why Angelo

was so pissed about getting his phone ripped off. But who the hell is this John McIntosh guy? And what's this 'East Bay outpost' shit?"

"Sounds like Angelo is certainly up to something. But hell, we're all into our own little scams."

"Scams are one thing, but I have a feeling this is something different." Patch looked over at Nine Inch again and shook his head. "Maybe a little investigation is in order here."

15

Along Comes Mary

Even with a war brewing, life went on for Angelo. He had a family unit—himself and Hollister—to maintain. He had worries. An FBI agent on his back. No job. No old lady. The club was on the verge of a fierce war. He was buried beneath a mountain of bills. When he felt close to rock bottom, he did what lots of red-blooded American men do. He went fishing.

Angelo steered his motorcycle off the main road and parked in the rocky lot next to the Outrigger, an old-time bike-rider bar along the water in the tiny fishing town of Crocket, thirty miles east of Oakland. Lots of his riding pals were probably already bellied up to the bar, blind drunk in the afternoon. The Outrigger sat right along the straits that emptied into the San Francisco Bay, and had a panoramic view of the giant Richmond San Rafael Bridge in the distance. The spot where he fished was a short walk from the bar.

Many an afternoon Angelo spent at Point Molate fishing for striped bass, alone with his cheap ten-foot rod and reel, his tackle box, and the grate from a barbecue grill. He rarely caught anything except an appetite and a thirst. Once he got hungry, he'd dig a small pit, gather a few sticks and build a fire, add charcoal briquettes, put the grate on top and roast sausages, and wash them down with a couple six-packs of Pabst Blue Ribbon. Heaven on earth, an afternoon on Point Molate was the perfect time and place for Angelo to contemplate his proper place in the universe.

Angelo cast his line with a six-ounce sinker and a heavy chunk of bait about fifty yards out and sat stoically facing the water. The current was strong and the water rougher; he could see whitecaps. The water was unusually cold ever since Fish and Game started feeding the strait with freshwater overflow from the northern delta region. That meant the fish were probably not biting. A man walked by with his young son. It was probably his weekly visitation day. Noticing Angelo's patch, the man turned his head the other way. The boy, however, managed a slight smile, so Angelo gave him a nod.

Between his ninth and tenth cast, Angelo built a fire, broke out the sausages and buns, and popped open his fourth beer. Then he had an epiphany. There was a way out of all this guilt and shame. Another way of looking at things. A flip side to his fucked-up situation.

Angelo had made his deal with J.W. and the FBI that night he was handcuffed to the interrogation chair. He didn't want to go back to prison or stand trial, so he promised he would implicate the club and its members as a criminal enterprise by instigating drug and weapons buys. This would allow J.W. to carry on his vendetta with the bike clubs.

J.W. had let him walk. Now it was time for Angelo to dance, to fulfill his part of the bargain. He would have to arrange the specifics of two deals, guns and drugs, setting the location and recruiting the characters involved. J.W. would fund the operation, and then have his agents swoop in on each site to make their arrests whenever appropriate.

151 **«**

In Angelo's mind, he wasn't selling out as much as he was cashing in, resetting his personal priorities. *From now on, I look out for my son and me. What has the club brought me lately? Poverty and jail time. Turning doesn't have to mean loyalty to the FBI, either. Fuck it,* Angelo decided, *play them both, the club and the feds, for all they're worth. Against each other.*

Using the government's money, he would be free to wheel and deal, operating under a protective cloud, funded by the U.S. taxpayers. He and the government were now partners. Thanks to J.W., the government would provide the money for Angelo to make money, stay out of prison, then simply disappear.

That was the positive aspect of turning over that Angelo hadn't originally realized. No wonder members ratted out. Reel in a few club guys for J.W., then, when the time came, he and Hollister would enter Wit Sec, Witness Protection, and disappear. The U.S. marshals were already setting that up. The future could be a helluva lot worse.

Angelo felt a tug on his fishing line. He saw that welcome splash in the distance. Then his reel started to whirl and click. He jumped to his feet and reeled in a twenty-inch striper, a " 'tweener" in size, but man, she was a beauty, and damned if he would throw it back. He'd take the sucker home to Hollister and panfry it. Tonight was day one of their new life.

» 152   **I**T DIDN'T TAKE MUCH CAJOLING ON ANGELO'S PART TO GET club members, first Eight Ball, then 12-12, involved in securing a substantial quantity of pot to buy and sell. His plan was to supposedly set up a network, a small army of members to move the merchandise around town on two wheels. Although the club was doing well, some of the members were in the same financial straits as Angelo was. Dismal. Angelo's scheme guaranteed a generous payday all around, tax-free. Angelo promised months' worth of wages for a few days of work, a chance to mule the first fifty pounds of processed Big Bud Sativa to the Bay Area for sale. There was money to be made selling the stuff on the streets. No problem there. In these times of economic stress, pot sales were brisk. "Customers" would include undercover FBI agents.

The whole thing had to be juicy enough for J.W., too. The

bastard was really turning on the heat. J.W. had phoned Angelo at home a couple of times the day before, checking up on his progress. He had news, having squared away the paperwork for the Witness Protection deal with the U.S. marshals. Either J.W. was testing the waters to make sure that Angelo wasn't backing out, or else he was tightening the leash. *Or was it a noose?*

To set the wheels in motion, Angelo needed to flush an old stoner buddy named Merle out of his Humboldt County digs. Merle was a longtime acquaintance of the Infidelz and had become a valuable pot supplier. Angelo's plan had to be sexy enough to get a lot of people on board. Eight Ball and 12-12 were greedy for the dough; they would enlist more members once things got rolling. J.W. needed evidence to get the RICO ball rolling; Merle thrived on moving fresh merchandise on a regular basis. Government dough would make it all go.

Following J.W.'s instructions, Angelo had become quite organized. He recorded and logged every piece of correspondence. He jotted down meticulous notes in a small spiral pad after each meeting and phone call, then transferred all the names, dates, meeting places, and small details into a secret file on the home computer Hollister used for his schoolwork.

"Let's meet at Bradley's in Jack London Square," he had told Merle earlier in the week. "It'll be good to see you. It's been a coon's age."

Bradley's was the kind of joint where Merle would feel comfortable meeting, nothing fancy. It was busy that afternoon, with tables spread far apart and enough tourist action and crowd noise to obscure any incriminating conversation.

"You guys grab a table. I'll go order up the beer," Angelo told Eight Ball and 12-12.

Angelo spotted Merle's 2002 Dodge Ram through the pub's window, circling the block. Merle never changed. He was a successful and braggadocious pot farmer from the north, and here he was, too damned nervous to park in a pay garage. The surveillance cameras worried him. When Merle walked into the restaurant, he removed his cap. Angelo rose from his chair at the bar to meet him.

At first Angelo barely recognized him. Merle was now clean-shaven, with a military buzz cut. He wore thick glasses and seemed wrapped in a perpetual marijuana haze. To get his attention, 12-12 waved his giant tattooed arms from the table in the far corner.

"Jesus Christ," Angelo muttered to himself as he ambled toward Merle, "nothing low-key about this meeting."

» 154

Merle and Angelo hugged, and then they headed to the table. "Dude. What happened to the beard? And you chopped off your hair!"

Merle smiled blankly. He was reverent about his cash crop. He called it Mary, his greatest and only love. His life was measured in time before and after he "met Mary." He was dressed in hemp cloth from the cap on his head to the shoes on his feet. He might look like a rube, but Merle was no country hick. He'd grown up on the East Bay boulevards of San Leandro, a hang-around with the Delz. Chucking his day job as a welding foreman, he moved north to Humboldt County for the scenery and tranquillity. What he found was anything but. He grew interested in raising hemp, but new-comers to the Northern California pot counties like Humboldt and Trinity were often mistrusted as potential

competition or undercover federales. Angelo unclipped a
beeper off his belt and set it on the table.

"Winning those guys over took some doin'," Merle told
the men at the table. "But if you're good with a gun and you
ride a motorcycle, they consider you a good ol' boy. Plus, I
showed up during harvest season. That's the most important
but dangerous time for growers. And that's about the time I
got started in security."

Merle helped the growers patrol their patches of green
cannabis on rolling hillsides. He recruited armed guards and
set up elaborate booby traps in their fields.

"We invented traps using trip wires and fishhook devices
that hung at eye level. I'm now the premier name in Humboldt hillside security."

Merle took a long swig of beer and continued his story.
Eight Ball and 12-12 were on the edge of their seats, riv-
eted. Angelo had heard the rap before.

"CAMP was a federal program, Campaign Against Marijuana Planting," said Merle. "The fucking government
strafed the hillsides with planes and helicopters. It was all-
out war sometimes. The California Highway Patrol clamped
down on anybody who habitually drove up and down the
Highway 101 corridor. But the locals loved us, especially the
merchants and the car dealerships, with guys coming out of
the hills buying new trucks and four-wheelers with paper
bags full of cash."

Merle had become a folk hero because of his uncanny
ability to evade the law. He had planted a thriving blend of
Skunk No. 1 Amsterdam seedlings on federal acreage that
was so remote, he often looked like Jeremiah Johnson, the
famous mountain man, when he reappeared every few

months for basic provisions and supplies. In just a few years' time, Merle had accumulated unimaginable wads of cash.

"The money is amazing. I literally 'canned' mason jars with laundered cash—tens, twenties, and fifties, even hundreds. I store them in a large pantry cupboard where I can keep an accurate cash inventory simply by counting the stacks of paraffin-sealed Ball jars."

Merle constantly modernized his operations. As the planes and helicopters forced the weed trade indoors, he built eight windowless compounds masquerading as residential houses on his squat of land.

"We call it living off the grid," said Merle, his eyes shining. "In the eyes of Pacific Gas and Electric, I don't exist." A diesel generator large enough to power a small hospital powered eight hydroponic greenhouses. By investing most of last year's cash crop, he was on his way toward installing wind-powered generators that would drastically cut his overhead.

And that was how Angelo got him to show up. Merle had already been scheduled to hit the Bay Area. He'd just come from a meeting where he ordered generators from a new company near Palo Alto.

"The company's owned by a couple of hotshot Stanford grads"—Merle laughed—"and they know damned well what I'm doing with their shit."

It was now time for Angelo to break in and get the deal rolling; otherwise Merle would hold the floor all afternoon with his pot stories.

"So, how's biz?" Angelo asked. "Mary must be bringing in bang-up bucks in the Emerald Triangle," he said, referring to the tricounty area of Mendocino, Humboldt, and Trinity.

"Can't complain. She's been good to me. I'm up to three Harleys I never ride, a big-assed boat I never sail, and as of a few hours ago, the proud owner of four fifty- to two-hundred-and-fifty-kilowatt wind generators. I'm in expansion mode, developing a whole new product line of affordable weed, which puts me in direct competition with the medical marijuana growers."

Merle's life wasn't all easy street. He would have to stay one step ahead of not only the DEA, FBI, IRS, ATF, CHP, and the National Guard, but also rival growers who continually ripped off one another's prime booty.

"Just last week," he said, "the feds valued a bust at two grand per plant. Can you believe it?"

Eight Ball and 12-12 sat stone-faced behind their beers. It was up to Angelo to keep the ball rolling.

"Merle, my friend, we're looking to move fifty pounds of primo weed, as top grade as you can get, sometime in the next two weeks. Then more, lots more, after that."

Angelo saw the wheels turn inside Merle's head. Angelo's affiliation with the Infidelz meant there would be only a minimum amount of front money involved. It didn't really matter how much Merle demanded. Getting the cash was going to be J.W.'s problem.

"Fifty pounds of Mary in two weeks? Could do," Merle said as he calculated Angelo's deal paying for a portion of the generators he'd just purchased. "Perhaps even sooner."

"That's why I brought Eight Ball and 12-12 here as your contacts. They'll be the guys who will pick up the stuff and move it on to the customers. Ain't that right, guys?"

"12-12 and I will personally oversee the deliveries and make sure you get your money," said Eight Ball.

Angelo continued, "I've already got plenty of interested parties—and all I need to make it happen is the product. Who's gonna stop us? We could arrange a pickup and meet in some out-of-the way place, like Redding?"

"Don't see why not," Merle said. "Redding is cool. Let's say next Wednesday. A friend of mine has a feed store there. We can run this whole operation through them, loading dock and all. I'll set you up with a nice price and a convenient time for pickup, cash on delivery. Afterward, we can set up volume discounts. Deal?"

Angelo nodded. Money was not discussed. Exactly what that price for the first lot would be, he knew Merle would let him know outside the restaurant.

"Great. Now let's order. I'm starved," said Merle.

Not bad, Angelo thought. The deal was done before the burgers hit the tabletop. Trust and respect in an otherwise ruthless and risky business. But as the food and condiments arrived, Angelo felt a wave of nausea attack his body, making it difficult for him to eat and exchange trivial small talk for the rest of the meal. Fortunately, he could tell that the city environment was already starting to make Merle squirm. He had a long drive back to his northern paradise. On the way out of Bradley's, Merle put his arm around Angelo.

"Angelo, I trust you know what you're doing," he said. "Give my love to the club. It's always nice doing business with you guys." Merle gave Angelo a tight hug and whispered, "Twenty grand. A bargain to set you up."

Locked inside Merle's embrace, Angelo didn't like what he spotted over the other man's shoulder. Sitting at the end of the bar, nursing a fresh pint of ale, was J. W. McIntosh.

He seemed oblivious to a gaggle of attractive girls standing near him. When Angelo's eyes connected with his, J. W. gave only the faintest gleam of recognition. Angelo made a mental note. He would have a word with the agent about his surveillance tactics. One more stupid move like that, and Angelo could be pushing up pot plants deep beneath the Garberville outback.

16

A Fistful of Dollars

Patch roared south on the highway out of Oakland. Traffic was light, and he took advantage of the late night, darting from lane to lane over ninety miles per hour. Twenty miles down the road, he pulled off the freeway onto a frontage road. A mile farther stood Trader's Roadhouse. Patch pulled into the bar's parking lot. He cut the engine and coasted to an open parking spot by the front door.

I hate this dive, he thought.

Patch nodded at the brawny tattooed bouncer standing out front and entered the noisy tavern. He inched his way through the crowd to the packed bar. He interrupted a large man in a ten-gallon hat ordering a round of drinks.

" 'Scuse me, partner," he said to the hat. The cowpoke was annoyed, but noticed Patch's MC colors and backed off.

"Lookin' for Jerry," Patch yelled to the bartender over the clamor of the customers. "He in his office?"

"The boss?" asked the barman.

"Yeah."

"He's busy."

Patch turned and walked toward the side of the bar, over to a big gray steel door. A curled piece of paper taped on the outside read *Employees Only. No Admittance.* The door opened. A beefy security guy exited the office and disappeared into the throng.

Patch walked up and beat on the door five times.

No answer.

He rapped on the door five more times. Harder and louder. The door cracked open. A redheaded man in his fifties stuck his head out. Patch pushed the door open wider, stepped inside the small office, and slammed the door behind him.

"Jerry," said Patch, without a smile. The cramped office smelled of stale cigar smoke. "How's biz?"

"Patch Kinkade," Jerry responded from the side of his mouth. He held a fat wad of cash. He walked back over and plopped down on the chair behind the desk. Short stacks of currency sat on the desktop. He was counting up the takings from the previous shift. "What brings you round?" he asked.

"I think you know why. One of our members got shot and killed here. Out in the parking lot."

"I was off that night."

"Any details?"

"Cops showed up. Asked a few questions. Ain't heard nothing since."

Patch took two steps closer and loomed over Jerry. "Really?"

Jerry glanced up nervously, then looked back down at the cash neatly arranged in denominations of ones, fives, tens, twenties, fifties, and hundreds. He resumed sorting the bills.

"Listen, Patch. Can we talk about this tomorrow? I'm kinda busy."

"Let's talk now."

"Okay." Jerry sighed. "Some bikers got in a punch-up. 2Wheelers, Soul Sacrifice."

"Gun Runners?"

"They were there. A couple of gunshots. A few heads bashed in. Over in a flash."

"Your guys see anything?"

"Nope. Happened too fast. Nothing we could do about it."

"That's all?"

"Listen, Patch, give me a day to ask my staff. I'll get back—"

"No. *You* listen." Patch lunged forward and swiveled Jerry's chair around, picked him up out of the seat, and grabbed him by the throat. A picture frame on the wall fell to the floor and glass shattered. "Don't jerk me off!"

Jerry struggled to breathe under Patch's grip. Patch squeezed tighter. Jerry looked uneasily over at the desktop.

"One of my guys is dead." Patch's eyes widened with rage. "Dead, Jerry. And Ahab and the club haven't heard word one from you." He shook the bar owner forcefully. Jerry's face reddened.

"Thursday Bike Nite," Patch scoffed. "Rip-off biker bar. It's a license to print money." He loosened his chokehold.

"Take it easy." Jerry shuddered. "We can work something—"

"Don't fuck with me, asshole. What do you know about the shooting?"

"Nothin'. Swear to God. I was off that night."

"I'm running out of patience."

"Okay, okay. The black guys got beat up pretty bad and arrested. The Wheelers and the Gun Runners left before the cops came."

Patch let go of Jerry. "Tell me somethin' new, you money-grubbin' little scum."

Patch cocked back his fist and landed a direct punch on Jerry's nose. Blood spurted from his face. Patch followed with a sock to his jaw. The impact of the combination sent Jerry reeling backward on the desk, scattering the money.

Patch looked down at the bills littered on the desk and the floor by the chair. He bent down and scooped up the larger notes, leaving the ones and fives. He angrily shook a fistful of dollars in Jerry's bloodied face, then grabbed the remaining wad clutched in the man's hand.

"I'll see to it that Marco's old lady gets your generous contribution," he said as he stuffed the money inside his jacket pocket.

Jerry reached for the security button under the table. Patch grabbed him by the hair. "Don't try it."

Jerry, spitting blood and his nose bleeding, nodded and moaned. Patch turned and opened the door, slammed it behind him, and weaved through the reveling crowd, outside to the Mean Machine. He jumped back on his bike and turned the key in the ignition. As he sped off, a trio of bouncers ran out into the parking lot. It was too late. Patch was gone.

Checkmate!

Patch had his doubts about the Soul Sacs. *How innocent are they in all of this?* He knew enough to know he was missing something. He knew he wasn't going to get his answers from his brothers. *When in doubt, look outside.* If it all started with Marco, then it all started at Trader's. And the Delz weren't the only ones who had suffered losses. Maybe the Sacs had access to info the Delz lacked. Maybe they had some answers.

Patch rode the Mean Machine uptown to a part of Oakland where young black men lost their lives daily, some gunned down in broad daylight. Despite the presence of a storefront church on nearly every block, these were mean streets. The local evening news tabulated an ongoing body count, and the totals rose from year to year. The bike clubs weren't the only ones shooting at one another. There was serious drug and gang shit going down in this part of town, and the cops weren't making a dent in the mayhem. In the middle of the combat zone sat Soul Sacrifice's Ninety-fifth Avenue headquarters. Lately, the newspapers had been quoting Soul Sacs' leader, Rollie George, who had pledged the manpower of the club to help try to control the indiscriminate gunplay plaguing the ghetto neighborhood.

Patch approached the Sacs' clubhouse, which was painted purple and yellow, Mardi Gras colors. It was a bright, bright, sunshiny day. A pair of beautifully customized chopped vintage Knuckleheads were parked out front. Patch backed his bike into the curb next to them. *Fucking museum pieces*. He got off his bike and pushed open the unlocked clubhouse door.

"Anybody home?"

Nothing. Patch eyed the barbecue joint across the street. No bike riders eating inside.

Man, these guys sure are loose about their HQ. Nobody even said "Boo." Patch walked in anyway; his eyes adjusted to the dark clubhouse.

One man sat alone in the corner behind a two-tone onyx chessboard with ornate cast metal pieces. He jiggled a nearly empty, tall can of Olde English "800" and studied the board. It was Rollie.

"Patch, my brother," said the dark figure in the corner. "Been expecting you. Sit down."

One of Rollie's boys must have spotted Patch rolling into town. There was no escaping Rollie George's Oaktown radar. Soul Sacrifice had their side of the city wired 24/7.

Patch took a seat at the table. The two shook hands straight, no jive.

"Game?" asked Rollie.

"I'm not in your league."

"So why you here?"

"Information."

"How about this: You talk, we play."

"And what do I get if I win? Will you answer my questions?"

"Maybe there's nothing I can tell you. Maybe you'll learn how the game is played."

Patch looked down at the chessboard. Years ago, in prison, he could devise a strategy. Now all he saw were pieces and squares. Patch was the first to break the ranks. He moved a silver center pawn two squares ahead. Rollie followed by inching out one of his pawns.

After a few moves, Patch moved out his knight.

Rollie quickly countered with his gold knight.

Patch noticed Rollie's hands on the chessboard. They were smooth, dark brown, barely creased—at a glance, the hands of a younger man. Rollie kept himself in tip-top shape. He looked thirtyish, slim, about half his age. Patch respected anyone who kept his body as strong and his mind as alert as Rollie did. Outside of a social toke of weed now and then, Rollie was totally clean, and hadn't done a lick of coke in ages. He'd served thirteen months in San Quentin during the early nineties. For what, no one was sure. Even in the joint, with its no-weight-room policy and starchy food, Rollie stayed loose with a diligent regimen of isometrics and yoga.

Rollie looked up from the chessboard, smiled, and shook his head. "You and me go back, back to the days when we lumped on the docks together. You lasted all of a couple of weeks."

"You had kids to raise. I had nothing but time and a bike."

"Three, all from the same mama. I put all their asses through college. My oldest is a lawyer. That comes in handy at times."

"You do run a tight ship. When one of your guys fucks up, all you have to do is glare at him, and he's hup-two. I wish I had that kind of control."

Rollie loved to customize Harleys and Camaros. He had amassed a wall of car- and bike-show trophies behind the Soul Sac clubhouse bar. He also treasured the free-ridin' life he'd created for his Soul Sacrifice club members, now going on thirty years. He named the club after his favorite Santana song. Rollie dubbed himself "semiretired," although nobody knew exactly what he was retired from.

Patch and Rollie exchanged a half dozen more moves on the board.

"So, you miss Oakland?"

"Haven't exactly had the chance to," said Patch. "The minute I leave here, all hell breaks loose."

Patch pondered his next move. He slid his silver bishop into position.

"Tell me about it," said Rollie. Then he moved *his* bishop.

"No, Rollie, *you* tell me. A few of your boys ran into a buzz saw out at the roadhouse, right?"

Patch moved his knight farther up toward Rollie's back line.

"Shit happens," Rollie said as he advanced his gold queen. He was smelling blood.

"What happened out there?"

Patch took Rollie's gold knight.

"A few of our boys got their heads busted by a bunch of white folks is all," Rollie said. "Things haven't changed that much."

"Aw, c'mon, Rollie. Don't play with me." Patch figured the Soul Sacs' leader wouldn't be so smug if revenge hadn't been in the works.

169 «

"We lost one of ours that night, too," Patch reminded him. "Then my guys end up playing duck and shoot with the 2Wheelers at Santa Paula behind poker tables and slot machines." He left out the part about the clubhouse shooting, though he was sure Rollie was well aware of that, too.

Rollie eyed the chessboard, then beamed again. He didn't even look up as Patch spoke.

"Tell me about the shootings on the estuary, the night before the poker run. You know anything about that?"

Patch realized he had made a stupid move taking Rollie's knight. A trap. He tried to regroup. Rollie drummed his fingers on the chessboard. "Maybe you should ask a few less questions and pay more attention to your game."

"Fess up. Did you put the hit out on those 2Wheelers at the estuary?"

"Listen, brother, it don't break my heart none having two less out-of-town white boys out there ridin' on our streets."

Three more moves were exchanged before Patch noticed his own queen in Rollie's line of fire.

Rollie smiled a tight-lipped grin. Patch couldn't tell if he was happy about the progress of the game or if he was just glad that a couple of leather-vested 2Wheeler peckerwoods were now playing checkers with Elvis.

Patch made a vain attempt to save his queen as Rollie tightened the net and made a few more decisive moves.

"Check," Rollie announced.

Patch tried to protect his king with his rook. Nothing doing.

"Checkmate."

Rollie's smile widened, this time revealing two rows of porcelain-white teeth that contrasted with his dark skin. As Patch laid his king down in defeat, he realized that Rollie loved having all his angles covered, a sly, quiet control freak. There would be no piercing the black curtain tonight. Or was there?

"Son of a bitch," said Patch, pounding the table.

"You know how I beat you, Patch?"

"Because you play this game a lot more times than I do."

"No. That's why I'm the better player. The reason you lost this game is because I had you focused on the front lines when the greatest threat was sneaking up on ya from behind."

"So I need to watch my back closer? Know who my real friends are?"

"Read your *Art of War*. Sometimes brothers with the best intentions have the most devious motives. Distraction. Diversion. That's the shit that wins wars. So ends the lesson."

18

Four Sergeants and a Captain

Implicate the Infidelz with weapons and drugs. Rile things up with the biker gangs operating all over Northern California. That's what we gotta do. That's what *you* gotta do," J.W. said authoritatively during a clandestine conversation with Angelo. "I'm out on a limb for you with the U.S. marshals and the DEA."

Angelo had all of the preliminaries for

the pot network set to go and ready to implement. That part was easy. The weapons and explosives business would prove a lot harder to engineer on short notice. He anticipated a few brick walls and dead ends. He had followed every lead he could think of, and got lucky inside his own club.

Angelo had stumbled onto some promising info through a club brother named Beaver Cleaver. Beaver rode with the Infidelz chapter in Ukiah, a small redneck dot on the map, three counties north of Oakland and San Francisco. The Ukiah Delz were stockpiling heavy arms for themselves and had the best line on what was available in the remote Northern California encampments, where the truly scary hillbilly gunrunners also ran their rural meth labs and country crack kitchens. Angelo knew he'd hit the jackpot with Beaver Cleaver. He was the man.

"I'm looking for some firepower to buy to move around these parts," Angelo said to Beav, who was calling back from a roadside gas-station pay phone. "Any leads?"

173 «

"You mean Oakland?"

"Yes. I'm lookin' to buy further north on your turf. But whatever we'd score would absolutely stay down here in Oaktown, way out of your territory."

"I could live with that."

"So, Beav, whattya got? Anything?"

Angelo stopped talking and let the pause in the connection sink in for a moment. Sometimes silence got results.

"Okay. Let's do this. Why don't you ride to my part of the country tomorrow and come along with me to check out a potential score?"

"That's good for me, Beav. What are the particulars?"

"I'll tell you when you get here."

Bingo, Angelo had said to himself as he slammed the receiver down and rubbed his palms together hard. *The shit is on.*

The next day he rode alone from Oakland a couple of hours north toward the Russian River, a cozy rural resort area in Sonoma County. He and Beaver Cleaver met and discussed the next leg of their journey while gassing up at the filling station.

"Here's the deal," said the Beav. "There's this tight-knit gang of Northern California leathernecks, four sergeants and a captain, stationed out of Fort Pearson."

"That's outside of Ukiah, another few hours north from here."

"They're primed to move a large cache of stolen military weapons."

This sounded okey-dokey to Angelo.

"That's genius. Whatta they got? Explosives? Guns? Automatic weapons?"

"All of the above."

"No shit?" Angelo couldn't believe his luck. The club was in. And he would have no problems attracting enough anxious buyers from nearby friendly motorcycle clubs. He'd be fighting them off with a leaded pool cue.

It was unquestionably a seller's market. 1%ers would buy and sell almost any kind of pistols, explosives, or automatic rifles they could get their hands on. They were determined to improve their proficiency in using automatic weapons, blowing things up, and staying on top of the latest artillery craze.

"What kind of explosives we talkin' about?" asked Angelo.

"I dunno what their total inventory is exactly. That's why

we're going there today," said Beaver Cleaver. "Lots of guns. But I did hear they're well stocked with C-4 and det cord."

Detonation cord? C-4? Whoa, baby, my lucky day, Angelo said to himself. He and the Beav roared out of the gas station and merged back onto Highway 101 for the trip north to Ukiah.

C-4 was in superhot demand. It came in long bars, a puttylike substance, wrapped in olive drab cellophane, ready to be cut and molded to fit any shaped container. An ounce was easily enough to blow a hole through a wall and came in handy for bank jobs, late-night warehouse break-ins, that kind of thing. The guys in Vietnam used to heat C rations with tiny pinches of the stuff. It was relatively safe to handle, being resistant to impact and fire, almost idiot proof. But C-4 could also be deadly. A pencil-size piece properly strung up with det cord could obliterate a tree trunk one foot thick. Det cord came in rolls to serve as a fuse for C-4. Along with a triggering device, det cord usually sold as a package on the black market for premium dough.

When Angelo and the Beav reached Ukiah, Beaver gave the hand signal to pull off. The pair rolled into a Texaco station on a rural street that ran alongside the freeway.

"We're real close now, but let's gas up before we get there. After we check out the goods and negotiate the deal, you can ride straight out of town and back home."

Angelo quizzed the Beav as he topped off his tank. "So who's the main wheeler-dealer here? And what's his story?"

"I've only talked to the guy on the phone. The Marine captain is a reclusive fella named Spivak," said Beaver. "He works out of the Marine Reserve Center near the Fort

Pearson barracks. He's the ringleader. He came out here after serving a hitch at Camp Lejeune in Carolina."

"We aren't riding into Pearson army base dressed like this, are we?" asked Angelo, tugging at his Infidelz colors.

"Nope. Spivak's got the stuff stashed off base. We're meeting there."

Beaver Cleaver screwed on the gas cap of his ride and set the gas nozzle back in its cradle. "Spivak does all the 'show-and-tell' while his partners stay completely in the shadows. Four sergeants and a captain. That's all I know. One's a staff sergeant, a gunnery sergeant, and a couple of drill sarges. Captain Spivak and his boys gathered their little arsenal over the past several months. They've had access to the Pearson storage dump. They trucked their stolen weapons and ammo over to Ukiah under Spivak's watch. And that's where we're goin'."

The rest of the trip was a nice backwoods putt to Spivak's place, not too far from the reserve center at Fort Pearson. Then Angelo and the Beav steered their bikes onto a heavily wooded dirt road driveway, covered in pine needles and leading to a small ranch house. They knocked on the front door and were greeted by a short, sinewy gentleman in camouflage uniform, complete with spit-shined black leather boots. Angelo and Beaver towered over the jarhead.

Spivak wore his fatigue hat down low, the brim practically touching his nose. As a result, Angelo never really saw the whites of his eyes. He wore a 9mm holster clipped to his belt.

At first, Spivak was coy about the specifics of his deadly booty, so they talked about motorcycles instead. The Marine captain stared at the patches on the riders' backs. "The Infidelz, eh?"

"That's right. We got a few Marines in the club. Semper fi."

Spivak cracked a faint smile. "Yeah? My dad rode an Indian when I was a kid. I'd ride on the back with him sometimes. I'll never forget the looks he got from people when we'd roar into the Dairy Queen parking lot on that thing."

"You'd be surprised, Cap'n," quipped the Beav. "We still get looks like that."

"I used to shoot pool in North Carolina with a bunch of you biker types. Those guys were a little grimy lookin', unkempt, but they were dependable guys. Men you felt you could trust."

That broke the ice. Angelo got to the point.

"Wanna show us what you got?"

"Follow me."

Spivak led the Beav and Angelo out the back door. Twenty yards outside of the ranch house stood a small structure surrounded by Douglas firs. The storage building had a hidden cellar entrance. Angelo, Beaver, and Captain Spivak climbed downstairs and eyed the goods, all neatly crated, stacked, and organized.

"Nice, Cap'n." The Beav gawked.

"What's on the menu?" asked Angelo.

Spivak cleared his throat and pulled out a wrinkled list from his shirt pocket.

"Let's see here. Two fifty-caliber machine guns. A couple of mortar launchers. One handheld B-40 rocket launcher. Two crates of grenades. That's twenty-four units. Canisters of all the ammo you need. Short-barreled MAC-10s."

"Nice." Angelo smiled. "I've never fired a MAC-10 before."

"Gotta be careful. Sixty rounds at once," said Spivak.

"You need an easy trigger finger on those suckers, so you don't blow your ammo load. Listen, any you guys interested in a restored World War Two jeep?"

"Hmm . . . we'll pass on the jeep," responded Angelo.

Spivak referred back to his list and pointed at each corresponding wooden container. "Over there we have a few land mines, a case of M14 rifles, an M203 grenade launcher, lots of ammo for that, and all along that wall is the cream of the crop. C-4 plastic explosives and rolls of det cord."

The Marine stockpile was a smorgasbord, more than enough to give any law enforcement officer like J.W. McIntosh a professional hard-on.

"Awesome, Cap'n," said Beaver Cleaver. "Whattya think, Angelo? You game?"

"We'll take the whole lot," said Angelo confidently.

"I was hopin' you'd say that. My partners are antsy to flog the entire arsenal in one chunk. Plus there's more from where this came from."

» 178

The timing was perfect for Angelo. This deal with the Beaver would include members from the club's Ukiah chapter and others farther north moving and buying some of the merchandise.

"Gimme a minute, sir, while I consult my partner," Angelo said to Spivak.

Angelo and Beaver conferred. "The Ukiah club would be most interested in the C-4 and the det cord," said Beav. "I'd like a couple of those MAC-10s for myself. How about it?"

"Let's do the deal," said Angelo. The two rejoined Spivak.

"What are we talkin' here?" asked Angelo. "Me and Beaver reckon we'll split the goods fifty-fifty. What's your price, Captain Spivak, sir? I'm talking about the full monty. Lock, stock, and both fuckin' barrels."

"Watch your mouth there, son," said Spivak. Then he smirked. "Forty-five grand, cash and carry. That's a bargain, boys. You load the gear right out of this place."

Beav looked over at Angelo and gritted his teeth. "Too much," he mouthed. Actually, forty-five grand was a steal. The haul was easily worth ten times that amount, even more on the open market.

"Much too much," Angelo replied. "We're thinkin' more like thirty-five." Beav grinned when Angelo looked back over at him.

"Now, that's too low for me, fellas. How about an even forty?" said Spivak.

"Thirty-seven five."

"You got yourselves a deal. I think a small Ryder truck will suffice for this gear."

"Cap'n, we ain't rentin' no wheels."

"Suit yourself, guys. Now let's arrange a pickup time that works for everybody." Spivak clapped his hands. "Are we happy, gentleman? You guys want a beer or something back at the house?"

After the meeting, Angelo and Beaver Cleaver shook on their fifty-fifty deal. Then the satisfied duo sped out and headed back south on Highway 101. Angelo gave Beaver Cleaver the peace sign when they separated. Beaver rode off his exit and Angelo stayed on 101 farther south toward Oakland. On the way home, he pulled off the road for a quick meal at a pancake house. Sitting in a booth, he pulled out his beeper. Only it wasn't a beeper. It was a miniature tape recorder. After paying the bill, he rustled up some extra change from the cashier for the pay phone.

"McIntosh."

"J.W., it's Angelo."

"What do you have for me today?"

"You're gonna shit, dude."

"Meaning what?"

"Well, I just haggled with a Marine captain who's part Sergeant Rock, part Rambo. And I got it all on tape."

"Meaning?"

"Evidence. The weapons buy I promised is a go, courtesy of one of our northern chapters. I've struck pay dirt. We found a group of Marines with everything but nerve gas." Angelo was careful to be vague with J.W. when it came to details to avoid any end-arounds.

"Where are you?"

"All in good time. I'm just checking in to say we're steady on course. I've got the club involved. I'll check in later to let you know what kind of cash we'll need on my end."

"Keep me in the loop and we'll talk soon."

Then J.W. was gone.

The call to J.W. put Angelo on track. Things were happening fast, even ahead of Angelo's timetable. He felt a long way emotionally from that awful night when he was handcuffed to the chair in the interrogation room. Now he was riding a wave of lucky breaks.

On the pot network, a bunch of Infidelz and a major grower would go down. But this weapons deal, Angelo's coup, would be page-one news above the crease. INFIDELZ LINKED TO WEAPONS CACHE. The follow-through process would be a cakewalk. Plus, Angelo would also nail a half-dozen more MCs, including the Warthogs, the Darkness MC, the Zeros, and even the Soul Sacs. Maybe he'd stage an auction.

Angelo had a weapons deal that would ordinarily have taken months or a year to piece together, ready to gel in a matter of days. J.W. would get him his capital from the federal piggy bank. Set up the buys, some involving agents and the club. Angelo would procure a little more money than needed, and skim some off the purchases for himself, and then make even more when he resold the weapons to the other MCs. That would bankroll his escape, and with J.W.'s help, he would finalize plans to get out of town, the state, wherever, forever.

After a long, smooth ride back to Oakland, Angelo's next stop was the Infidelz clubhouse. There he found Ahab sitting at a table drinking a bottle of beer and eating a hoagie. The club prez motioned him over.

181 «

"Just the man I need to see. We gotta talk."

"What's up, boss?"

"You gonna be round here for a while?"

"As long as you need me."

"Great. We're hitting the 2Wheelers. It's on."

"It's about time."

"I got a few ideas on how we're going to do it. I want to run battle plans down with you first. You ready?"

"Lay 'em on me, Ahab. I'm all ears."

Pumping Iron

Patch decided to nose around Lock N Load's neck of the woods. Rollie George had been cryptic about what happened at Trader's. Maybe the Gun Runners would be more forthright. Patch put out the word that he'd be stopping by the Gun Runners' home turf. He fired up his Road King and cruised fifty minutes south down Highway 880. He knew the way to San Jose.

The Gun Runners' clubhouse wasn't much to speak of, a small run-down Victorian in the Rocksprings section of town. Based in the San Jose barrio, the Gunners rubbed shoulders on the streets with members of a prison-run Hispanic mob that controlled the neighborhood's drug dealing. Patch recalled reading in the papers about how the mob masterminded a series of San Jose bank robberies using pistols, sawed-off shotguns, and pepper spray. A few of the Latin guys who rode with the Gunners were rumored to have been involved. Either way, Patch conceded, for the Gunners to put down roots in this section of the jungle took balls.

LOCK N LOAD LED THE GUNNERS' NORTHERN CHAPTERS. Lock was easy to pick out of a crowd. First you heard him. He had a high-shrieking, spun-glass voice that couldn't be considered an obvious match to his body. When he was amused he screamed like a hyena. When he was angry he screamed like a hyena. Green-and-orange flames were tattooed to the side of his shiny bald skull.

Lock guzzled beer straight out of the pitcher, but a rigid program of strength training, power lifting, and sprinting kept his gut trim and well off his club belt buckle. He stood about six-four and weighed in at 270 pounds. He was as strong as a bull and mean as a crocodile. He had arms like tree trunks and could lift a Panhead onto the bed of a pickup solo.

Lock hadn't been the Gunners' South Bay chapter president all that long, less than a year. The Gunners went through officers like paper towels, since the club attracted a lot of guys who were not exactly known for staying in one place for long. Since their system for background checks of new prospects was one notch above shoddy, cops and feds regularly infiltrated their club chapters, resulting in numerous busts and mass arrests. For a while, the Gunners were endangered. The law nearly broke the MC apart. They were now on a campaign to regain the membership strength and size they'd lost over the past few years while squirming under law enforcement's thumb. Now, in order to fortify their ranks, the Gunners recruited non-bike-riding street-gang members and quickly put them up on stolen bikes. Lock N Load needed to build up a strong and devoted inner sanctum. Eventually he did: a group of four guys he called his "Ring of Fire"—Razz, Juice, Dawg, and Shadow. They made up Lock's elite guard.

PATCH BLINKED AND MISSED THE GUNNERS' CLUBHOUSE AS he rode by. Except for a small iron insignia hanging over a side door, the place was inconspicuous—a contrast to the enormous sign that hung in front of the Oakland Delz HQ. It was late morning when Patch doubled back the Mean Machine into the Gun Runners' driveway. Only a couple other bikes were parked outside. One was obviously Lock's ride, a new FXT Sport with the same gaudy orange-and-green flames painted on the tank and fenders that Lock had tattooed on his head. Emblazoned across the tank in block letters was *Death Trap*.

Patch walked up to a gray wooden side door and slapped

its surface four times with the flat of his hand. He heard heavy-booted footsteps on the other side. The door creaked open and a large bearded fellow greeted him. Stitched onto his vest, over his heart, was the name *Razz*. Underneath, another smaller orange and white patch: *Ring of Fire*.

"I'm looking for Mr. Lock N Load," announced Patch.

Razz shook Patch's hand and snorted, "Don't mind if I pat you down, do ya?"

"Do whatever you have to do." Patch figured the guy was more worried about wires than weapons, since he didn't look twice at Sharpfinger hanging off Patch's belt. *If this mook could feel a wire, he's a fucking genius*, Patch figured. Since the Gunners was a club that only a few years earlier had found itself infested with rats, informants, and infiltrators, he understood their caution and raised his hands well over his head.

"What's behind your belt buckle? Push it down for me," commanded Razz.

"Nothin' but my sexy belly," Patch deadpanned.

"I wanna see behind that buckle." Patch permitted the search and was allowed in.

Razz led him to the rear of the house, into a converted weight room and gym. German marching music blasted from a boom box. Lock N Load was lying on his back, on a cheap flat board, huffing and puffing, bench-pressing a fat chrome-plated bar with a foot-wide stack of jumbo, made-in-China Weider iron plates loosely clamped on each side. Hanging nearby, slung over a wooden chair in plain sight, was a denim vest with Lock N Load's three-piece orange-and-green Gun Runners patch.

"Gimme a minute," Lock grunted, ". . . eleven . . .

twelve . . . thirteen . . ." Then, after a brief pause: "Four-teen . . . fifteen."

If this little show was meant to impress Patch, it hit the mark. Lock was pressing a shitload of weight. Shirtless, Lock acknowledged Patch's presence again with a slight nod. Lock's physique was unmarred by body fat or body hair. His tattoos gleamed with sweat. The Gothic images inked on his skin seemed almost three-dimensional as he flexed his muscular arms. He toweled off the sweat before grabbing his patch off the chair and slipping it over his huge torso.

Another Delz member usually came along when Patch visited friendly clubhouses, in case a guy like Lock N Load began to feel his Cheerios. Lock forced a smile, turned off the marching music, and greeted Patch with a vise-grip handshake.

"Brother Patch."

Patch squeezed back hard. For a couple of ill-at-ease moments, the two stood facing each other, eyeballs locked, joined by a prison-yard handshake of mutual respect. Everybody was right about Lock's high, squeaky voice. It just didn't fit in with the man's physique.

Lock nodded toward the bar resting on the bench. "You work out?"

"I suppose I can bench-press my IQ," said Patch with a modest grin.

"Then be my guest, bro. I'll spot you." Lock began to remove the collars as he prepared to take off weight. Patch waved him off.

"Leave it. I can handle what's on the bar."

Lock chuckled under his breath. Patch was at least six

inches shorter than him. As Patch positioned himself on the bench, he lined his hands up, spreading his arms a little wider than his shoulders. He evened up his forehead with the chrome bar and planted both feet flat on the floor.

With one sure motion, Lock lifted the bar off its stand and released it into Patch's control. Patch bore its full weight, but it nearly overwhelmed him. There was no turning back. Careful not to bounce the weight off his sternum, he bore down, grunting through the first rep.

"Why are you here?" Lock asked. "I'd heard you left California."

Patch dipped and guided the bar carefully through a second rep.

"Not officially. Not yet"—his voice reflecting the strain of the tremendous weight on the bar—"not with all this shit that's going down."

Patch looked up at Lock looking down at him, his arms folded. With his tattooed bald head, he looked like a sinister Mr. Clean.

"Yeah, all this fightin'. It's no damned good for anyone. It's bad for business, too. Like I told Ahab, if you all need us to help settle something between Infidelz and 2Wheelers, we're there."

By the third rep, the bar felt even heavier. Patch continued to raise and lower it with controlled movements—down to his chest, slightly touching, then exploding the weight back upward. Somehow he had to get through fifteen reps.

"What do you know about the Trader's incident? All I know is that I ride out of town and one of our guys goes down. What do you know?"

"Not much."

By the sixth rep, Patch felt a burning strain on his pecs and delts. As his energy ebbed, his muscles nearly gave out. His forearms trembled and shivered. Yet he couldn't, wouldn't break stride. His glutes stayed glued to the bench.

"Guys who live by the patch die by the patch," said Lock. "You know that. It happens all the time. Why is one of your guys dying such a big fucking deal?"

"Say what?"

Lock's comment rekindled Patch's energy, giving him a second wind. Adrenaline shot through his body. Suddenly the bar lost its leaded mass.

"Eight . . . nine . . . ten . . ."

If Lock was looking to spot, he would be sorely disappointed. Patch was on a roll. He had found his mantra—hatred for the other man's blatant disrespect for a fallen Infidelz brother.

"Twelve . . . thirteen . . . fourteen . . ."

By the time he hit the fifteenth rep, he was ready for more. But the voice inside told him it was time to rack it. Pride aside, showing someone up in his own clubhouse wasn't a wise move, not with so much iron hovering over one's own neck.

After racking the bar, Patch inhaled deeply, then let out a long exhale and climbed to his feet. His whole upper body was drenched and his muscles pulsed and quivered involuntarily. Lock threw him a clean towel like a Roger Clemens fastball, with lotsa mustard on it.

Then the two bike riders stood face-to-face in the cramped hallway outside Lock's pint-size makeshift gym.

"Why don't you show me around your place?" Patch asked.

"Ain't much to show," replied Lock. "We don't have fancy digs here. Not like you guys in Oakland."

"Well then, I'll leave you to it, Lock. Oh yeah, and thanks for the offer to mediate. We'll pass for now."

"You figure you got the Wheelers under control?"

"We're the Infidelz, man. We got everything under control. I'll see myself out."

» C H A P T E R «

20

This Old
Porch

Patch shut off his bike in front of the tiny house on Rampart Street in the East Oakland foothills, just below the towering Mormon temple on the hillside. He stomped up the wooden front-porch steps, where pink fuchsias now hung from blue ceramic planter boxes. He'd been gone barely a week and already the place was beginning to take on a new personality. He rang the bell. No answer. Eve was at work. She'll be off around four, he remembered. It was a quarter till, so he'd just chill on the porch. Take a load off, sit a spell. Patch could while away a half hour kicking back before Eve made her way home.

Man, I could murder a ham and cheese sandwich. If anything, an ex–old lady ought to be good for a sandwich. Then it occurred to him that he still had his key. But when he jiggled it in the lock, it didn't fit. *Jesus,* he thought, *she changed the locks already.* Another funny thing: her car was in the driveway. *Maybe she rode her motorcycle to work,* he thought. *Fat chance.*

Stranded outside, Patch ambled around the porch for a few minutes. He cupped his eyes on the glass and gazed through the front picture window. As he peered through the lace curtains, he realized there never used to be lace curtains. Looking into the front room, he thought it seemed empty, roomier for such a tiny house, and the walls were now bare, clean, and freshly painted. She must have worked day and night to make all those changes. *The white walls make the room look bigger.* Patch's presence hardly seemed missed. In fact, his absence was an improvement. Eve's place, not theirs, was becoming just like the rest of the houses on Rampart Street—orderly, well kept, quiet, picket fence, flowers, a straight home instead of a bike-club hangout.

The retired woman who lived across the street was working in her front garden as usual. She noticed Patch out front. They knew each other only by sight, and in the past they had exchanged pleasantries, though he couldn't exactly recall her name. *Wanda, Evelyn, one of those "little old lady" names.*

When Patch put up a hand to acknowledge her, she averted her eyes and pretended not to see him.

At least his lawn chair occupied its usual place on the wooden porch, on top of the same loose, creaky board. Patch slumped his butt down onto the chair's wooden slats and leaned back. He put his boots up on the banister like he always had, closed his eyes, and inhaled deeply. *Somebody's freshly cut lawn.* With the smell came a flood of memories. How many hours, days, had he spent in that goddamned chair, days when the front yard was filled with cycles and his brothers kicked back on the green grass and swilled cans of cheap beer? At first the neighbors had freaked. Then they got used to it and realized some of the positive implications. Since Patch and Eve had moved in, a rash of burglaries and car thefts mysteriously ceased. OPD cruisers routinely prowled the block. *Rampart Street is now safe as mother's milk.*

It was on this old porch that Patch had reveled in his Oakland roots. Had his best ideas. Sorted out nuts, bolts, bike parts, and ideas. Averted catastrophes. Got catatonic on a variety of strange drugs. Worried about shit. Made bad decisions. He'd even been arrested a few times on that porch, back when he was club president.

This was where Patch and Eve's kid brother, Corky, used to get tight. *Good kid, but a bit soft, slow, and dim.* He taught the kid how to ride a cycle on this street. And how to smoke reefer and drink beer when his motherly older sister wasn't looking. But he could remember very few times when he and Eve sat alone together on this porch.

Just as Patch was getting comfortable, a late-model Aerostar minivan pulled up in front of the house. His eyes widened. Eve was sitting up front on the passenger's side with the window rolled down. A younger man, early thirties, neatly groomed, was behind the wheel. In the back sat a little girl about four years old.

Eve noticed the Mean Machine first, and then saw Patch reclining in his chair on the porch. He smirked. As the three got out of the vehicle, she shot him a look of horror, somewhere between *what-the-hell-are-you-doing-here?* and *tell-me-this-isn't-happening*. This was going to be a tricky situation for her. *I'm going to enjoy this,* Patch thought.

"John." Eve snarled under her breath as they approached. She didn't call him Patch and certainly never risked calling him Everett. "I didn't . . ."

Her voice trailed off.

The minivan driver stood behind Eve with his hands resting protectively on her shoulders. He wore a tweed sport coat, a blue cotton button-down shirt. Beige slacks. No tie. Black-rimmed glasses. Behind him, the little girl shyly buried her face in her father's sport-coat tails.

Patch made his way down the porch steps and stopped short of giving Eve a hug. With her back to the minivan man, Eve rolled her eyes and mouthed Patch a "don't you dare" message.

Patch wasn't much of a lip-reader, but he could tell that Eve was annoyed and embarrassed. The man in the sport coat seemed caught off guard, too. He could tell there was more between Patch and Eve than a casual friendship. Patch could easily have hotfooted it to his bike and taken off as he had done so many times before during more unpleasant confrontations and arguments. But this wouldn't rate such a response. Eve wasn't going to be let off that easily.

Patch reached past Eve and extended his hand to the man.

"I'm Patch."

"Uh, Charles."

"Charles and I work together," Eve piped up. "This is his daughter, Jessica. We were on our way out for pizza. We stopped by to drop a few things off. I'm, uh, really, uh, surprised to see you."

Charles glanced over at the Mean Machine. Then he surveyed the tattoos on Patch's arms. So did his young daughter.

"Daddy, that man has writing on his arms."

Charles's face reddened after the child's comment. *Leave it to the children to break the ice*, Patch thought.

"They're tattoos, honey," said Charles.

Patch was used to little kids running around the club-house. *They shoot from the hip, no bullshit. Speak their curious minds.* He liked that. Patch approached the little girl, down on his knees, eye to eye with the youngster.

"They never go away. See this one here?" He gestured to his right biceps, a cobra ready to strike. Patch flexed his muscle. The snake danced. The child giggled. "I was in a chair for four hours in Mexico getting that one. This one, the devil riding a motorcycle, I got in Anaheim near Disneyland from a guy named Teardrop. See this one? You have to do something really stupid before you're allowed to get one of these." It was his 187 mark.

"Eve," Patch said, looking over at Charles, "why don't you show Jessica *your* tattoo?" His eyes narrowed. "She's got Mickey Mouse right on her ass."

Patch smiled and the little girl laughed again, the only ones who found the moment humorous.

"That's enough, children. I'm sorry, Charles, he's as bad as the kids."

"So, where are you coming from John, uh, Patch?" Charles asked, inching himself between the child and Patch.

Obviously Eve hadn't yet discussed much of her personal past with good ol' Charles.

"I'm living in Arizona. But I'm in town right now—under the radar, you might say." Patch looked over at Eve. "I'm crashing with Tony, you know, Big Jab's boy. I meant to call, but . . ." He shrugged.

Charles cleared his throat. "You know, Eve, perhaps we ought to take a rain check on that pizza." Jessica frowned at the suggestion. "Make it another day?"

Patch was surprised when Eve took the out.

"That's sweet of you, Charles. I'll see you tomorrow morning." They then kissed awkwardly.

The summit on the lawn broke up. Charles lifted his young daughter into the backseat of the Aerostar van and with a wave he quickly jogged to the driver's side. Speeding off, he even burned a little rubber. As they were leaving, the little girl waved enthusiastically and yelled out the open window.

195 ««

"Bye, Patch."

"Bye, Jessica," he replied with the same innocent eagerness.

Eve shook her head and smacked her ex on the back of the head with the rolled-up *Oakland Tribune* she had picked up off the lawn, a smile on her face. "What Mickey Mouse on my butt? You never let me have any tattoos. Oh, and by the way, that was my boss. I hope you're satisfied."

"You usually kiss the boss?"

Eve let the question pass and unlocked the front door as Patch held the screen door open. He stared at the light hairs on her neck, then down at her ass, and reached for it, but backed off as she pushed the door open and quickly stepped inside.

"Eaten yet?" she asked.

Patch hesitated before entering Eve's new domain. It wasn't his home anymore.

"C'mon. Get inside and I'll whip you up something."

The fireplace mantel was like a shrine. There were photographs of Eve and Corky as youngsters, Eve the doting older sister. The two, nearly a decade apart, looked more like mother and son than brother and sister: Corky and Eve playing in the snow, horsing around. Corky and Eve on horseback. And not a single snapshot of Patch or a motorcycle. He had been exorcized from the house. Patch was evidence expunged.

FOR NEARLY A DOZEN YEARS, PATCH HAD JUGGLED THE club, his wife, and his marriage until everything unraveled. Until a year ago, he could ride and fistfight with the boys while living with and loving Eve. He succeeded at keeping the two most important aspects of his life, his club and his old lady, in harmony with each other.

But the trouble in their marriage started a year ago, sixty miles from home, in Sonoma County. The Delz had just "flipped" the patches of a local 1%er support group, the Jackyls MC, into their own. After months of riding and hanging out, the Jackyls became full-fledged, hell-raising Infidelz patch holders, but only after Patch, Ahab, and Angelo helped thin out the herd.

As a general rule, most national MCs incorporated outside support clubs into their ranks en masse. Not the Infidelz. Rather than guaranteeing blanket membership to the entire Jackyls mob in Sonoma, the Infidelz picked and chose only the best riders and toughest fighters. Those selected wore an Infidelz bottom rocker and prospected for a year or so before earning their full orange-and-black Infidelz patches. It was a long and cautious process, calculated to avoid law enforcement infiltration.

In the case of the Jackyls, a couple of members had been passed over, including the prez, who founded the club. He didn't take kindly to being among the rejected few. As if rejection wasn't humiliating enough, a stiff beating and a severely bruised ego accompanied his unceremonious ouster. The bloodied ex-prez was forcibly dragged from the clubhouse as he shouted threats and promises of revenge.

That same year, on a sunny and cloudless Sunday, Patch, Eve, and Corky were cruising a straightaway patch of Highway 12 on their bikes, just outside of the small town of Kenwood. To their left, sprawling green pastures. To their right were disciplined rows of grape vineyards and plum trees. Patch was leading on his Mean Machine. Eve rode the blue Sportster he had built for her from scratch. Corky, who had just entered junior college, rode a borrowed Softail. The three had spent a good part of the day hanging at the new Sonoma Jackyls-turned-Infidelz clubhouse.

An oncoming red Ford pickup truck approached them on the highway. Patch noticed a large Harley-Davidson wings decal on the window. At first he assumed the truck was merely speeding. Then he saw the front wheels of the truck jerk into his lane and barely miss him. His reflexes were lightning fast. So were Eve's. But not Corky's. The oncoming truck clipped his front wheel and sent the boy sailing, flipped off the bike, airborne, coming down hard, scraping across the pavement, immediately transformed into a mass of torn flesh, spilled blood, and shattered bones. The red truck was long gone—no name, no face, no license number.

Amid the chaos of the accident, Patch laid his bike down and sprinted to Corky's aid while Eve stopped her bike, ran back to the scene, then wandered hysterically, mumbling and crying, then screaming.

"No, no, no, no, no."

Patch had seen more than enough death in his day, but this one cut deep. Corky had been like a son to them both. As he took the boy in his arms, he brushed the gravel and dust from his forehead and dirty brown hair. Patch fought the urge to hold his lifeless body close, but instead he gently laid the boy back down on the warm pavement and checked his pulse and breathing. When he felt nothing, he covered the boy's face with his club sweatshirt.

When the cops arrived to investigate and write up their report, Patch stayed tight-lipped. The EMTs loaded Corky's body into the ambulance. On the roadside lay the Softail, a twisted heap of scrap metal, chrome, and rubber. Eve sat near a row of rural mailboxes, silent, her mouth agape. Her eyes were empty. She barely blinked, too stunned to cry.

Neither Patch, Ahab, nor Angelo had been able to positively link the accident to the ousted Jackyls. But they suspected it. Unfortunately, so did Eve.

» » » « « «

YOU KNOW, I DON'T EVEN MISS YOU," EVE SAID SOFTLY, flipping over a grilled ham and cheese sandwich on the stovetop. "And I'm doing well since you left.

"No, really. I know what you're thinking, but . . . I'm doing well. I have my own life now. I'm helping to write computer programs. It's a little tedious, but I like it. I work with nice people. Sometimes we all go out for drinks."

Patch merely nodded as he chewed his sandwich. *Eve will soon be on a tear.* He knew when to shut up. He'd learned how to become a good listener in prison. His style was to let people spill out their guts as their inner emotional coils, ratcheted tight, came completely unwound.

"We were together—what, twelve years? I was alone for over half of them. You were in jail. I cleaned toilets and motel rooms. I barely paid the bills. The lawyers. The writs. I could have gone to law school for all the legal work I did for you on the outside. Okay, I'll admit I was a little messed up on drugs. Well, a lot. But drugs are what got me through. And the club guys, most of them abandoned me. Every so often they'd come by to help out, or let me ride with them on short runs, but mainly, I was alone, broke, and, god-dammit, I was scared."

Eve reluctantly started to cry. Her hair was already starting to grow out of the blond dye. Dark roots were beginning to show, as was her age, but to Patch, she looked terrific. Young, nubile hard bodies like the ones Nine Inch brought home were one thing. But to Patch, even in sorrow, there was nothing like an older, smarter woman who was willing

199 ««

to share the ride as an accomplice, a partner in crime. As he always said, the better the old lady, the better the MC member.

Eve soon stopped talking, wiped her tears, turned on the television, and dropped herself onto the couch. Patch walked over, sat next to her, and put his hand on her knee.

"I don't miss you," Eve repeated. "But I do miss my little brother. After my mother died, I was the one who was supposed to protect him, not get him killed."

"What else do you want from me, Eve? I packed my gear. I left. I'm gone."

"You're still coming around."

"Hey, let's try to be civil. I left on such a bad note. I want us to be friends, and give you a chance to start over."

"Start over?"

"Yeah. And fix your pain. Deal with your brother's loss. Then move on. That's what I do."

"Typical guy talk. I lose my brother. You say 'fix' it, like it's a motorcycle or something. It's not that easy."

"You'll see it through. Look, the main reason I left California was—" Patch paused.

"Why?"

He looked down at the floor.

"Why, John?"

"I left to protect you. Give you space. Let you grow on your own. Out of my shadow. The club's shadow. Eve, in this stage of your life, you're better off with a guy like Charles."

"Then why are you here?"

"I don't know. I'm through with Oakland; I'm only here for business. I'm not trying to get back together. I know I may not be the best thing for you now, but I wanted you to know I left because of what happened, not how I felt. I couldn't come back to town without setting the record straight."

A silly comedy was on TV. The actors guffawed about love and marriage. It was the same old, same old. The guys were the jerks; the ladies were the wise and crafty souls.

The phony laugh track hung over the room. Patch and Eve watched the comedy for twenty minutes without saying a word. Patch held her hand. Together they had experienced "bipolar," "dysfunctional," and "codependent" long before they became family-counseling buzzwords.

"Look, I may not be the best thing for you. Call me self-ish, but you're still the best thing for me."

"Dammit, Patch. Haven't you heard anything I've said during the last hour? I'm readjusted. We're over. History. Finito."

"I understand *that*, but maybe I ought to stay awhile, at least a little longer. You seem pretty emotional right now. You need someone to help calm you down." He held her hand.

201 **«**

Eve wiped her eyes again, blew her nose into a tissue, and stuffed it into the pocket of her jeans. Then she smiled sadly.

"Patch, in all our time together, calming me down was never one of your specialties."

"Then how come we clicked so well?" he asked.

"You had a lot of other . . . talents," she said, her smile broadening. "They just weren't the kinds of talents that calmed me down."

"Oh, really," he said, his own grin spreading. "You know I always felt a man should go with his strengths."

"Words to live by," Eve agreed, pulling the shades on her window.

» CHAPTER «

21

A Visit
from the Godfather

Wake up, Tony. We need to run an errand."

It was past noon, closing in on one o'clock. Nine Inch was asleep, dead to the world. Patch had gotten in around seven that morning. He kicked around the loft. Reading the papers. Pacing the floor. Thumbing through bike magazines. Washing his T-shirts and underwear in Nine Inch's high-tech washing machine. He nearly used the kitchen sink. Patch wondered, *Is there anything conventional in this place?* He remembered the days when he would sleep half his day away; Eve couldn't wake him for anything. Patch would have mercy on Nine Inch. He'd been staying at his loft for nearly a week now. He knew he was cramping the kid's style. With the setup the way it was, the boy probably hadn't gotten laid, at least not since Patch rolled into town, unless he brought someone home last night while Patch had been at Eve's. Today Patch would start putting Nine Inch's nervous, pent-up energy to good use.

As he lifted his face off the mattress, Nine Inch's hair was standing on end. His face was contorted in a paralyzed snarl and marked with bedsheet-fold patterns.

"Man, what time is it?"

"Quarter past one . . . in the afternoon. Half the day is gone, although I'm sure it's still morning somewhere in the world."

"Where'd you crash last night? I waited as long as I could, then the boys and I went out ridin'. We blew around town and went clubbin'."

"I need to return this cell phone," Patch said, waving Angelo's phone. "Wanna come along?"

"Give me twenty minutes and I'll be showered and shaved and ready to roll."

AS THE TWO TURNED INTO ANGELO'S DRIVEWAY, PATCH remembered when the place had been in better shape. Angelo used to be fanatical about his front yard. Every blade of grass had to be in place. He swept up constantly. Sometimes the boys would mess with his landscape by mixing the bark chips with the ornamental stones. Or switch the flowerpots and concrete planters around. It drove Angelo ballistic. None of the club guys enjoyed hanging at Angelo's because he was so fussy about his house. Angelo explained it was because he grew up a damned poor Texan with sand and soil. Greenery was luxury. Then the wife ran off, and after the divorce and a bitter custody battle for Hollister, he was strapped for cash. Angelo was left with the boy and the legal bills. The house had gone to seed.

Patch pressed the doorbell, expecting Angelo. A young teenager opened the door instead.

"Hollister, what's up? Where's the slob of the house? Angelo around?"

"Godfather," Hollister greeted Patch.

"God, why do you always call me that?" Patch asked. "Like I've ever been a godfather to you. What does a godfather do anyway? You look good, kid. Grown a bit. Say hello to my friend Tony," he said, gesturing to his partner. "His friends call him Nine Inch. I don't."

"Hey Nine Inch," said Hollister.

Hollister looked downright preppy. He was dressed neatly, conservatively, button-down shirt and khaki slacks, nothing like his father, whose idea of dressing up was to wear a clean sweatshirt. Not a hair was out of place on the boy's carefully groomed head.

Hollister was sandy-haired, like his old man, and wore a small hoop earring in his left ear. He was tall and skinny like his mother. His appearance seemed to clash with the rest of the house, which was in total disarray. Patch had always thought if he would have a kid, he'd want one like Hollister, a good kid, reliable and with heart.

Patch and Nine Inch followed the kid inside the living room as Hollister quickly cleared off the cluttered couch. The three sat among the household rubble, strewn clothes, dirty dishes, stacks of magazines, and empty soft-drink cans scattered around the place. The television was on with the volume all the way down.

"Anyone want a Coke?"

"I'm cool," said Nine Inch.

"None for me, kid," said Patch. "So, Hollister, how old are you now?"

"Fifteen," Hollister yelled from the kitchen.

"Girlfriends?"

"A few that I study with. Nothing heavy."

"How's life treating you?"

Hollister sat back down on the couch with his two guests. Patch was expecting him to reply with the perfunctory "fine," but instead his dark eyes took on a pained expression. He said nothing.

"What's the matter? You look bummed."

"I'm worried about my dad. He's not his usual self, or maybe I should say he *is* his usual self. You know what that means."

"No, I don't. Tell me."

"I don't know. He's not sleeping much. He crashes on the couch in front of the TV. He's typing away on the computer a lot, which is okay, I guess. But I don't know what he's up to. He's in and out a lot. His moods are up and down. I can tell when he's high on different pills and stuff."

"Hollister," Patch began. He admired a kid who was

intelligent, whom he could level with. "What do you think he's up to?"

"I don't know. He doesn't leave anything on the computer's hard drive. I feel bad spying on him. He takes all his calls on a cellular these days. Our regular phone never rings. When it does ring, whoever is on the other end usually hangs up. I figure the cops are after us. Dad's been talking to someone he calls J.W. When he calls, he gets up and takes the call outside. Maybe he's selling weed again. I guess that's okay. But what's up with all the secrecy?"

Nine Inch noticed it first. Scattered across the coffee table in front of the couch was a stack of mail, including, near the top of the heap, a bill from Horizon, Angelo's cellular-phone carrier. Nine Inch nudged Patch while Hollister was downing the last of his can of Coke.

"Speaking of which," Patch said, picking up Nine Inch's signal, "they found your father's cell phone down at the clubhouse. Here it is. Sorry it took a couple days to return it. He'll be glad to get it back."

He looked down at the phone bill on the table. "Just make sure you check the next bill so you guys don't get whacked for a bunch of bogus calls."

"Yeah, thanks." Hollister set the phone on the table. "Dad was pissed when he lost his phone. He tried calling it, and got really mad at someone who answered. I got smacked for laughing."

Hollister looked down at the mail sprawled across the coffee table. He picked out the Horizon wireless bill.

"Look. Here's the latest cell bill. It just came in. We can check it out now."

He tore the envelope open and sifted through the printed matter and announcements and extracted the bill. He tried looking at the numbers and wrinkled his face in confusion.

"This stuff doesn't mean anything to me. See if anyone's tried to rip us off."

Nine Inch pulled a small slip of paper out of his pocket with a phone number written on it. He leaned in and checked the call record. It was hot off the press and up-to-date. Under the "outgoing calls" information was the same phone number he'd jotted down for Patch that night, the one they retrieved from the cell phone after the club meeting—the 2:34 P.M. call to 510-555-9178 from this John McIntosh guy. And there were a lot of calls made to that same number, over a dozen within a couple of days.

"Hollister," Nine Inch asked as he looked up from study-ing the bill, "who was the guy you said that's been calling your dad a lot?"

"I'm pretty sure Dad called him J.W."

Patch and Nine Inch looked at each other. "J.W.," Nine Inch whispered to Patch. "John W. McIntosh on that voice-mail greeting. Gotta be the same guy. Probably his dope source or something."

According to the Horizon bill, this John McIntosh char-acter kept in constant contact with Angelo. The calls ranged from one minute to twenty-five. Patch and Nine Inch no-ticed the bill was past due, bordered in red ink. Angelo was in debt to the company for $246. It must have been a cou-ple months since he last paid them.

"This looks okay to me, Hollister," said Patch. "No calls

for the last couple of days." He and Nine Inch stood up and headed for the front door.

"We gotta run, kid. Tell your Pa we came by and we're sorry we missed him." Patch paused. "Don't worry about your dad. He probably has a lot of stuff floatin' around in his head that he doesn't want to trouble you with."

"Let's keep all this stuff between us," said Hollister, "in case it all turns out to be typical Dad. You know, nothing too bad."

"I understand."

Before Patch and Nine Inch opened the door, Patch stopped.

"Hollister. If something comes up, here's a number you can reach me at while I'm here. Anything at all, just call. I know I haven't exactly been there for you, being your godfather and all."

"How long you staying for?"

"For as long as it takes. I want to get a few things cleared up and out of the way. Then I'm off, heading back to Arizona."

"That's right, you're in Arizona now. Hot weather. Maybe I could visit for a week or so. We could spend time in the desert, riding bikes."

"Sounds great, kid." Patch wished he was lounging in the dry heat of his empty backyard on a chaise longue or riding down Carefree Highway into another beautiful Arizona sunset.

Before they started their motorcycles, Nine Inch looked over at Patch and shook his head in disgust. To Nine Inch, there was almost no sin greater than mess.

"Nice kid. Too bad things are so fucked up here."

"Yeah," Patch said, "and it's too bad he's got a father up to his neck in God knows what."

"Patch, this McIntosh character is your key. He might have something to do with why Angelo is acting so strangely."

Patch nodded, already thinking ahead.

22

Swingin' @ the Starlight

Angelo sat alone, in his regular booth, at the Mexican coffee shop, blowing smoke rings and pushing around a fat breakfast burrito with his fork. His mind was racing, going over the details of the pot deal and the weapons buy. He was searching for holes, anything he might have overlooked. It was time to set up the funding. Seventy Gs would fuel all his

DEAD IN 5 HEARTBEATS

projects, with a little extra off the top for himself. Just then, his reclaimed cell phone vibrated. He was glad when Hollister had handed it over. It was J.W.

"I was just getting ready to call you, man. My shit is set up. We need to talk money, real soon."

"Okay then, let's meet," said J.W. "How about tonight? I'll call you later with the where and when."

"Splendido. See ya."

ANGELO'S POWWOW WITH J.W. WAS SET THAT NIGHT AT, OF all places, the Starlight Motel, a swingers' palace down the road from the Oakland airport. J.W. had his usual room reserved: 12F. Seven o'clock. Angelo promised himself he'd lay off the applejack, reefer, pills, and powder. This was an important negotiation. He needed all his wits about him. He also needed his pistol, which he packed inside his jacket pocket.

The Starlight had been Oakland's premier motel and Triple-X playground since the 1970s, when Jim and Artie Mitchell candy-coated live porn at San Francisco's famed O'Farrell Theatre. Three decades later, it seemed like an odd place for Angelo to broker his brand-new life. He had conducted his drug deals and scams in more unsavory environments. Particularly in San Francisco, in places like a Russian nightclub in the Richmond district, a Seventh Street tattoo parlor, North Beach S&M sex shops, Tenderloin strip joints.

Oakland had its own seamy underbelly, but not so much these days. The city's vice scene had fizzled compared with

Frisco. Black crack whores and low-rent massage parlors operated, mostly. By comparison, the Starlight seemed self-contained and certainly a bit cheesier.

Just down the street from the Starlight was the Harley dealership. Angelo stopped on the way and picked up gaskets and filters he'd put off replacing on his bike. Later on, he'd have it looked at thoroughly. Depending on how things went with J.W., he would be in the market to sell his Harley when it was time to leave town.

Angelo pulled into the Starlight's parking lot twenty minutes early. He thought this was a place worth reexploring. Relive the old times. He hadn't been "Starlighting" in ages. When the Infidelz formed in the seventies, a few of the club members partied at the place, a clothing-optional adult playpen. Back then it catered to nudists, celebrity swingers, local sex addicts, trashy politicians, and other East Bay deviants who were "exploring the lifestyle." During the swinging seventies and the cocaine eighties, it wasn't unusual to walk in on pro football players, or whatever visiting team happened to be on the road, in midorgy, gangbanging hookers dressed as cheerleaders or cheerleaders dressed as hookers.

In those days, to have a good time, all you needed was a couple of drinks to lose your inhibitions, a pocketful of drugs, and a stiffy to play hide the salami. While the clothing-optional downstairs nightclub and bar thing was a pleasant diversion, the hard-core action took place in the sixty-four rooms attached. Angelo remembered the hallways, bustling and hustling like a Middle Eastern bazaar as couples frequently changed partners and positions. During the seventies and the eighties, nobody paid for anything except booze and a room to do it in. Different rooms catered to different scenes—S&M, leather, group sex, girl-on-girl, assorted fetishes, voyeurism, and musk-oil massages.

Angelo and the boys used to laugh about the Snake Room, where a twelve-foot python had lived, courtesy of a white girl with a permed Afro hairstyle who wore nothing more than red cowboy boots. Whatever lit your wick, it was all a go-go at the Starlight.

While retaining its seventies motif, the new Starlight had certainly changed since the old days. It wasn't funky and reckless as it had been in the pre-AIDS days. Rather, the joint was antiseptic in a humorless and soulless new-millennium kind of way. The elite strippers with exotic names like Goddess Fontina or AfroDeity had been replaced with surgically enhanced B-team girls with names like Angel and Tina. They systematically worked the tabletops on all fours, efficiently separating lonely and delusional men from their hard-earned cash. In a slick place like the new Starlight, there was no such thing as free love or free pussy.

What J.W. was doing in a place like this, Angelo didn't even venture a guess. Actually, it was a stroke of genius. There wasn't a uniformed cop in sight. The place was mostly inhabited by out-of-towners from the airport, desperate for a layover before returning to their wives and kids. A flyer posted nearby advertised the services of a traveling Russian stripper from Modesto available for hire every Friday at the Starlight. There was a bachelor party in one of the small ballrooms, where Nadia, an oblivious law student by day, stripper by night, did the bump-and-grind to a mundane R. Kelly hip-hop pop tune. The bar served cold beer, seven-fifty a bottle.

Angelo peeked inside. *Man, used to be you could bounce quarters off a Starlight girl's ass, especially the fine black fillies. This place has sure strayed from the days when ballroom literally meant ball-room.*

At seven straight up, Angelo picked up the powder-blue house phone. It reeked of some Persian's sweet aftershave, so he held it away from his ear and cheek.

"McIntosh's room, please," he instructed the desk operator.

The phone sounded a burst of five tones until J.W. picked up.

"Hello?"

"Yo, I'm down in the lobby, the bar or whatever."

"Pretty swinging place, eh?"

"Yeah. Real groovy," Angelo droned.

"C'mon up. Twelve-F." *Click.*

Angelo navigated his way through the hallway maze of rooms just like the old days, twenty years gone. The memories whizzed by. Twelve-F wasn't too far from the Snake Room. *Whatever happened to the Snake Woman, anyway?*

He rapped on the door.

"Enter and sign in please," J.W. said after opening the door, seemingly in a jovial mood. He was dressed in a Chicago Bulls warm-up suit. He looked like a cross between Hugh Hefner and David Caruso. Something about seeing J.W. in basketball sweats instead of a business suit made Angelo feel even oilier. One desk lamp burned on a nightstand while a Lava lamp glowed on the other side of the bed. The dimly lit atmosphere was way too intimate and cozy for two guys to meet. It made Angelo feel queasy. The desk was stacked with paperwork and a laptop computer that hummed quietly. Stray floppies and CD-ROMs overflowed onto the floor. The walls were a dark chocolate brown. The bed was made up with dark satin sheets topped with a fake brown fur comforter.

"I'm working undercover on a sex racket thing."

Oh, sure. Angelo was unconvinced.

"Mainly," J.W. confessed, "I come here to get away from the riffraff and the office politics. I can't get shit done in my office. Plus, if I'm tensed up, I can get an escort outcall to come up and give me a hand job."

Angelo winced. *Too much information.* But it sounded more plausible than J.W.'s "sex racket" explanation.

"Okay, let's see what you've got. Give me a progress report," J.W. said brusquely, losing part of the good mood he had conveyed when he opened the door.

"Here's where we are, and here's some tapes of what went down," Angelo said, handing J.W. the microcassettes. "Two deals are set, a day apart."

215 «

"The first one being?"

"Listen to the tapes. A pretty hefty pot network ready to set up, fifty pounds for the first shipment, fully processed. Guys from the club will sell it on the street. We pick up in Redding on the twenty-third of the month. That's next week. Like I said, mucho club guys involved. As for the source, you might know him as Humboldt Merle. He's a pretty big operator."

"I'm not familiar, but I'm sure he's big kahuna."

"He's been a ganja pipeline for the Infidelz over the past two or three years. Plus, I'm sure he's a doorway to more growers if you want to go in that direction. That's up to you. All I need is money up front. Twenty-five."

"Grand?"

No, you idiot, cents. "Yes, J.W., twenty-five grand."

J.W. seemed too preoccupied on other matters to give Angelo any shit back. He wasn't fully tuned in. Yet he kept shaking his head in agreement, so Angelo continued his pitch.

"Now for the good part. Like I told you, I got five leathernecks up north. They've been looting a Marine munitions dump for about eighteen months. Machine guns, mortars, rockets, C-4. We split the whole dessert tray with one of our chapters up north; maybe even bring in one or two more. Less than twenty grand on our end. Plus I've got a long list of guys from about eight bike clubs that will buy the stuff. Like I said, the deal is scheduled to go down the next day. Lots of street interest."

"Sounds like you've been busy, Angelo."

"Which is why you need to clue me in on the basics. I need to know how your boys operate. How *do you* intend to stage the buys and busts?"

"Buys and busts?" J.W. asked.

"Yeah, buys and busts. Won't my guys be selling some of this shit to undercover agents?"

J.W. cast his eyes to someplace far away.

Angelo felt a thud of pressure hit his chest. His head throbbed. *So this is what happens when you deal with cops.*

"What's goin' on here, J.W.?"

"A change of plans. You got a coupla lousy drugs and weapons buys. That's small-time shit, Angelo."

Angelo's stomach dropped to his shoes. He would have swallowed hard except his mouth was dry. Sweat bathed his forehead. He thought about reaching for the gun in his pocket.

"I don't understand."

"It's simple. I need more information on the Infidelz."

Angelo was flummoxed.

"What about the busts?" he asked as the pitch of his voice rose.

"Look, I'm looking at cleaning up these streets. You and me, we can play a huge role in that."

"You and me? What the fuck are you talking about?"

J.W. laid down his trump card.

"You and I work as a team, we agitate and aggravate, behind the scenes, of course. Not only can we clean up the streets, but with your help, let's say I intervene between the Infidelz and the other clubs before you and your friends kill each other. Whattaya think?"

"Look, asshole. I just wanna do my deals and disappear. Fuck this law-and-order shit." Angelo scowled as he tightened the grip on the hidden revolver. His finger was on the trigger. *This guy is not only changing the deal, he's living in a dreamworld. Clean up these streets?* J.W. was a pubic hair away from getting whacked.

"Angelo, I need your help. And you need mine. Either we work together or else maybe the club gets wind of your involvement with the government."

"Are you threatening me?" Angelo let go of the gun stashed in his pocket. Then he grabbed J.W. by his red warm-up shirt, swung him around, lifted him off his feet, and slammed him up against the wall. J.W. could feel Angelo's hyperventilated breath in his face, his eyes bugged out and his teeth clenched like a lunatic's.

"It's not so much a threat as a fact. I don't really have to go over your options, do I?" J.W. said. "Just suppose the club got an eyeful of the Witness Protection paperwork sitting on my desk? Or if they heard what's on the tapes you just gave me? Imagine the wrong stuff getting into the wrong hands? If the club even knew we were having this conversation, you'd be killed. So are you on board or what?"

Angelo let go of J.W. and paced the length of the motel room clutching his gun. Doing prison time and losing his son was one thing, but if the club found out what he'd been up to, pure and simple, he *was* a dead man.

J.W. straightened himself up in the mirror. Recent events between the warring MCs were working in his favor. Tensions were pretty high. The shit was ready to fly.

"Tell me something, J.W. What's your piece in all this? You gotta be gettin' your beak wet somehow."

"I look good to my people. What's so terrible about that? So we both get something out of all this before you disappear. The night you got busted I saw opportunity. Honestly, I don't see how you can walk away from all this. You're up to your ears in it now, buddy. Think about your balls hanging from the Infidelz flagpole."

J.W.'s threat hit home. Angelo let go of the pistol in his jacket pocket.

"How do I know I can trust you, you fuckin' weasel?"

"Angelo, like I said, you have no choice. This fucking weasel is your only salvation. It's either you and me together, or you take your chances out on the street. Suit yourself. There's the door."

"Like I have a fucking choice?"

"Like I keep tellin' ya." J.W. laughed. "No. I need you out there on the inside."

Angelo would play ball. He'd have to. The clubs were on

the brink of war anyway. "Okay, listen," he said. "There's stuff going down with the club tomorrow night that could be, uh, convenient to your plans."

"Our plans. That's the spirit. Remember, Angelo, information is power. No doubt the tapes you've given me are powerful."

Angelo felt sick. Things at the Starlight had not gone quite as he'd planned. *Maybe I oughta waste this guy after all.*

He blinked as he pondered his next move. *Two choices. Either walk out the door and play along or end it now, kill the motherfucker and turn the place into a crime scene.* The headlines alone were tempting: FBI AGENT FOUND SLAIN IN XXX MOTEL. But he couldn't do it—he was already on record as J.W.'s informant. If the fed was killed, Angelo knew he'd be at the top of the list of suspects. He couldn't risk it—not with Hollister still needing him.

"I think we're done, Angelo." J.W. forced a smile. "Now get the hell out of here. I'm expecting company. Remember. You need to keep me in the loop. Like I said, you're my eyes and ears, brother."

Angelo cringed again. "Listen, you sad fuck, don't you ever 'brother' me again."

Angelo's predicament placed J.W. under a protective shield. The agent was in a fortuitous position. The violence and the vengeance between the MCs were already festering. Sides were being taken; lines were being drawn even as the two of them spoke. Angelo headed for the door.

Out in the hallway, he reached for his beeper. He'd gotten everything on tape.

"That little cunt," he muttered under his breath as he slammed the door behind him. Standing in the motel hallway,

219 «

he had a mind to go back in and blow J.W.'s brains all over that Lava lamp. *That prick tried to play me.*

As Angelo rode home, he tried to sort out the details of what transpired. Whatever scheme J.W. had in mind, he had to play along. He couldn't help but think J.W. had a backup plan in place with somebody. Whatever or whoever it was, he did know that the agent had him by the short and curlies. He had no choice but to play along.

Angelo's tape collection was his thin line between life and death. A balance of power. An insurance policy in case J.W. had a mind to abandon him.

23

Crunch Time

Patch arrived at the clubhouse just as Angelo was pulling off his helmet and gloves. He angled his bike next to his partner's.

"Looks like we got another full house tonight."

"We better," Angelo said, surveying the long line of bikes. "Big meetin', I s'pose."

Inside the clubhouse, a raucous quorum

had already assembled. Laid out on the front table were the Wheeler colors that Patch had pulled off the dead shooter. It was all the evidence the Infidelz needed to pursue vengeance. If their last meeting had consisted of questions, doubts, and hesitation, this one would be an agenda of decision, action, and execution.

Ahab pounded his gavel and called for order. He had fresh news to pass on to the members.

"Listen up! An important piece of information came our way, courtesy of one of our members' old ladies. There's going to be a big 2Wheeler hoedown in Oakland. Game time, tomorrow night. All their California charters will be there."

The news was greeted with loud yelps and cheers.

"It's at the Ashland Court Motel. Chino and his boys own the place. It'll be the perfect place to ambush those bastards—in our town, but on their turf. After their meeting, before they bring in their girls to party—*bam!*—that's when we hit 'em.

"Tomorrow night, instead of getting fucked, the 2Wheelers are going to get *fucked up*.

"I scouted the place out. Access points. Escape routes. Everything looks good. We go in. Strike hard and fast. We go out. *Bada-bing!* Those fuckin' guys won't know what hit 'em.

"Vans and cars have already been lined up. Drivers are assigned, too. Tomorrow, Brother Streeter will do more surveillance and get an extra read on things just before we head out."

The raid was set.

"Meet here tomorrow night. Ten forty-five rollout. Bring your weapons and whatever else you need. Guns, knives, shotguns, whatever. Use your imagination."

After the meeting adjourned, Patch walked outside past Lester. He was patched up from the shooting and his arm was in a sling. Now he had to master the art of riding one-handed.

Angelo was sitting on his ride. He stared intently at the lines on the street and finished his cigarette. Patch walked over and tapped his partner on the shoulder.

"Ready for tomorrow?" he asked.

Angelo shrugged. "Ready as I'll ever be. They got it comin'. War is war." He lit up another smoke. "The younger guys seem a little nervous."

"They should be," said Patch. "They've only known peace and prosperity."

Choosing the club over family was one of the most diffi-cult choices a member was required to make before he donned the patch. Crunch time was the hardest time to wear your colors. Some of the club's best members had joined up after doing time in prison or the armed forces. They'd experienced brotherhood and camaraderie through violence and confrontation. Patch had warned the newer members numerous times. Join the club and maybe your own flesh and blood—your family, your parents, your sib-lings—might turn their backs on you. What then? He knew from experience. His own loyalty to the club had already cost him his wife and longtime soul mate, Eve.

"Did Hollister tell you we came by?" Patch asked Angelo. "They found your phone at the clubhouse."

"Yeah, he said something. Sorry I missed you guys."

"He's practically a grown man."

Angelo hung his head and puffed on his Viceroy. "Yeah, I'd catch a bullet for that kid." He laughed. "I don't know whether I'm taking care of him or he of me. The lines get kinda blurry sometimes."

"I don't know what to tell you, Angelo. I'm certainly not one to lecture."

"Sometimes I ask myself," Angelo continued, "what means more, my club or my family? It's weird."

"It ain't weird, Angelo. It's just tough, sometimes. I had to make the same choice with Eve. It's great when the club and the family fit, but it doesn't always work out that way. Shit happens."

"You gettin' back together?"

"Who knows? I need to get myself together first. Then I can worry about other people."

Angelo flicked his lit cigarette butt all the way to the centerline of East Fourteenth Street. Patch looked at his friend, sadly hunched over his motorcycle. He seemed a million

» 224

miles away. Angelo was a good man to have by your side during the heat of battle. Patch admired the guy's physical strength but wondered about his mental stamina. He wanted to believe everything was okay with Angelo.

"See *you* tomorrow night," Patch said, reaching over and poking Angelo's chest with his finger before starting his bike. "And be on time for once, will ya?"

Angelo, the great procrastinator. He smiled back at Patch and started up his bike. Patch slipped on his helmet. Both men rode off in opposite directions, straight into darkness.

A BLACK HARLEY SPORTSTER WAS PARKED BY THE DOOR of Nine Inch's compound. He had company. Patch checked out the chrome and paint job on the bike as he rode up. He instantly recognized Sammy the Greek's flame designs. Top-shelf work. Sammy's Oakland bike shop was legendary up and down the coast for its custom paint jobs.

Tonight, the night before battle, Patch was keyed up. He wanted nothing more than a warm bed, a cold beer, and soli-tude. Read a little *Art of War*. Practice a bit of meditation.

Inside the loft, Nine Inch sat at the couch and sorted through another stack of proof sheets, preparing to spend some time inside his stuffy, chemical-laden darkroom.

"Hey, brother. Got a little surprise for you upstairs," Nine Inch said without looking up from his work.

"I hate surprises."

"You'll like this one."

Patch climbed the stairs to the bed on his side of the loft. He thought about a workout on Nine Inch's gym equip-ment. Iron out the kinks and tightness that tensed up his neck and shoulders. But his plans were about to change. Sit-ting on the mattress, cross-legged, was LiLac.

"So, that must be your horse out front."

"That's me," she said, suggestively patting the mattress with her hand.

The girl amused Patch. Not much more than half his age, smart and cocky. He stretched out next to her, kicked off his boots, and clasped his hands behind his head. She lay down next to him.

From below, Nine Inch hinted loudly about his extended time developing photos.

"That's it, folks," he called out. "I'm going in the dark-room now. Could be in there for hours."

The compound door slammed shut. Then the walls

vibrated to the muffled sounds of Tool blasting from the darkroom stereo. Patch and LiLac laughed.

"He totally admires you," LiLac said.

Patch shrugged, his mind not entirely settled down. *This time tomorrow, the shit will be on.* He always left the possibility open that there would be problems. Arrests. Fuckups. Something deadly—or worse, utter defeat. He kept those thoughts at bay.

"What's the saying?" LiLac asked. "A penny for what you're thinking?"

"You mean a penny for my thoughts? You don't wanna know."

Patch wrapped his arms around LiLac's thin frame and squeezed her tightly. A young body in his arms on a night like this was a fair consolation. LiLac unbuttoned the fly of his pants. He reciprocated and worked on the top button of hers. It didn't take much nudging to get LiLac out of her tight black jeans. She wore a loose, purple silk button-down top.

"I hope I'm not intruding," she said.

"Not at all. I've had enough of being alone."

LiLac started to unbutton her top.

"No, no. Leave it on."

They made love quickly, as if time were at a premium, LiLac on top, Patch's hands lost under her shirt. He ran his palms up and down the silky skin of her back. With a soft and low purr, LiLac came first with a quivering shake, faster than Patch had seen a girl come before. *Ladies first.* A few minutes after, he spent himself. Then LiLac laid her head on his shoulder.

"You're still a mystery to me."

"Yeah, well." Patch sighed. "I told you enough already, unless . . ."

"Unless what?"

Patch had caught his second wind; he was suddenly game for a little night riding.

"Unless you feel like heading out for a drink and a bite to eat somewhere. I know just the place."

Making love with LiLac hadn't tamed the adrenaline that flooded Patch's system. Some steak and ale in a dark place would help do the trick.

"Jeez. Don't you have things backward? Aren't you supposed to wine and dine me *first?*"

Patch got up and pulled on his jeans.

"Are you coming or not?"

"Honey, I already did."

227 **«**

IT WAS JUST PAST MIDNIGHT. ANGELO POKED HIS HEAD IN-side the refrigerator and grabbed the milk. He finished it off, washing down a couple of Percodans. A trickle of milk dribbled down the side of his mouth, which he wiped off with his sleeve.

He had put off a call to J.W. as long as he could. Dark thoughts and hard choices were clouding his mind. He thought about not making the call at all. Fess up to Ahab and Patch, own up to his betrayal, take whatever punishment was decided upon. Be it expulsion, a beating, whatever. But it was too late. He had gone too far. Plus, there was Hollister. He owed the kid some kind of life.

Angelo pulled out his cell and hit the speed dial. "You're

hanging out at the kinky motel, aren't you? On second thought, don't tell me."

"Actually I'm in my office," J.W. said. "What's up?"

Angelo breathed out a long resigned sigh. "Okay. Ashland Court Motel, Oakland, ten forty-five P.M. tomorrow. The Infidelz move in on the 2Wheelers. There's gonna be an invasion."

"That's perfect! Just what we needed. That means you and me, we're in business."

Yeah, right, you and me. Then he thought of something more reassuring. "The 2Wheelers," Angelo said to J.W., "are gonna be toast." He paused. "So, J.W., that shit that went down at the Starlight? Where you talked about the arrests and stuff?"

"Yeah."

"That's all on the level. Like, the Infidelz aren't going down, outside of a little jail time."

"Absolutely."

"Dammit, this is important, J.W. No bullshit. I don't care what you do with those other guys so long as my boys come out okay in the end."

"That's the deal, Angelo. Everybody wins. You go away with your boy. Your guys get off with light time. And I clean up the city and still avoid a war. We're both heroes, *capisce*?"

"I hope so."

Angelo's stomach was churning. He felt a lot of things—regretful, anxious, uncertain, guilty—anything but heroic.

A LITTLE BEFORE FIVE IN THE MORNING, IN THE MIDST OF a dream, Patch, alone, bolted upright in his bed, eyes open, heart racing. He'd dreamed of his father, the commander. He'd invented a face and a voice for him. Most of the details of the dream vanished when he awoke. He felt disoriented and his heart pounded.

Patch could only imagine his father's reaction to *his* life thus far. Being a military pilot, would he have understood the brotherhood his son was fighting for? If Patch bought the farm later that night, a 2Wheeler shiv mortally lodged in his gut, would he measure up to the old man's expectations?

What did Patch have to show for his forty-plus years on the planet? A broken marriage and enough motorcycle mileage to orbit the earth several times over? Like his father, conceivably he would also leave this earth in a blaze of glory, with the only thing he had to show for life—his freedom. Death. It was an eerie but oddly comforting thought. Then he drifted back into a deeper doze.

24

V-Rod

As Angelo tinkered in the garage with Hollister's bike, his phone rang. He was expecting a follow-up call from J.W.

"Angelo here."

"Angelo, it's Ronnie."

Ronnie was an old riding buddy. A citizen, and a fairly decent guy. He lent Angelo a few bucks on occasion. Was this a collection call?

"Angelo, I'm stoked."

"What's up, Brother Ron?"

"You doin' anything just now, Angie?"

Angelo scowled at being called that. "Nothing that can't wait. Just replacing the plugs on Holly's bike. Changing the oil. Almost done."

"C'mon over to my crib. I just cleared the waiting list. You're speaking to the proud owner of a new Harley V-Rod."

"That's great. I'm happy for you, bud." Angelo had read about the new machine. The V-Rod's motor was water-cooled and manufactured by Porsche. It was Harley's clos-est stab at the Jap bike market. Who'da thunk?

"Get over here," Ronnie yelled into the phone with ela-tion. "I need your 'yea' or 'nay' on this baby after you take it out for a spin."

Angelo roared up to Ronnie's pad and spied the virgin cycle parked in the driveway. Ronnie stood next to the V-Rod like a proud father, grinning, his hand resting on the deep arc of the bike's plush black leather seat. It had a svelte aluminum body and fenders, glinting solid disc brakes, and high-rise handle-bars, a stunning combination of modern and retro.

"You're the first guy I called, Angelo. I wanna know what a club guy thinks of my new machine. I've been out riding all morning."

Angelo looked up and down at the Harley's curvaceous design. "Whoa, baby, nice bod." He whistled and ran his hand across the silver-brushed aluminum cowling that housed the gas tank. "About as shapely as Pamela Ander-son's ass."

Angelo swung his leg over the new bike and settled onto its low seat. He pushed back the kickstand and bounced his weight up and down repeatedly, checking the cycle's suspension, and leaned it from side to side. It felt at least a hundred pounds lighter than a Road King.

"It's eleven hundred and thirty cc's, a five-speed beauty," bragged Ronnie. "Go on. Get outta here; I'll see you back in an hour."

Angelo reached down by his right thigh and lit up the V-Rod's ignition after watching its high-tech display go through its checkout sequence. He gunned the accelerator a few times and noticed the crescent-shaped tach showed the bike responding with very high rpm's. Even then, the V-Rod didn't have the blustering, deafening sound of his regular ride. He kinda missed that, as only a civilized whirring sound escaped the pipes of the V-Rod. But once he was rolling, the new motorcycle cornered smoother than his own beater. He revved the Porsche motor and opened up the throttle on a deserted frontage straightaway. Zero to sixty in under five seconds. *Not bad.* Angelo was quietly impressed. He rode surprisingly low on the bike with his feet stretched out in front of him. It didn't have the wobble of so many other new Harleys. But was it worth such a high price, a few grand over sticker and a four-month wait?

Angelo kicked the bike into high gear and merged onto the 580 freeway. He headed east for a few miles.

Let's see what this motherfucker can do.

He pulled the V-Rod off the freeway and onto the Golf Links Road exit and maintained constant speed. He saw no cars waiting at the stoplight intersection up ahead, so he jacked up his speed, ran the red light, veered the cycle left, and roared up into the hills toward the Knowland Park Zoo, all in one smooth motion.

Not bad, not bad at all.

After a few minutes scurrying up side roads past the zoo, he turned around, opened up the throttle again, and sped down the hill, back toward the flatlands. Angelo shifted his body from side to side, digging into each twist of the road. At the bottom of the grade, he redlined the bike toward 9,000 rpm's and hung a sharp left off Golf Links and skidded onto Ninety-eighth Avenue toward the Oakland airport.

Angelo guided the V-Rod a few more miles down Ninety-eighth Avenue, then pulled into the lot of his favorite hot-dog joint. He ordered a couple of chili dogs and took a seat on top of one of the picnic tables outside. He gazed over at the still-pristine V-Rod and listened to the crackling sound the alloy metals made as the engine cooled after his brisk ride. He devoured his first dog in four bites and reached inside the bag for the second one.

A fellow motorcyclist putted into the parking lot.

"Yo, brother! That your bike?"

"Yup."

"First time I've seen a V-Rod. How's it ride?"

"Like a dream."

"Man," the guy said, "ain't life grand?"

"Sure is." Angelo gave him a halfhearted thumbs-up sign and the guy rode off.

A brand-new bike was symbolic of a brand-new life. You start from scratch as you rediscover the open highway. Each twist and turn of the road seems fresh and exciting. He longed for that feeling again.

Just as he had done the afternoon he spent fishing for stripers off Point Molate, Angelo experienced a moment of clarity. He knew he had reached a point of no return. His problems with the club and the feds could not be solved with reason or cunning. His younger, hopeful days were now behind him.

If the battle with the 2Wheelers was going to be curtailed by the feds, what was the point in showing up? Angelo was through with the club. His days riding as a 1%er were over.

He stared intently at the long and low contours of Ronnie's sweet machine and pondered the landscape of self-preservation, a chance to start anew. He would rediscover another open highway. His life.

I**T WAS TWO P.M. ON A FRIDAY AND THE BUREAU OFFICE WAS** abandoned, a law enforcement ghost town. Most of the other agents already had a jump on the weekend. J.W. was just getting in. He tossed his briefcase into the corner of his beige cubicle and slipped off his sport coat. He loosened his tie and reached immediately for the receiver of his telephone and punched up an outside line.

J.W.'s desktop was part fed command post, part minibar and medicine cabinet. In one locked drawer were two small half-empty bottles of vodka and tequila. In another, various psychotropic remedies. Uppers and downers and stuff designed to keep him even-keeled. Orange plastic bottles contained Black Beauties, Valiums, Percodan, and a few grams of speed, prescription mood meds, mostly samples he wangled from a doctor friend. J.W. gave him the usual line, having to do with the debilitating stress associated with fighting crime.

J.W. popped an upper and pulled out his loose-leaf organizer, thumbed through the pages, and looked up the latest number for one of his MC contacts. He'd been trying to reach the guy since Angelo dropped the news of the invasion. As he stabbed out the digits of the phone number with the eraser side of his pencil, he snickered at the thought of storing the personal number of a 1%er prez, or any of his other snitches for that matter, into his Bureau speed-dialing phone system, as instructed. J.W. hated his outpost chief as much as he did his cubicle. He was nothing but an incompetent political kiss-ass. Fat, soft, and weak.

After several rings, a voice picked up, tense and pinched. "Lock here."

"Lock N Load, it's J.W."

"Man, ring me on this other line." He gave J.W. another number. "Five minutes." *Click.*

J.W. scrawled the new number into his dog-eared organizer. Now the Gun Runners prez had four different phone numbers next to his name.

"Lock, it's J.W. again. We have to meet."

"Where and when?"

"It's your call, Lock."

Lock thought a moment. "Actually, I'm in your town right now. I know just the place. Got a pencil?"

25

The Everglades

J.W. wasn't familiar with the shabby little hole-in-the-wall bar that Lock N Load had chosen for their meeting. The Everglades. Must have been quite the Polynesian dive in its heyday. Fortunately, the place was empty in the late afternoon. The Gunners' leader was already seated in a booth, alone, with a bottle of Corona in front of him. He was not prone to small talk or hospitality.

"Whattaya got for me?" Lock asked.

"Tonight the Infidelz go to war."

An extended pause. Lock rubbed his chin. "Says who?"

"Says my sources, that's who."

"Who's getting clipped? Which club?" Lock's tone was truculent and confrontational.

"What's it matter?"

"I'm in no mood for guessing games."

"The lowdown I'm giving you . . ." said J.W., "the gang squad doesn't even have this, and between you and me, they aren't gonna get it, either. Not from me. As for our financial arrangement—"

"Yeah, yeah. Don't fucking remind me again. I've cleared everything with my people. We have an understanding. No worries. You'll get your monthly piece of the pie. So what the fuck's goin' on?"

"The Infidelz are hitting the 2Wheelers in Oakland. Just like we figured. Ten forty-five tonight."

Another long pause. Lock's face froze like stone. Then a high-pitched snicker. "Christ. Chino's gonna get creamed. Payback for the casino. Hmm. That's good."

"Listen, Lock. Here's how I wanna do this. First, tip off the Wheelers that it's happening. But leak it anonymously to Chino and his boys so they can't trace it back to me, not to you, not to anybody."

Lock N Load scratched his bald pate. "Okay. I'm keyed in. Can do."

"Next," continued J.W., "I want you guys to be on the sidelines and out of sight until it's time. Infidelz and the 2Wheelers fight to the death. The Gun Runners have to roll in and take out the winners. That's essential to our plan, do you understand? The Gunners move in. Can you call your guys and get crackin' on this?"

Lock N Load exhaled a long gasp of air. He knew what was at stake here; it was his biggest challenge to date as a club prez. He and his boys could soon have the run of the whole state. But playing with a renegade FBI agent was high-stakes poker.

"There's not enough time to get reinforcements up from SoCal." Lock thought out loud.

"Lock, are you with me on this, or what?" J.W. squirmed in his seat and moved closer. He was eyeballing Lock, face-to-face. J.W. was persuasive. He could talk smack with the most hard-boiled wiseguys. But he hated dealing with Lock's aloofness and curt responses.

"Once we cut out both the 2Wheelers and the Infidelz, think of your position here. The Gun Runners will be the top dogs. Everything will run through you guys. This is it. But you guys need to be able to pull this off on your own. I know what you're capable of."

J.W., of all people, knew what Lock was capable of. The agent had access to every file of every club member in California. When he first came up with the idea of pitting the clubs against one another, he had wanted to approach the most influential member of the strongest club. But that man was Patch, and he had just bailed out of Oakland, out of California.

The next best candidate on J.W.'s law enforcement list—Lock N Load.

The leader of the Gun Runners tried to cultivate the image of a plainspoken musclehead, but he was far more clever than he let on. During the brawl at Trader's, he had realized what a perfect opportunity he had when Marco pulled into the parking lot. It had been his S&W Python that had ended Marco's life. Lock knew that in the confusion of the brawl, no one would be able to tell where the shots had come from. And he knew that the shooting would cause widespread suspicion that another club had the Delz in their sights.

But he had to make sure the war was fought between the Gunners' biggest rivals. That meant the 2Wheelers had to be involved. But how do you get the Wheelers to war with the Delz? Lock's next move was to target Hank and Reload on the Oakland estuary. He figured that the deaths of the two Wheelers would be blamed on the only other club to have lost a member recently—the Infidelz. The subsequent fire-fight in the casino was just what he had hoped for: the Wheelers assumed that the estuary shootings were some kind of retaliation by the Delz for Marco's death. But after the dust settled, war still hadn't been declared.

239 «

It was just another opportunity, as far as Lock was concerned. He knew that he would be suspected of being behind the attacks. So he did what anyone would do if they were suspected of planning war—he campaigned for peace. By offering to be a mediator between the Infidelz and the 2Wheelers, he avoided suspicion, looking like the great peacemaker, while at the same time making the two clubs seem all the more eager to fight by rejecting his offer. But Lock had underestimated Ahab's coolheadedness. The man wouldn't break the peace until he had no choice. So Lock, with J.W.'s help, made sure they gave Ahab no choice.

It wasn't that hard. J.W. had plenty of tools at his disposal. One of them was Frank Peterson, an undercover member of the LAPD's gang squad who was as freewheeling and "open-minded" about the law as J.W. himself. It only took a little talk, and some under-the-table cash, and the cop, already having infiltrated the Wheelers and posing as a prospect, came on board. Peterson was then able to convince a very new and very drunk member of the Wheelers that they'd be heroes to the club if the two of them shot up the Delz clubhouse as payback for Hank and Reload.

After the job was done, Peterson simply had to ensure that the Delz got a good look at the Wheeler patch his buddy was wearing. He hadn't counted on Patch getting right on his tail. When Peterson realized he might not be able to get away, he put a bullet in the Wheeler's chest, partly as a way to make sure the Wheelers got blamed, partly as a way to elude Patch during the chase. It wasn't enough. Peterson became just another stain on the roadway, but his mission had been accomplished—the Delz had their evidence.

Now there would be a war. But whoever emerged as the victor wouldn't live long enough to celebrate.

"We need you to make this thing happen tonight," said J.W.

Lock loved the sound of a begging federal agent.

"We'll knock those motherfuckers out," said Lock. "I'll get my guys together. We'll be ready."

"The Ashland Court Motel in Oakland. Ten forty-five. Don't fuck it up. Call me on my mobile after everything goes down. I'll be waiting to hear from you."

J.W. didn't care how anxious he sounded to Lock N Load. This shit needed to be done.

"Done." Lock drank his beer down, got up, and walked

out of the Everglades. J.W. heard a motorcycle start and the roar of straight pipes. Then Lock was gone.

BACK IN HIS OFFICE, J.W. SAT UP IN HIS SEAT, ROLLED HIS chair back, and opened up a freebie real-estate magazine he had stashed in his briefcase. *California land, baby. Here's one: 4,500-square-foot house, Mediterranean style, four bedrooms, bayside view, 1.3 mil.* It was only a matter of time until he moved out of his rented apartment and began livin' large. Like a player. Right now he drove a Buick. Before long, it would be nothing less than a Benz or a Beemer. Prosperous times were just around the corner.

As a reward for a job well done, J.W. would head down to the Starlight and have a few celebratory drinks. Then he'd treat himself to 12F, kick back, order up room service, a little company, and for the rest of the night he'd wait for Lock's call to tell him that everything had gone down according to plan.

J.W. gathered up his stuff. He threw a few orange prescription bottles into his briefcase. Then he headed for the elevator and pushed the down button. On the way to the Starlight he would drop by the liquor store for a big bottle of Cuervo Gold.

241 «

» CHAPTER «

26

Marco's Night

A towering four-wheel-drive Monster pickup truck rolled to a full stop outside the Infidelz clubhouse. Its body was customized and jacked up high. It rode on oversize tires. The cab was stickered with decals and emblazoned with painted flames. *Grave Digger* was scripted in fluorescent colors on the side of the massive vehicle.

A figure wearing a 2Wheeler patch jumped out of the cab. It was quite a leap, a long drop, like jumping off the roof of a regular-size vehicle. Streeter signaled the driver by slapping the side of the cab. The four-wheel monster drove off into the night. Streeter slipped off the 2Wheeler colors he wore, which Patch had taken off the dead shooter a few nights before. Then he walked inside the clubhouse, looked around, and smiled amid the noise and commotion.

Ahab whistled to him from the bar and motioned him over. "Streeter! Talk to me, brother. How's it looking over at the Ashland?"

Streeter, a ten-year member, had finished his reconnaissance mission over at the Ashland Court Motel. It was past ten P.M., less than thirty minutes before the Infidelz would take to the streets and storm the 2Wheeler stronghold. The Ashland Court was an easy ten-minute drive, right off MacArthur Boulevard, one of the main arteries that ran through the east side of Oakland.

243 «

"Pretty big place. There are no citizens staying there, just 2Wheeler club guys everywhere. I counted forty-seven bikes and not one cop," Streeter told Ahab as he pulled off the XXXL 2Wheeler support shirt he also wore as a disguise and dumped it into the trash can by the bar. He replaced it with a huge Infidelz tee and his own patch and vest.

"Plus, there's another fifteen vehicles, mostly vans and trucks, parked in the main lot—you know, that big common area where all the rooms are circled around. Looks like all their California chapters are here. I'd put them at about sixty guys, seventy-five tops. They must be still meeting, 'cause I didn't hear any loud music or see any chicks walkin' around."

"Sounds good." Ahab clapped his hands and let out a loud whistle. "Okay, quiet down. Listen up! I'm sending out the advance lookout guys right now. Dum-Dum, Ace, and Willy, hit the road."

Ahab gave each scout a walkie-talkie, a firm bear hug, and sent him off with a hearty slap on the back. "Get over there and take your positions. Make sure you stay in touch with each other. Call us if anything weird comes down. Do us proud.

"The rest of you, let's get this show on the road. Everybody front and center. Brutus, Duffy, Eight Ball, Patch, that means you. Hurry up, dammit. This'll only take a few minutes."

Ahab was prepared to address the whole chapter, about forty men strong. He looked over at Brutus.

"Where the fuck's Angelo?"

Brutus shrugged his shoulders.

Ahab yelled over the assembled members, "Anybody here seen Angelo?"

No response.

"Shit," Ahab muttered under his breath. "Motherfucker's late again. We can't wait. Let's get started. We're outta here in ten minutes."

He waved his enormous arms. "Listen! All of you got your group numbers. We got five vans and three cars. Will the drivers put up their hands, so's we know that you're here and accounted for?"

Eight men put up their hands as Ahab gazed around the room. The plan was to surround and invade the Ashland Court from all corners—north, south, east, and west—with eight separate bands of fighters. Each group would include at least one member of the 187 Crue. In drawing up the ranks, Ahab and Angelo decided to spread the best 187 street fighters among the groups. The Infidelz would leave their motorcycles behind. The high-decibel rumble of forty pissed-off, high-throttled iron horses would literally be a dead giveaway.

"Each group has four guys and a driver. You all know who your wheelman is? Groups one through four will drop off their troops and park their vans down on Speer Road, about a block and a half north of the Ashland Court. Groups five through eight—that's the fifth van and the three cars—will circle in at Shaker Court, a block to the south. Drivers remain inside your vehicles throughout the entire operation. Keep your engines running. We won't be long. After the fight, each group member will return to his designated van, and once each van is full, you split. There's also one more roving van in the area, just in case we need to cart off anybody. Except for the rover, no van or car leaves unless everyone is accounted for, dead or alive. After the fight, the vans will take us directly to the safe house. Everyone steer clear of the clubhouse. Am I understood?

"Any questions?"

Ahab surveyed the room and saw no confused looks or raised hands. But he did see a spectacular array of weaponry.

As an armed band of warriors, the Infidelz were a street mob with weapons of various shapes, sizes, and origins. All wore knives. Brutus holstered a sawed-off Remington twelve-gauge as a sidearm, and held a Winchester repeater rifle in his arms. Hambone waved a Dirty Harry .44 Magnum pistol. Eight Ball carried an authentic WWII German

Luger and a razor-sharp Japanese dagger. Duffy, a trained martial artist, was a follower of Bruce Lee's Jeet Kune Do techniques. He rarely fought without his Nunchakus and Philippine rattan Escrina sticks. A few members toted deadly jagged throwing stars and quick-toss spikes. The rest of the members settled for more conventional weaponry, a Smith & Wesson six-shooter, a serrated hunting knife, or a fat metal pipe. Ahab surveyed his troops and swung a thick, heavy chain as he felt his confidence surge.

"Excellent. Fucking excellent," he said through a broad smile while he made his final inspection. "Stick together so we don't lose track of each other. Just in case, there are extra slapjacks, ax handles, and baseball bats packed inside each vehicle. And there's lead pipes, too."

"Guys," added Brutus, cradling his rifle. "I'd like to get them pipes back afterward. Quality lead pipe is hard to find

these days, so wipe them clean."

The room erupted into laughter at Brutus's finicky request.

Ahab looked over at Patch. "You've been through this before. Any last-minute words of wisdom?"

Patch shook his head. "Just go in and get it done. We've lost five guys already. They killed us. Now we kill them."

"Okay, let's do it," yelled Ahab.

Outside, Patch circulated among the men as the vans and cars loaded up. All members were armed to the teeth and most were gung ho, breathing hard, with stern faces and furrowed brows. Only a handful of riders felt uneasy about being drafted into the night's skirmish. They thought about their loved ones, their livelihoods, their old ladies and kids. They understood that they could be jailed, injured, or killed should the invasion go bad.

"I hear we're outnumbered, like two to one," whispered one member tensely. "Where the fuck are the guys from Richmond, Frisco, Sacto, or Vallejo?"

A couple of Delz nodded in agreement.

Patch approached his concerned comrades.

"Gentlemen, this is *our* chance."

He faced the doubting member and looked around at the crowd of serious men. Then he jumped up onto a wooden table and waved his arm.

"Some of you are worried about being outnumbered. Well, don't be! Frankly, I don't give a shit if we're outnumbered two to one. Or three to one. I don't care because we don't need one more motherfuckin' guy. One Infidelz is worth ten 2Wheelers any day."

A member in the back ranks let out a holler.

"Infidelz don't cut and run like other clubs," Patch added. "We fight to the end. And that's what we'll do tonight. And that's why we'll win. Sure, we'll spill some blood tonight. But so what?"

Patch stripped back his sleeve to show a long scar on his right arm.

"See this? I got this scar from a couple of guys who tried to knife me to death. Hell yeah, I got cut. But I won the fight. The same thing will happen tonight. We'll suffer gashes and bruises, but years from now they'll be trophies when people see us on the streets and say, 'Man, those are some tough, crazy motherfuckers.'

"Brothers, this is an important standoff for the Oakland chapter. We're talking self-preservation. We're either gonna win this battle tonight, or our power disappears. Our street rep is on the line. It's that simple. Think of this as a do-or-die night for the club. Let's call it Marco's Night. It will be a night when the Oakland Infidelz take all the glory, while the other chapters miss out on all the action."

Patch pointed out various members of the crowd clutching their weapons.

"Look around you. These are the only men you'll need. Guys like Ahab. Brutus. Streeter. Eight Ball. We're the best. The hardest. The bravest. The toughest."

Patch jumped down and walked back over to the doubting member. He put his hands on the man's shoulders and shook him in a playful manner.

"We're gonna pound those assholes into the ground."

He smiled broadly as his comrade shrieked out a loud war cry.

"So," said Patch, "you don't think we need to call up Richmond, Sacto, and Frisco?"

"Fuck no," he shouted to Patch. "The two of us alone could take on all those fuckin' 2Wheelers if we had to!"

The doubting member's eyes lit up and he yelled to the men: "I pity the poor bastard who has to deal with us tonight."

Streeter ran up to Patch and the horde.

"Time to move, bros. The 2Wheelers are wrapping up. The scouts say there must be over sixty of them now."

Patch walked up to the Infidelz clubhouse door, where a square polished plaque commemorated the formation of the Oakland chapter. He put his left hand on the plaque, his right on his heart. Then he turned around, faced his angry brothers, and shook his fist in the air.

"Okay, men," he shouted. "Let's find these guys and fuck 'em up. Revenge! Victory! Let's go!"

27

The Battle of Ashland Court

Patch rode over to the Ashland Court Motel, assigned to group five. He sat in silence in the back of a black Chevy van, cracking his knuckles and doing breathing exercises. Geordie, group five's wheelman, steered the Chevy vigilantly through Oakland's potholed backstreets. It was a bumpy ride. Geordie was the only one riding up front.

The other passengers, Patch and three armed Infidelz fighters dressed in black, all wearing stocking caps, huddled together. They sat on large overturned plastic buckets on the paint-splattered floor in the back of Geordie's van.

Patch momentarily flashed on Angelo. He hadn't been there for load-out. Ahab had been looking for him, too. Angelo was an official no-show, which was not a good thing. He faced serious consequences, deserving much more than a simple fine. *What the fuck is up with this guy?* Angelo had been the one most eager to lay waste on the 2Wheelers.

Patch popped open his cell and fired off a quick call to Nine Inch. He spoke amid the murmur of the other men.

"Tony. Patch. Can't talk now, so just listen. I want you to put a tail on—"

"Don't tell me, Angelo Timmons."

"Exactly. You remember his address?"

"Tell you what. I'll get LiLac on it."

"Fine. I'll check in later to find out what you come up with. Keep your phone on."

Patch looked around at his three brothers-in-arms in the back of the van. Eight Ball was sliding a loaded magazine into his backup pistol, a Walther PPK. His Luger fit smoothly into a tooled leather shoulder holster; his ancient Japanese dagger hung from his side. While heart rates increased and blood pressures rose, Eight Ball whistled as he caressed his piece.

Wrangler, another passenger, was an amateur kick boxer who had placed top three in various statewide competitions. His longest match, two minutes; shortest, thirty-three seconds. He was limbering up and stretching his taut, muscular arms. Sitting across from Wrangler in the back of the panel van was a younger member named Steve-O.

Steve-O flashed Patch the "V for Victory" sign when their eyes met. He was an athletic and agile kid for two hundred pounds, and had a small Infidelz tattoo on his neck.

"Patch," asked Steve-O, "what makes a great fighter?"

Patch replied without hesitation. "The guy who *acts,* not reacts. Gets started quick and finishes quicker."

Patch gave Steve-O the thumbs-up sign as he kept the fight talk going. It was a good motivator.

"The ring has rules, the street sure as hell doesn't," he said. "Ain't that right, Wrangler?"

"Damn straight, I've gone toe-to-toe with guys who scared the living shit out of me. But face 'em in a back alley, and they're scared and shakin'. They freeze. Rules of the ring don't apply to the street."

"How long do you reckon tonight's fight is gonna last?" Steve-O asked.

Patch rubbed his chin and thought for a moment.

"Fair question. The Sioux Nation had an old saying about Custer's Last Stand at Little Bighorn. The battle lasted as long as it took for a hungry man to finish his dinner."

Patch had picked out what he thought was the most combat-worthy piece of lead pipe from Brutus's collection. The grip had to be just right. Eighteen inches was a popular length. Some guys preferred shorter. Patch preferred lead to steel. One whack with a cold steel bar and at best you've made a quarter-inch dent into an unlucky bastard's skull. But sock him with a soft, fat, vintage lead pipe and you'll get up to eight bonus inches of wraparound contact from the more flexible metal. One or two whacks and down they go. Then it's on to the next victim.

The van slowed down. Geordie turned around to his passengers.

"We're here. Grab your gear. I'll be waiting across the street with the back door unlocked, motor running. Slap like hell on the side of the van when you're all back inside and we'll kick it outta here. Good luck."

It was a chilly night. A large mound of dirt from a major landscaping job in progress blocked the sidewalk from the front of the Ashland Court Motel and its large asphalt parking lot. The dirt hill provided handy cover before the Delz commenced their attack.

Patch left the boys at the van and crossed the street to where Ahab and four other Delz were crouched in front of the motel. The rest of the groups surrounded its perimeter, waiting for the signal to charge.

Patch and Ahab peered over the dirt mound and surveyed the situation. From this vantage point, the motel resembled a fort. Behind the dirt mound, they held an impromptu pow-wow. Patch and Ahab expressed their concern.

"Our scouts ain't seen nobody leave or enter in the last twenty minutes," said Ahab. "Plus there's no guards posted outside. That's kinda weird."

"This place is entirely too quiet," Patch agreed. "If this were a typical 2Wheeler meeting, you'd hear it a mile away. Music blasting, bikes revving, people shootin' guns in the air. Cops all over. The place would be crawling with Chino's bitches. There's nobody in the office. Something stinks here."

"I'm seriously considering calling this whole thing off," said Ahab, scratching his head.

"Don't," Patch replied. "I've got an idea. You all stay here. Get ahold of the rest of the groups and tell them that when I give the sign, we attack. Gimme two minutes. Wait for my signal."

"What signal?"

"You'll know it when you see it."

Patch crossed the street to where Geordie sat parked in his black Chevy. He took a final drag off his smoke as Steve-O, Wrangler, and Eight Ball were gathered outside the vehicle.

"Out of the van," said Patch. "There's been a change of plans. You'll all need to figure out some other way to get back."

Patch pointed down the road. "Hook up with Ahab. He'll reassign you. You, too, Geordie. Now give me your keys." He snatched them out of Geordie's hands and opened the driver's-side door.

253 «

"What the fuck, Patch! That's my company's van. You can't . . ."

Before Geordie could utter another word, Patch slid behind the wheel of the Chevy, slammed the door, and rolled up the window. He pulled out his cell phone and made a hasty call as Geordie thumped on the window. After a short conversation, Patch folded the phone, started the van, and gunned the Chevy. He rolled the window back down and stuck out his head.

"Report this baby as stolen," he yelled to Geordie.

He roughly threw the van into gear with a grating, harsh grind. The tires squealed as he made an abrupt U-turn across four lanes and aimed the truck around toward the motel. An approaching car skidded ninety degrees to avoid a broadside collision. Patch stomped the accelerator to the floor and headed straight toward the entrance of the Ashland Court.

"Hey, wait a minute, Patch!" Geordie yelled out. "Careful with my ride. I need it for . . . work . . . tomorrow . . ." His voice trailed off.

Patch full-throttled the van up the motel's driveway. He waved his arm wildly out of the driver's-side window. Ahab and the rest of his guys staked out in front caught the signal.

Patch skidded and screeched the van into the parking lot of the Ashland Court. He heard the *ping, ping, ping, ping* of .38 bullets raining on the reinforced roof of the van as he weaved through the grounds. It was a 2Wheeler rooftop lookout.

Patch was a high-speed moving target as the black van squealed toward the large picture window of the motel's check-in office. He clutched the steering wheel with white knuckles and braced himself. In seconds, it was sudden impact. As the van met the plate-glass window of the Ashland Court office, he screamed at the top of his lungs.

"Let's get it on!"

The sound of the crash was enough to draw the 2Wheelers out from their hiding places inside their rooms. They revealed themselves, fully armed, clutching knives, ax handles, pistols, and clubs.

As decoys, Ahab and his small band of Infidelz charged up and over the dirt hill. The first throng of 2Wheelers jumped out from behind the doors and barricades of the motel and stormed toward them.

Patch wrestled himself free of the van's wreckage, kicking the windshield out with both boot heels. The van had turned over on its side from the violent impact. Patch wiped the sweat and blood that had streamed into his eyes. He threw off his stocking hat and brushed off the cubes of broken tempered glass that stuck to his clothes. Then he charged out into the parking lot. He kicked over the first bike in a long line of motorcycles. The rest toppled like dominoes. With Sharpfinger in one hand and a lead pipe in the other, he yelled out to his 2Wheeler adversaries.

"All right, you motherfuckers, come out and fight!"

A swarm of 2Wheelers emerged from their motel rooms and ran down the hill, with weapons drawn, toward Ahab and his small crew. Streeter had been right. There must have been sixty of them. Then the full army of Infidelz fighters moved into position and invaded the remaining 2Wheelers from behind. The pitched battle spilled out into the Ashland Court parking lot, two hordes of modern barbarians locked in lethal combat.

The 2Wheelers, expecting a face-to-face, head-on battle, waved *their* pipes, knives, and ax handles and shot pistols in the air in the hope of scaring their outnumbered opposition into retreat. But the Infidelz, rallying from all sides with their own show of force, disoriented and confused the other club. 12-12 drew his six-shooter from his holster and shot into the 2Wheeler throng. The rest of the Delz who came strapped opened fire with their pistols, rifles, and shotguns. With the battle only seconds old, the first 2Wheeler casualities crumpled facedown on the ground, their backs riddled with bullets and buckshot.

The 2Wheelers, ambushed from behind, watched in horror as more of their prized fighters fell from the next volley of smoking gunfire. A cloud drifted over the battleground.

Outgunned and outmaneuvered, the remaining 2Wheelers turned and sprinted back toward the safety of their motel stronghold. There they were intercepted by more Infidelz muscle, wielding baseball bats and pipes.

Club-wielding Delz swatted the Wheelers across their knees and shins. They crunched baseball bats over heads. Wheelers and Infidelz slugged it out on the ground floor and on the second-story walkways of the motel complex. Infidelz enforcers stomped up and down the walkways, searching out any 2Wheelers who were hiding in their rooms.

Brutus fired both rounds of his sawed-off Remington into the door of one of the upper-level rooms. The blasts splintered the door into a hundred wooden shards as three oversize 2Wheelers bolted out the room and jumped him, working him over. Brutus took the first round of punches before Streeter ran up, took aim, and winged one of the assailants with his pistol, then he jumped in and joined Brutus in the punching fray as they knocked the two remaining opponents over the edge of the balcony.

Hambone raised his large hunting knife and charged, whacking and thrashing into a group of screaming 2Wheelers. In a far corner, Duffy and Wrangler fought off a half-dozen Wheeler prospects. The click and clack of Duffy's Nunchakus accompanied Wrangler's whirling, kicking blows. Wrangler and Duffy's flailing arms and legs left bodies in their wake, broken arms, busted legs, and cracked skulls.

Infidelz casualties mounted, too. As 12-12 reloaded his Smith & Wesson revolver, he felt a searing rain of lead penetrate his left arm and chest. He convulsed and slumped to his knees, then fell motionless onto the pavement. Nearby,

Steve-O took a bullet through the middle of his right palm. As he doubled over in agony, clutching the bleeding hand between his thighs, a 2Wheeler armed with a tire iron finished him off with a blow to the head. Red ran to Steve-O's rescue and chased off his assailant. A look of horror darkened Red's face as he looked down at where Steve-O lay, bloodied and battered. Patch tackled the fleeing 2Wheeler and stabbed him repeatedly. Patch then whirled around with pipe in hand and clubbed a burly, bald-headed biker twice his size. Ahab yelled out to him.

"Behind you. Look out!" Patch heard a loud blast.

As Patch spun back around, he felt the impact of the bullet slug slam into his chest. The force knocked him backward. He looked up and, as if in slow motion, saw both Ahab and Geordie, faces aghast, running feverishly toward his falling body. The back of his skull crashed onto the hard ground, bounced up, and smacked down again. His brain jarred inside his head and the world went black. Moments later, Ahab's face was looking down at him screaming, but there was no sound coming out of his mouth.

Patch came to after a few seconds. The roar of the battle surged back into his ears. As he rolled over to get back on his feet, he saw Ahab kicking a 2Wheeler repeatedly in the head. It was Chino. The 2Wheelers' chief lay groaning on the pavement, blood gushing from a broken nose and jaw. Then Ahab swung his chain at the chrome pistol clutched in Chino's right hand. Patch saw the silver Smith & Wesson six-shooter fly from his hand and skate across the lot. A nearby Infidelz member scooped up the piece and shoved it behind his belt.

"Patch," screamed Geordie as he pulled Patch back to his

feet by his vest and shook him briskly. "You okay? Speak to me, brother."

Patch rubbed his chest. He had felt the impact of Chino's shot—it knocked him flat on his back—but he hadn't felt the deep flesh-cutting burn that should have followed such a traumatic jolt. He had tasted the elixir of Lady Luck. His flak vest had saved his life.

Patch got up and surveyed the parking-lot battlefield. The 2Wheelers had put up a valiant fight, but the momentum had shifted in the direction of the Infidelz. Casualties from both sides littered the parking lot. But the Wheelers had retreated. A few hopped-up Infidelz swung their bats and broke down the remaining doors of the motel rooms, in search of more hidden foes. None were found. The survivors had pulled their bikes from the pile or had already taken off on foot for the hills. The Delz loaded their casualties into the roving van.

Ahab raised his weary arms victoriously. Judging from his euphoric grin, he could have been the modern incarnation of a victorious gladiator.

"Let's round up our guys and get outta here! You men got the job done." The Infidelz erupted in loud whistles, whoops, and hollers. But just as Ahab barked out his jubilant command to fall out, a loud thunderous rumble interrupted their triumph. Another pack of chugging Harleys descended on the parking lot.

"What the fuck?" yelled Streeter as he drew his six-shooter. But before he could fire, one of the invading riders aimed his gun and winged him on the arm. He grabbed his bloody limb and collapsed.

Patch, standing not far away, looked over and saw two

dozen chopped Harleys skidding to a stop. Their patches blazed green and orange. He recognized Shadow, Juice, Razz, and Dawg first—Lock N Load's Ring of Fire.

"Son of a bitch," Brutus yelled out to his comrades. "It's the fuckin' Gun Runners! We gotta kick their motherfuckin' asses, too?"

Lock N Load jumped off his bike and stomped to the front of his posse. He stood poised with a bowie knife in one hand, a pistol in the other, ready to slash and shoot. Every muscle in his face, neck, and shoulders was tensed. Steam rose off his sweaty bald dome. Only his colors, stitched onto his denim vest, covered his mammoth tattooed torso. Patch, small and lean by comparison, staggered to the front of the Infidelz ranks. He defiantly raised Sharpfinger, anticipating a new round of cold-blooded mayhem.

"You figured you'd get a chance to pick at the bones of the winning club, eh?" Patch said. "Interesting strategy. Do you really think we're gonna lay down?"

259 ««

Lock and his troops seemed unfazed by Patch's battle-weary taunt. The Gunners waved sharpened machetes, semiautomatic pistols, and slapjacks. They menacingly swung thick-linked chains.

"Die, you fuckers," snorted Lock N Load, wielding his piece. "We're takin' over your turf. We own this town now."

A second shot rang out and another Infidelz member, Willy, standing next to Patch, grabbed his chest. Just like Marco, Willy caught a round from Lock N Load's cold blue steel S&W Python. After another shot, this time to the left leg, Willy hit the pavement like a felled tree. Ahab, momentarily stunned, ran over and knelt down next to him. Just like Marco, Willy died in the sights of Lock N Load's pistol.

Patch ran toward Lock N Load and signaled to his brothers. The next round of battle began. Chains and fists swung freely. The Infidelz dug in, but their ranks were weakened as more members fell. Down went Duffy, then Hambone, then Geordie.

Patch confronted his nemesis with Sharpfinger. Lock boasted the much larger, gleaming bowie blade. Each stared angrily into the other's bloodshot eyes.

Lock swiped and drew first blood, gashing Patch's forearm with the bowie knife. Blood spewed from a bone-deep slice across one of Patch's faded blue tattoos. Patch spun a full three-sixty, the kick connecting to the side of Lock's face with the crushing weight of his steel-toed boot, fracturing Lock's jaw. Clearly smarting and bent down on one knee, Lock rubbed his chin hesitantly. He kept his bowie knife up to keep Patch at bay.

Lock leaped to his feet, screaming with rage and charged headfirst into Patch's chest, knocking him to the ground on his back. The impact sent Patch's Sharpfinger tumbling just out of reach. Both fighters hit the pavement hard, and then began to roll around, struggling savagely to gain advantage.

Lock was a skilled wrestler, and was soon dominant. He had Patch pinned facedown with his knee on his back. Next he delivered a series of blows with the butt of the bowie. Patch's skull throbbed. His forearm was bleeding from the deep wound. Then Lock grabbed him by the hair, poised to run the blade's razor edge across his throat. Patch held back the knife with all the strength he could summon, but it drew steadily closer.

Just then a new round of motorcycle thunder entered the battle arena. Razz screamed out to Lock N Load, who looked up as he held the knife close to Patch's throat.

"We've got trouble."

It wasn't the rumble of any bike made in America. It was the deafening roar of a herd of monsters, extreme monsters, Ducati Monsters. A wave of charging Bushido Blades crested airborne over the dirt mound. The dozen helmetless renegade riders, yelping like Sioux warriors, wore red bandannas covering their mouths and chins. Each rider brandished a taser as they roared toward the Gunners. Black teakwood billy clubs hung from their belts.

The Blades swiftly and aggressively penetrated the front line of Gun Runner Harleys. Jumping off their bikes, the Blades stunned their opponents with electric-shock taser blasts.

The tactics of the Bushido attack was systematic. They worked in pairs. One touch from the open spark of a taser and each Gunner victim collapsed instantly, writhing and twitching to the ground. After each debilitating zap, another Blade finished the victim off with forceful billy-club swings to the head and kidneys. Energized by the Blades' reinforcements, Ahab and his men found renewed strength and complemented the sting of the tasers and the walloping billy clubs with beatings and stompings of their own.

Patch barely registered the arrival of the reinforcements. He was too intent on fighting for his life under Lock N Load's iron grip. He could feel his muscles weaken as he tried to hold back the razor-sharp blade nearing his throat. As he was about to succumb to Lock's brute strength, the Gunners' leader was brutally blindsided with a solid kick to the right side of his head. Nine Inch had landed a direct punt to the Gun Runner's dome. The bowie knife dropped from Lock's hand. The force of the kick was enough to free

Patch from his grasp. Patch jumped back to his feet and leveled his own boot kick from behind into Lock's bloodied cranium, sending him facedown into the mound of dirt. He ran over to the felled Gunner prez.

"I'd normally take an ear or a nose," Patch growled to a semiconscious Lock, "but I'll settle for this."

With a few strokes of the Sharpfinger, he sliced the sacred orange-and-green Gunners' patch off Lock N Load's back. Sirens in the far distance grew louder as Lock lay facedown in the dirt.

Patch bent over and whispered into his bleeding ear. "I figured you out," he said. "It wasn't luck that you showed up here just in time to pick off the winners. You planned this all along, didn't you?"

Lock groaned.

"But you'll get what's comin'," said Patch. "I'll make sure these colors make it to your boys in L.A."

With the cops now on the way, most of the Gun Runners had already fled. Patch looked over at his fellow Infidelz hunched over, dazed, breathing heavy, and barely standing. Four Infidelz died at Ashland Court; dozens were injured. No member was left unscathed. Ahab let out a loud whistle. Clutching Lock's severed patch stained with blood, Patch shouted out to his club brothers.

"C'mon. Let's get the flying fuck outta here."

The Infidelz headed toward their assigned getaway vehicles. They whooped and screamed like savages, fists and weapons thrust in the air. Some ran, most hobbled, while the brawnier members like Wrangler and Brutus carried the dead and wounded over their shoulders back to the transports. Without a single word or parting gesture, the Blades started up their bikes. Crouched low over their Ducatis, the dozen Blades, unhurt from the rumble, sped away in a small pack and disappeared.

The police sirens grew louder and louder. Soon the Ashland Court Motel was bathed in orange, red, and blue swirling police lights. The cops tended to the few conscious Gunners scattered around the parking lot. By the time Lock N Load came to and sat up, he saw that most of his fellow riders had deserted him. They were long gone, the parking lot strewn with the remaining 2Wheeler and Gunner bodies and bikes.

Patch and Ahab had jumped into the same getaway van, which was now snaking through the unlit dark Oakland backstreets. Their destination was the secret outpost miles from the Infidelz clubhouse. Both club members lay sprawled in the crowded van, dog-tired and breathing hard. Patch could barely keep his head up. He used a red handkerchief as a tourniquet on his bleeding forearm. His face was swollen. He'd suffered one black eye and probably a concussion. Slumped and lying on his back, he felt dizzy and nauseous. He would have passed out then and there, but Ahab punched him lightly on the shoulder and gave him a crooked, saw-toothed grin.

"Man, how close was that?" He beamed. "And Geordie's truck. Truly awesome. Who called in the kids riding those extremes?"

Patch managed a weak shrug. "That was me. I called in the cavalry after I hijacked Geordie's truck."

Patch was in no mood to celebrate. He stared down at his bloodied and torn clothes. The club had lost four men. Among the dead was 12-12 and Willy, fifteen-year club veterans, and Steve-O, a young rider who, like Marco, had shown early leadership potential. Patch shuddered as he recalled the victory sign Steve-O had given him in Geordie's van on the way to the rumble.

The wheelman swung a sudden turn, mashing together all the Infidelz fighters sardined in the back of the van. A few groaned as the unexpected shift of bulky humanity aggravated deep sprains and broken bones.

But nobody had the energy to complain. Another page in Infidelz history had been written that night: they had endured serious, nonstop hand-to-hand combat against not one, but two major clubs. But as Patch had promised during his clubhouse speech earlier, many members from the other chapters in the area would curse the night they weren't at the Ashland Court.

The exhausted and battle-scarred passengers felt a surge of velocity as the van merged onto a freeway. A sharp migrainelike jolt ran through Patch's skull like a pneumatic drill. There was a swelling, pounding sensation in his right knee and lower back. His forearm stung and tingled. He'd get the wound wrapped and dressed at the next stop.

Patch looked over at Ahab. "Angelo was a fuckin' no-show."

"I know." Ahab's face wrinkled. "What's up with that shit? Something's not right. We sure coulda used him."

Patch could only shake his head in agreement. *Angelo had better have a fucking good explanation. Hopefully LiLac will have something new to report to Tony. Tony "Nine Inch" Naylor. Yeah, that son of a gun saved my life.*

28

Take It
to the Bridge

J.W. lay sprawled, half asleep on the motel double bed watching three "barely legal" nymphettes frolicking and writhing on the TV screen. *Lesbian Dorm Teens #3*. Earlier, he had requested some Starlight outcall action. Then he felt a buzzing sensation at his side. It was his cell, vibrating. It had to be Lock N Load with the news.

J.W. checked his watch. Well past midnight. He grabbed the TV remote and muted the moaning and groaning sounds, then fumbled clumsily for the buzzing phone.

He answered on the seventh ring. "Yeah." He expected to hear Lock's voice.

Instead of a voice, he heard shouting and commotion in the background. J.W. suspected a party or celebration. He sat up on the bed and shouted into the cell to compete with the noise at the other end.

"Hello?"

"We shoulda never hooked up with any of you fuckin' cops."

"Hello?"

"I said, *'We shoulda never hooked up with any of you fuckin' cops.'* " It was definitely Lock N Load, fuming.

"What the hell happened?"

"We got knocked out. The ones who didn't cut and run on me. I don't even know if I have a chapter anymore."

"Whattaya mean?"

Lock's voice lowered to a whisper. "We got wiped out. The 2Wheelers got wiped out. The Infidelz pulled my fucking patch. Motherfuckers coulda killed me. After they wipe their asses with my colors, I know they're gonna send them down to L.A. to my officers in SoCal. Probably with bullet holes. I just know it. That tells my guys that we didn't stand up for the club or ourselves.

"The Infidelz are way fuckin' pissed off. They're gonna take this whole thing personal. Heads are gonna roll and blood will run. Count on it."

J.W. gulped.

"You cost me my charter, maybe my club," Lock continued. "When I get my hands on you, you're a dead man."

"What about our deal?"

"Deal? Are you crazy? Fuck off."

Lock was gone, for now anyway. So was J.W.'s house on the hill, his new BMW, and his monthly piece of the action.

The agent's hands shook uncontrollably. He and Angelo were probably on the Infidelz hit list right now. Number one with a bullet. He reached for the orange bottle of pills sitting next to his watch on the nightstand and washed down three Percodans with a long slug from the tall bottle of Cuervo Gold.

He dialed up Angelo. He answered on the first ring. "Yeah."

J.W. spat out a staccato order.

"Meet me. Downtown. Same place. Right now."

His next call was to the front desk.

"Cancel my outcall. I'm outta here."

PATCH CALLED NINE INCH AND THE TWO MET AT THE SAFE house. Nine Inch pulled up on his Ducati. After Patch's arm was dressed and taped up by one of the club's old ladies, the two walked over to Nine Inch's bike. An incoming call rang for Nine Inch.

"It's LiLac," Nine Inch whispered to Patch. "Yeah," he said into the phone. "Great. Be right there. Hold on a sec."

He turned back to Patch.

"LiLac's tailing Angelo. It looks like he's making a move. She says he's headed downtown on his bike with a bag. Looks like your guy is ready to bolt."

"Tell LiLac to stay on his trail," Patch instructed. "I'll ride with you back to the Oakland clubhouse. We'll pick up my bike and call her when we get downtown."

Nine Inch yelled back into the phone. "Don't lose him. Back in fifteen, Li. Later."

Nine Inch fired up his ride. "Wow," he cracked, "Patch Kinkade riding bitch on *my* extreme. Imagine that."

"Don't flatter yourself, wiseguy. Let's roll."

The pair raced back to Oaktown. The dark night was clear and the air was still. The ride was barely tolerable. Nine Inch rode like a maniac. Minutes later, they picked up Patch's motorcycle and his colors, and headed downtown. The bikes pulled over to the curb in front of City Hall. Nine Inch phoned LiLac back for the exact location.

"Angelo went into a parking garage at the corner of Tenth and Webster," he reported to Patch. "LiLac is staked out in the UPS lot across the street. She's hiding behind one of the trucks. So far, Angelo hasn't left."

As Patch and Nine Inch approached the corner, they cut their engines and rolled silently into the UPS lot. They spotted LiLac, dressed in black, next to a yellow Ducati, concealed behind one of the shiny brown delivery trucks. She gave Patch and Nine Inch the skinny.

"I've been here about twenty minutes. Your guy on the bike is on the first floor of the parking lot over there." LiLac pointed across the street. "Another guy driving a maroon sedan pulled in about ten minutes ago. I think they're meeting. Nobody's left the garage since. I'm sure of that. There's just one way in, one way out. Except for the motorcycle and the sedan, the place looks empty. I heard your guy and this other fellow shouting. Somebody sounds plenty pissed off."

"Good work," said Patch.

"Hey, I heard I missed a good one. You guys okay?" LiLac smiled, noticing the tape on Patch's arm and the condition of his face.

"Next time," Nine Inch said. "I promise."

The sound of Angelo's Harley starting up ricocheted from across the street. Patch recognized that gurgle and rumble he knew so well. He and Angelo had torn that cycle down a dozen times during the rainy seasons. Angelo's bike darted out of the parking-garage exit, making a wide turn. A maroon, four-door Buick Park Avenue followed close behind.

"They could be headed toward the freeway out of town," said LiLac. "Either west to Frisco or east toward Sacto. Or north to Richmond or Marin County." Patch and Nine Inch jumped back on their motorcycles.

They blended into the traffic, following the two vehicles from a reasonable distance. Angelo's bike and the Buick turned into a brightly lit Arco station next to the 580-freeway on-ramp. The gas station/convenience store was a mass of cars and trucks. The bars had just closed. Arco was party central. Cars blaring distorted, trunk-thumping hip-hop bass lined up as they waited their turns at the gas pumps, ten cents a gallon cheaper than the deserted Chevron station across the street.

Patch and Nine Inch pulled into the quiet Chevron station. With a full view of the Arco lot, Patch saw Angelo in an animated dispute with the dark-haired driver of the Buick. At one point, it looked like the two were close to blows as Angelo gave the driver a firm shove into the side of his car.

» » » « « «

DON'T YOU GET IT?" SCREAMED ANGELO AS HE MANHAN-
dled J.W. into the Buick. "I'm a fucking dead man. I thought
you guys were gonna step in before the shit got heavy. What
the fuck happened?" J.W. staggered to regain his balance.
The Percodans had kicked in, complemented by the wash of
tequila he used to knock them back. The agent was beyond
medicated. He was having trouble standing up straight, let
alone resisting an irate bike rider who outweighed him by
eighty pounds.

"The club." Angelo gasped hysterically to catch his
breath. "They're probably out there looking for me this
minute. I can't be seen anywhere on a bike within a
hundred-mile radius. I'm a moving target. Dead man ridin'.
You gotta get me outta here. Remember, you didn't get the
only copies of the tapes I made. I even managed to record
our 'deal.' I got a nice stash of tapes the cops might be interested in hearing."

J.W. swallowed hard.

"Tell you what," he said. "I can put you up in Marin
County in the custody of the U.S. marshals for a couple of
days until you can leave the state."

Just then three loud Harleys stormed past the Arco station. The pair nearly jumped out of their pants. False alarm.
It was a small pack of RUBs.

Angelo grabbed J.W. by his lapels. The agent's feet nearly
left the ground. "Look, my nerves are shot as it is. I'm a
fuckin' wreck. You get me outta here right now or else I
swear I'll kill you. I'm telling you, fuckhead, *right now*."

"Okay, okay, okay," said J.W. "I'll take you over the bridge to Marin myself. Who's gonna look for you there?" He was more than glad to be rid of Angelo. The biker would soon be the marshals' headache.

Angelo pulled out his pistol from inside his jacket and stuck it in J.W.'s side. J.W. sighed and rolled his eyes. He'd been through Angelo's gun routine before.

"Will you fucking cool down? People are starting to stare. Look, we're in this together."

"Yeah, like two rats in a cage," said Angelo.

Patch and Nine Inch watched the shoving and commotion from the Chevron station. "It's getting lively over there. What are those two up to?"

J.W. had a live one on his hands. He had half a mind to cut Angelo loose, leave him behind, and run. But he was in too deep with this desperate character. If J.W. didn't take him into custody, then the guy might do anything to save himself—including turning himself in. If he started talking to the cops, he could easily link J.W. to the rumble that night that killed a bunch of guys. The only way for J.W. to save himself was to save Angelo.

The pills and booze continued their dance inside his bloodstream. He had a slight case of the shakes and cottonmouth. He could feel a panic attack coming on, but he needed to maintain his composure.

"Tell you what, Angelo. I've got to fill up my tank first. Then let me buy you a soda. We'll stash your bike here. In less than an hour, we'll be in Marin with the marshals and you'll be safe and sound. Then I'll send someone over for your son. It's all worked out.

"C'mon, we both need to calm down and think this

through," J.W. said, clapping him on the back. "Let's go inside."

"Don't you fucking touch me," Angelo warned.

ACROSS THE STREET, PATCH AND NINE INCH WATCHED AN-gelo and J.W. walk into the gas station's convenience store. They took their place at the end of a long line of customers and kept right on arguing. Angelo waved his arms violently as the driver shook his head, trying to keep him calm.

"I think the answers to a lot of our questions lie with this guy that Angelo's with," said Patch.

Then Patch slipped off his colors. He grabbed Nine Inch's stocking cap off his head and pushed it over his eyes. He dashed across the street to the Arco station, where Angelo had parked his bike next to the maroon Buick.

Patch walked around to the back of the Buick, aimed his right boot heel, and with one sure, swift kick smashed the car's driver's-side taillight lens into a dozen pieces. He bent over, picked up and pocketed the biggest red plastic fragments, kicked the rest of the particles away from the vehicle, and quickly ran back.

"What was all that about?" Nine Inch asked.

"Watch and learn."

J.W. AND ANGELO PAID FOR THE GAS AND SODAS AND CAME back outside. Angelo pushed the Harley behind the filling-station wall and stashed it near the car wash while J.W.

gassed up. Angelo shook his head and took one long, last look at his bike.

Angelo craved something to calm his raw nerves, but in his haste he'd carelessly left his stash at home. His hands quaked. His stomach tightened. He couldn't call Hollister. He wouldn't risk it. Club guys, perhaps Ahab, Patch, or Wrangler, were probably staked out at the house waiting for him. Or worse, combing the streets. All he had now to soothe his nerves was a bottle of 7Up, a few bucks in his pocket, and his gun. The thought of being seen riding with a cop, even a plainclothes one, made him shudder. What if he was seen? Bike riders could smell cops a mile away.

J.W. started up the Buick after Angelo ditched his bike. He unlocked the passenger-side door. Angelo stood outside the car with his arms crossed.

J.W. lowered the window and called out, "So? You getting in or what?"

"No way."

Angelo remained obstinate.

"The trunk," Angelo said.

"Whattaya mean 'the trunk'?"

"Put me in the fucking trunk, J.W. Now."

"The trunk?" At first, the absurdity of Angelo riding to Marin County stashed in the trunk of his car didn't compute. But as the fear set in, so did Angelo's logic. The Delz would be looking for two guys, one of them Angelo. Chances were they had no idea what J.W. even looked like. So far he was safe. The agent felt his confidence return. He and Angelo had to slip out of town, and fast.

"Okay," he said as he slid out from behind the driver's

seat. He reached down and popped open the latch of the trunk.

Patch and Nine Inch watched from across the street as Angelo tumbled into the Buick's trunk. The driver slammed the trunk shut, then tossed Angelo's bag into the backseat.

Back in the driver's seat, J.W. took a long swig from the tequila bottle. He dialed his cell phone and spoke in code.

"Marin County. DOJ. Witness Protection. Change of plans. We're comin' in. ETA, forty minutes."

The Buick made its way onto the 580-freeway entrance. Its broken taillight shined a telltale burst of penetrating white light. Tailing the car was no problem. Thanks to the busted light, it stuck out easily in the late-night flow of urban traffic. J.W. had no clue he was being followed as Patch and Nine Inch putted far behind and from a secure distance. The chase was on. J.W. headed north toward the bridge that would take him and Angelo to Richmond, then across the bay to Marin County.

29

Dead In
5 Heartbeats

Patch and Nine Inch stayed the course, and luckily the fog hadn't rolled in. The night was still clear. They followed the maroon Buick at a comfortable distance, guided by the brilliance of J.W.'s exposed taillight.

The double-decked Richmond—San Rafael Bridge linked two polar-opposite regions, the gritty, industrial East Bay cities of Richmond,

Berkeley, and Oakland with posh Marin hamlets like Mill Valley, Sausalito, and San Anselmo. It also spanned the San Francisco Bay. Eleven miles due west on the choppy bay stood the Golden Gate. Past that, the Pacific Ocean.

Even on a calm night, the crosswinds of the Pacific blew forceful gusts onto the gray-girdered Richmond–San Rafael Bridge, powerful enough gales to shove a speeding Harley-Davidson involuntarily into the next lane. But the stars sparkled above a distant panoramic skyline. It was a spectacle automobile drivers with solid roofs over their heads were deprived of.

As Patch and Nine Inch approached the bridge, Patch could see the turret lights of San Quentin State Prison. He thought of the handful of club brothers holed up on "the Hill" and in H Unit. To Patch, the inmates at "Q" were the only Marin County residents he knew, or for that matter, trusted.

CONSIDERING THE BOOZE AND THE PILLS BOBBING AROUND his system, J.W. did an admirable job of steering the Buick within the confines of his lane, though not careful enough to escape the hawklike attention of a lone California highway patrolman named Ronald Gibson. Sipping black coffee, he noticed the Buick's subtle but erratic weaving. Then the cop saw the broken taillight. This would be his first takedown of the night. Patrolman Gibson downed his coffee and switched on his flashers, passing Patch and Nine Inch in pursuit of J.W.'s maroon four-door Buick sedan.

Patch couldn't believe his eyes. John Law was doing their dirty work for them. The CHP cruiser easily overtook the Buick and signaled for it to pull over. Patch flashed a quick "pull over" signal of his own to Nine Inch. Just off the bridge and with little time for the riders to downshift, the two bikes fishtailed to a stop first, on the side of the busy highway. The roadside was littered with cans, broken bottles, and "road alligators," the strips of retread rubber thrown from blown-out truck tires.

The riders rolled their bikes behind tall bushes and stashed their helmets. Nine Inch pointed over to the flashing lights of the police car that had detained the Buick just ahead, a little farther up the road.

"Where's a cop when you need one?" Nine Inch laughed. "Right up there."

J.W. had panicked at the sight of the CHP cruiser. He pulled to the side of the freeway so suddenly that the flashing highway patrol vehicle had to stop a couple of car lengths ahead of him.

Patch pointed toward the two cars. While the paved shoulder of the freeway was level and flat, once you hit dirt there was a steep drop-off, then a ditch. A steel Cyclone fence topped with barbed wire separated the freeway from the frontage road that ran parallel to it.

"We gotta make a run for it and check out what's going on up there."

Patch and Nine Inch made a swift dash along the Cyclone fencing near to where J.W.'s Buick was pulled over behind the CHP car.

"Far enough," Patch whispered to Nine Inch as they huddled behind some brush. "Now we watch and we wait."

Cars and trucks lumbered by, shaking the ground, leaving behind a flurry of dust and grit. Patch checked his watch. It was nearly two-thirty.

Shit," J.W. SAID TO HIMSELF, THEN YELLED TOWARD THE backseat, hoping Angelo could hear him in the trunk. "A fucking cop just pulled us over. Stay cool back there. I'll take care of this in a jiff."

J.W. switched on his hazard lights. He got out of his car and walked just shy of where the officer whose nameplate read *Gibson* was parked ahead. As he approached the officer, another CHP cruiser veered onto the scene and suddenly parked a few yards ahead of the first patrol car. A sturdy, butch female CHP officer stepped out. Her nameplate read *E. Sanchez*. J.W. now had two law enforcement officers to contend with.

"Good evening, ladies and gentlemen," said J.W., laughing, extending his hand. The sour-faced female CHP was not amused.

"Good evening," repeated Officer Gibson, smelling alcohol on J.W.'s breath. "Sir, can I ask you if there's anything wrong with the steering in your car?"

"No. Why?"

"Then I'm gonna insist you step over to my vehicle for a routine check."

"What kind of routine check?"

"Listen, pal. I'll ask the questions, you'll answer them. Now step over to my car."

Patch and Nine Inch lay back in the bushes and watched

as J.W. attempted to appease the two suspicious officers. It was a familiar scenario for all riders who flew colors—getting pulled over and hassled by the law in the middle of the night. Especially when you're cold, tired, and nursing a buzz.

"I'm going to wanna see your driver's license and current registration for the car," Gibson demanded.

J.W.'s anger kindled at the officer's brashness. He fumbled for his wallet, pulled out his license, and tossed it at Sanchez. The license fluttered to the ground. Gibson and Sanchez looked at each other and visibly seethed.

"Very funny. Now pick it up. Or maybe you wanna spend the rest of the night in jail," Gibson warned. He bounced his ticket book impatiently off the palm of his hand as J.W. squatted down and stumbled awkwardly on his hands and knees to fetch the license.

"Fuck." J.W. cursed under his breath as he fumbled for the ID card on the ground. "Officers," he asked as he stood up, "can't we just work this out?"

"Your taillight is broken," said Gibson, "and you're driving erratically. We'll decide what needs working out here."

"Now hold on a minute."

J.W. reached into his coat pocket. Gibson put his hand on his gun. J.W. produced a silver badge and a photo ID from inside his sport coat. He waved it in both officers' faces.

"Look, you two. I ain't takin' shit. I'm a federal law enforcement agent."

The cops looked at each other and shook their heads. "Oh really?" Sanchez sniffed. "Federal?"

Patch heard J.W. yell.

"Yeah, federal! John Wilkes McIntosh, *Federal* Bureau of Investigation."

"That's him," Patch whispered to Nine Inch. "J.W. the man. The guy we found on Angelo's cell phone."

Patch and Nine Inch watched J.W. unravel as he dealt with the pair of sarcastic troopers. His G-man federal government act had already worn thin.

"Fed or not, McIntosh," said Sanchez, "we're gonna walk your federal ass back to your car. We'll need to see your automobile registration."

"All right, all right," J.W. argued back curtly. "It's in the glove compartment.

He opened the front passenger door of the Buick. As he rifled through the glove compartment, searching for the car's most up-to-date registration, the female CHP stood over him and cautiously shined her flashlight into the car.

"Give me a minute," yelled J.W. impatiently as he sifted through a handful of loose papers and old registrations. "It's in here somewhere."

Officer Sanchez looked down and much to J.W.'s chagrin saw the bottle of Cuervo on the floor of the car. She seized it immediately.

"Here it is." J.W. handed the officer the latest registration, trying to ignore the bottle. The cop studied the form, then unscrewed the lid of the bottle, sniffing its contents.

"Okay, McIntosh, I want you back at the patrolman's vehicle. Now."

"Fer crissakes, lady, I told you I'm a federal agent."

"Look, let's not complicate things," Sanchez insisted. "Walk with me back to the patrolman's vehicle."

"Okay, now you look here," J.W. said. "Lemme just explain."

The front door of the Buick was left wide open as J.W.

and Sanchez walked back to Gibson's cruiser. Amid the flashing lights, J.W. attempted to explain the bottle's presence.

"Lady—"

"That's Officer to you."

"Okay, Officer, that bottle belongs to a friend, who we, I, just . . ."

Sanchez pulled Gibson aside.

"This guy's bad news. Any idiot can carry around a mail-order badge and ID. His breath smells of booze. His speech is slurred. He can barely stand up. I say we test him."

Sanchez gestured toward J.W. "We're gonna need you to take a field sobriety test."

"Field sobriety? No fucking way," J.W. bellowed. "Like touch my nose, do the bunny hop, and recite the alphabet? I got your alphabet right here, baby." J.W. grabbed his crotch. "F-B-fucking-I!"

"Step up closer to the officer's vehicle," Sanchez instructed.

"Listen, I don't need this shit, and neither do you," J.W. shouted loudly. "I'm on my way to the federal marshal's office in San Rafael."

Patch looked over at Nine Inch. "What's he going to do at some fucking federal marshal's office?"

Sanchez nudged J.W. with her nightstick.

"I *said* step up to the vehicle."

J.W.'s face went scarlet. His eyes bugged out of his head. He flailed his arms wildly as he cursed loudly. FBI or not, he was ordered to assume the position. Soon his body was arched over the hood of the squad car, both arms sprawled out, feet spread far apart. To add to his humiliation, the female officer, Sanchez, patted him down and emptied out the contents of his pockets, finding his wallet, a key chain, a few coins, a tube of Chap Stick, and a couple of bottles of pills. Hunched over the car hood, J.W. looked back and sputtered another barrage of obscenities. Every "FBI this" and "FBI that" out of his mouth made him less and less convincing.

But not to Patch. *This son of a bitch isn't kidding.* The chase across the bridge was beginning to make more and more sense. *This loudmouthed motherfucker is FBI. Angelo's turning over to the feds.* Stashed in the trunk of a federal agent's sedan was one of Patch's closest confidants, now a rat and a sellout to his brothers. Patch's stare toward the Buick turned icy.

Patch eyed the trunk of the Buick as a rage stormed over him. A lot of information finally added up: The phone call during the club meeting. Hollister's suspicions. Angelo's no-show during the battles with the 2Wheelers and the Gunners. Patch's anger grew. *No way this motherfucker talks to the cops. No way he turns over to the FBI.*

"You stay here." Patch pushed Nine Inch aside and headed up the dirt grade.

Patch yanked Sharpfinger out of the sheath as he climbed to the level roadside. Crouching down low, he scurried commando style toward the back of the Buick. While J.W. and the highway patrol cops continued arguing, shielded by the open door, Patch ducked down and cautiously opened the back passenger door, sliding headfirst into the backseat. A friend of Eve's drove a Buick, and if he remembered right, it had a rear fold-down pass-through seat. That meant the backseat flipped down, providing interior access to the trunk.

Patch pulled down the seat.

"Surprise, motherfucker."

Angelo rolled over, cramped and drenched in sweat. The two Infidelz made eye contact. Angelo's face froze.

"Patch! Help me!"

Patch's expression was one of stone-faced anger. His jaw was clenched, his neck muscles bulging. Angelo was flushed and sweaty. Patch gripped Sharpfinger.

"How long have you been ratting for the cops?"

Angelo's eyes filled with tears as Patch squeezed Sharpfinger's handle tighter.

"Tell me!"

"I just wanted to save my boy."

"And make him live underground with a piece of low-life police-informant scum? What kind of life is that for a kid? You sold out the club. Four more guys died tonight, you asshole."

283 «

"Brother, I can explain. The club was supposed to be protected." Angelo put his hand up to cover his tear stained face. "Brother, help me."

Don't you "brother" me ever again, you fuckin' rat!

Without a word, Patch reached his hand up and plunged Sharpfinger deep into Angelo's armpit. Angelo jerked. As the knife tore through his body, Patch gave the blade an angry twist. The knife pierced through the chest wall, between two ribs, and sliced a main artery from the heart. The removal of the blade produced a torrent of blood. It was an old Marine kill technique he learned in the joint. Angelo bled out almost instantly.

He was dead. Dead in five heartbeats.

Patch slammed the backseat in place, slid stealthily out of the car, and scurried back to the brush, where Nine Inch remained in hiding.

"It's done," he said in a disconnected, faint whisper.

Patch wiped the blade clean with a red bandanna and slipped Sharpfinger back into its sheath. He stuck the bandanna, stained with the blood of his close friend, into the back pocket of his jeans.

An awkward silence hung in the air between Patch and Nine Inch. A cold, detached expression on Patch's face told Nine Inch to hold his tongue. Whatever he wanted to know would have to wait. Patch finally spoke in a subdued tone.

"We wait here until it's all clear."

A Three-Bridge Run

Two lanes of freeway traffic ground to a near standstill. As late as it was, motorists were more interested in the flashing lights and J.W.'s predicament with the cops than in moving ahead. Officer Sanchez had had her fill of J.W.'s insolence and, with her colleague's blessing, cuffed his hands behind his back.

"You're under arrest. DUI and an open container," she said as she applied the restraints tightly.

J.W. shuddered at the sensation of cold steel wrapped around *his* wrists. He finally realized he had to be more cooperative.

"Look," he reasoned, "this whole misunderstanding can be cleared up with a single phone call."

Gibson and Sanchez looked at each other. Gibson shrugged. J.W. seemed calmer and spoke rationally.

"Look, Officer, just dial the U.S. marshals' office. There's an agent waiting for me. He'll vouch for me. And if I caused you two any undue hardship, I apologize. It's been a rough week."

J.W. was gaining more ground with his apology than with his drunken antagonism. Gibson dialed the marshals and spoke with the dispatcher who picked up on the other end.

As Gibson talked, he ambled over toward the weeds and the ditch, not far from where Patch and Nine Inch were hidden. The agent on the line confirmed to the patrolman that yes, J.W., John Wilkes McIntosh, was actually FBI. They were expecting him. Yes, McIntosh was a bit of a hothead. Could he talk to him?

Officer Gibson was satisfied enough to motion to the female CHP to uncuff J.W. He handed J.W. the phone. "Someone wants to talk to you."

J.W. spoke nervously into the phone. "Sorry 'bout that. That's right, a little roadside misunderstanding. No, I'm okay. I can drive. I'll see you in a few."

The three had reached an accord. J.W. would walk. Gibson canceled all backup units. No one was going to be arrested. He dismissed the request for a tow truck. No vehicles would be impounded.

"Thank Christ," J.W. muttered as he walked back to his car, shut the passenger door, got in, and buckled his seat belt. Where had he put his keys? He panicked and felt inside his pockets until he noticed they were dangling from the ignition. He took one long deep breath and started up the car. Then he hit a switch on the door and lowered the front window to talk to the approaching cop.

"Agent McIntosh," Gibson said, now speaking in a civil tone. "We'll forget about the DUI and open container, but I'm gonna write you up a 'fix-it' for that taillight. I still have your license."

"Do whatever you need to do," said J.W., rubbing his wrists, still sore from the handcuffs. He was eager to leave this dramatic scene behind and get back on the road.

After taking a few minutes to write the ticket, Gibson walked back to J.W.'s Buick. He handed J.W. the ticket pressed onto a small clipboard. J.W. signed the acknowledgment and got his driver's license back. He remembered when he had been a rookie cop on graveyard, stuck on traffic detail, and how much crap he took from pissed-off drivers, drunks, and motorcycle riders.

"Sir, before you go," said Gibson, "I'd really like to help you with that taillight. Since it's shattered, it's liable to short out your electrical system, or worse, you don't want to get stopped again."

"No, sirree!" said J.W., trying to act cheerful.

Then J.W. jolted upright in his seat. Angelo! All this time, he'd forgotten about Angelo locked away in the trunk. The last thing he needed now was to explain to a patrolman why a hefty biker with a gun in his pocket had been hiding in his trunk.

"Officer, I'd rather not trouble you any more than I already have tonight. I promise you I'll get this taillight looked at first thing tomorrow."

"It's really no trouble at all, Agent McIntosh. One wire. These cars are so modularized these days, it won't take a minute to disconnect."

"Actually, Officer, it's not *really* necessary and I need to be on my way. Like I said, it's been a terrible night, and they're expecting me in San Rafael. It's late. I've gotten people out of bed and kept them waiting long enough."

"I understand," Gibson said, tearing off J.W.'s yellow copy of the fix-it ticket and handing it to him through the open window. "You be careful driving, sir. Have a good night."

"Yeah, right, fucko," J.W. said under his breath after he raised his window. Gibson walked back toward his cruiser. J.W. crumpled the ticket and threw it on the floor. He watched Gibson and Sanchez talking. Then the female CHP got into her car, merged into the traffic, and drove off.

J.W. put the Buick into "drive."

"We're on the road again, Angelo," he called toward the backseat. "Sorry 'bout that. Took a little longer than expected. We're nearly home free."

J.W. signaled and waited for a gap in traffic to reenter the freeway. He watched Officer Gibson stop, scratch his head, turn around again, and walk back toward the Buick. J.W. lowered the window *again* and stuck his head out, straining to remain pleasant.

"Is there something *else* I can help you with, Officer?"

"You know, I spoke to my colleague just before she left and she insisted the light be disconnected because it could be a hazard."

J.W. pounded his fists on the steering wheel in frustration, raising the officer's suspicions again. The officer took a more forceful, less apologetic approach.

"Sir, step out of the car."

J.W.'s anger rekindled. He yanked the keys out of the ignition, opened the car door, jumped to his feet, and kicked the door shut behind him. Okay, he'd open the trunk of the car. Okay, the CHP would find Angelo inside. Okay, J.W. would cop to having a two-hundred-pound rogue stashed in his trunk. What could they do to him? He wasn't breaking the law. He was transporting a witness. Later on, it would make a good story over beers.

"I'll warn you up front, Officer," J.W. announced as he walked back and unlocked the trunk. He turned toward the cop, lifted the trunk open, and stepped aside. "Officer, I can explain." The agent spoke loudly, hoping Angelo might hear and catch on. *Play it cool. Don't launch into another desperate tirade.* He didn't need another roadside episode.

J.W. shut his eyes. He needed a convincing excuse. Gibson pulled out his flashlight and shined it around the interior of the trunk. The beam settled on an unconscious lump.

The officer took one step back. "Agent McIntosh, raise your hands and step away from the vehicle," Gibson said, pulling his gun out of his holster. He then stepped forward and reached around to roll Angelo over onto his back. Angelo's eyes were glassy but wide open, his pupils unresponsive to the flashlight's intense beam. His face was smeared with blood and sweat. The front of his T-shirt was also drenched in blood. The floor of the trunk was damp and sticky.

Gibson swallowed hard, physically sickened by the unexpected gore.

"Jesus Christ," he gasped, and turned to J.W. "I'm gonna need more than an explanation," he said, pointing his gun at J.W. "You, sir, are under arrest for murder."

J.W. gazed down at the crimson-stained body. What was this? An hour ago in Oakland he had closed the trunk on a freaked-out, hell-raising desperado. Now here was a lifeless corpse, and J.W. had no idea how he got that way. The agent lunged toward Angelo's body and pounded his fists on the motionless chest.

"You crazy son of a bitch," he yelled as he shook Angelo's body up and down, then side to side. "Wake up, you sorry bastard, and breathe!" Gibson pulled J.W. off Angelo's body, handcuffed him, and then put him in the backseat of the patrol car. The cop made an immediate call for backup and a tow truck. And an ambulance. J.W., his hands cuffed behind him, held his head down. He shook as his eyes welled up with tears.

From his position in the bushes, Patch looked over at Nine Inch. "Let's get the hell outta here before more cops come."

In the darkness, the two men ran back to their bikes. They pulled their motorcycles out of the bushes and started them up as quietly as possible. With their headlights off, they inconspicuously darted into the traffic lane.

INSIDE THE PATROL CAR, CHP OFFICER RONALD GIBSON held his radio in one hand. In the other hand, his Miranda card. He recited the words carefully to the dumbfounded prisoner in the backseat.

"You have the right to remain silent. Anything you say can and will be used against you in a court of law . . ."

Gibson continued the familiar legal litany, raising his voice louder above the noise of a Harley-Davidson and a Ducati that were cruising by. Nine Inch was crouched low and kept his head down like a disobedient schoolboy. Patch, on the other hand, gazed over for one last look at his dead comrade. As the cycles passed by, J.W. looked out the window of the squad car and caught a glimpse of Patch's Infidelz colors.

Patch took the lead and throttled the Mean Machine. Nine Inch easily kept pace as they sped up to take the long way home, over to southbound Highway 101, across the Golden Gate into San Francisco, and then back to Oakland via the Bay Bridge. It had been one marathon night. They had ridden their bikes full circle: from Oakland to Marin to San Francisco and back to Oakland again. Including the rumble and the chase that followed, Patch and Nine Inch had completed a grueling three-bridge run of death.

One of
Our Own

Hollister checked his Swatch: 8:35 in the morning. It was going on two days and his father still hadn't called home. Usually he checked in after a day, even if he was out on a bender with the guys in the club. The couch, Angelo's favorite spot these days, was just as he had left it, his green army blanket wadded up in a ball and the cushions in disarray. He'd even left the fridge door ajar. Hollister cursed his father's carelessness when he found the milk spoiled and everything else decaying at room temperature. Once again the two had switched roles. Angelo was the out-of-control adolescent; Hollister became the concerned parent.

Hollister was due at school in less than half an hour. *I'll give him a little more time,* he thought to himself, half expecting Angelo to burst through the back door at any moment. *Why hasn't he at least called?*

He looked at the clock again nervously. Hollister decided he would check back at the house in the afternoon, hopeful he would find his dad crashed out on the couch or tinkering in the garage.

Hollister made it back home around three in the afternoon. He hadn't been there five minutes when the doorbell rang. He creaked open the chain-latched door just wide enough to see two black men in dark suits. One man wore a proper red power tie. The other held up his credentials. Badge and ID. Hollister gazed through the crack of the open door.

293 «

"I'm Agent Swill, Terrence Swill of the FBI," one of the men said. "We're here about your father, Angelo Timmons. You mind if we come in?"

"I'm—I'm—just—just on my way out," the teenager stuttered to the agents outside. "Come back when my dad gets home. He went out for a while. He'll be back soon."

"Hollister," the agent insisted, "let us in. We need to speak with you."

Hollister opened the door.

The agents didn't bother to search the house for Angelo. Not a good sign. Cops had been around the house before. They usually searched every room thoroughly.

"Son, sit down. We have something to tell you. Your father is dead. The highway patrol found his body last night."

THE INFIDELZ MADE IMMEDIATE ARRANGEMENTS TO BURY their member after the feds released Angelo's body a day after the coroner's inquest. On the evening before the funeral, Nine Inch and Patch sat at the table over coffee and fruit and said very little. They had spent over an hour lifting free weights, avoiding the fancy fitness machines. Patch and Nine Inch hadn't discussed Angelo's death that night on the roadside. It became the proverbial elephant in the living room neither would acknowledge.

Then Patch seized the moment.

"Tony, I'm assuming that what went down between us stays between us."

"Goes without saying."

"As far as anybody knows, Angelo Timmons was murdered by the FBI. And let the Gun Runners take the rap for the 2Wheelers rumble. They have a lot of explaining to do to their people, anyway. As for Angelo, he brought the police into the club's affairs and sold out our members. I believe his relationship with the feds caused the death of some of my guys."

Nine Inch stroked his goatee.

"From my perspective," he said, "the thing with Angelo takes a little getting used to."

"How so?"

"This is new to me. Patch, I'm an accessory to murder."

"No, you're not."

"Technically, I am."

"You would never go down for something I did. That's a promise, kid."

Nine Inch paused again and collected his thoughts before asking, "How do you live with it? How do you take another man's life, no matter how justified it is in your own mind?"

Patch's eyes went cold. Nine Inch felt the same chill he'd experienced at the roadside.

"All I can tell you," said Patch, "is that in my world, and in your father's world, you learn to take care of things your own way without involving the cops."

Nine Inch studied the lines on the other man's face. To him, Patch was like his father, fair and just, but capable of darkness and cruelty to anyone who crossed him.

"Tony," Patch said, "you say you support the club. Well, now you know a lot more about what it is you support."

295 «

He checked his watch, then fiddled with the bandage on his arm.

"As far as Ahab and the Oakland club and the rest of the bike riders in this town are concerned, the real cause of Angelo's death stays between you and me."

Patch extended his hand. Nine Inch nodded. Their bond of silence was secured with a handshake.

IT WAS THE DAY OF ANGELO'S FUNERAL. OUTSIDE THE GUN Runners' soon-to-be abandoned San Jose clubhouse, a small convoy of Harley riders was packed, mounted, and ready to roll south, back to L.A. Lock N Load, surrounded by his

Ring of Fire, looked around the neighborhood for one last time. Then he defiantly gave it the finger.

"Won't be missing this place anytime soon," he said to Razz. Lock scowled as he spoke. His bandaged and swollen face fit snugly and painfully inside his helmet.

All five bikes started up and gunned in unison as the orange-and-blue fleet made its way toward the freeway on-ramp that would steer them to SoCal. Five pipe-blasting motorcycles made a thunderous, afternoon exodus. First gas stop: the Little Panoche Road exit just before three hundred miles of agricultural desolation on Interstate 5.

As the bikes merged into a high-speed, wheel-to-wheel formation on the freeway, a black Cadillac Escalade SUV with dark-tinted windows followed close behind. Inside the SUV, a vintage Ohio Players bass line reverberated, masking the distinctive *pump-click* sound of three locked and loaded shotguns. They were poised and ready for their own lethal payback: revenge for the beatings and stabbings Soul Sacrifice suffered at the hands of the Gunners during the MC rumble at Trader's Roadhouse.

ANGELO'S FUNERAL DREW NEARLY FIVE HUNDRED MOURN-ers, more than half of them arrived on motorcycles. The responsibility of organizing the funeral service fell on the club. A sea of MC patches filled the rows of chapel pews at the memorial service. The Infidelz were represented from chapters near and far. Members flew in from all over the world. There was a contingent of Soul Sacs led by club prez Rollie George. The Bushido Blades were on hand. A few small, regional clubs showed up and paid their respects. A stray 2Wheeler, an old cycling buddy of Angelo's, rode in on a trike. Patch admired his *cajones* for doing that.

Patch noticed that the front row, reserved for Angelo's family, was empty except for young Hollister, who sat alone, his head bowed and eyes closed. Angelo's ex didn't show, and whoever was left in the Timmons family in Oklahoma and Texas was either too old or too poor to make the trip on short notice.

"1%ers are experts at enforcing territory and going to war," Patch said to Nine Inch in the vestibule of the chapel. "We're certainly tough on each other."

"You reckon there may be more fighting?"

"Dunno. We may be in for some crazy times ahead."

Just then Ahab walked up. He nodded at Nine Inch, who took the hint and backed away to give him and Patch room to speak privately. The club's prez had important news.

"There's going to be a sit-down with the Central Valley 2Wheelers and the Gun Runners up from L.A. on what to do about the cops," Ahab whispered to Patch. "It's typical. Shit doesn't happen till people die. *Then* it's time to talk." He paused. "This sucks. We've had to bury too many of our guys."

"I hear ya."

Ahab tugged at his mustache. "It sure was bizarre seeing the stories in the paper on Angelo's murder. I hope they fry that FBI bastard for killin' him. You know, we're gonna help Hollister file a wrongful-death suit against the government. I don't know how the feds can squirm out of this one.

"What in the hell could Angelo have been up to that got him whacked by the feds? I just can't figure it out. Got any theories?"

"Nope," replied Patch. "I hate it when we lose one of our own." He changed the subject quickly. "Have there been any developments on the casino shootings?"

"Our moles at the cop shop says 'the tapes are inconclusive.' " Ahab winked knowingly. "The cops can't make any sense out of the security videos. They don't have a fuckin' clue who started what and who reacted in self-defense. So far there have been no arrests."

Patch nodded toward Nine Inch and motioned for him to come back over. He put his hand on Nine Inch's shoulder.

"You know, Ahab, I'd hate to think what coulda happened if this guy's posse hadn't ridden in when they did at the Ashland Court."

"No shit, bro," seconded Ahab. "Which reminds me, Tony. I want to invite you and your officers over to the clubhouse one night as soon as all this stuff blows over. We need to talk. I'm thinkin' along the lines of possibly the Blades becoming an official support club for us here in Oakland, or else offering you guys a prospect chapter somewhere in Northern Cal."

Nine Inch looked over at Patch.

"Well, don't look at me," said Patch. "My Oakland days are over. Deal with Ahab on this one."

Nine Inch ducked outside for a smoke while Patch stepped inside the chapel, went to the front pew, and sat next to Hollister. He tried to play it upbeat and patted the kid on the back.

"So, you holding up okay?"

"It's crazy out there."

"I know. Just hang in there."

"Everybody says I'll get over this, but, you know, Patch, they haven't got a clue."

"If you need to call someone, you've got me."

"Don't even go there. I can't depend on anybody."

They were both staring straight ahead at Angelo's open casket when Nine Inch rushed in to join them. The front of the chapel resembled a flower shop. Elaborate floral arrangements surrounded the casket. It was the kind of os-tentatious display that made Patch bristle at bike rider fu-nerals. Hollister could have used the money that had been spent on flowers and other non-necessities.

"Shit, Patch. You ain't coming back. And I've got nothing. I've got nobody."

"What about buddies? Surely you have friends."

"It was always just me and Dad." Hollister gazed down at the floor.

Patch and Nine Inch exchanged somber glances. Nine Inch nodded sorrowfully and slinked down in the pew.

The kid was right on both counts. Patch wasn't coming back anytime soon, and the boy had nothing and nobody. He would probably be taken into foster care. Child Protec-tive Services. The boy was fifteen. The three years before his eighteenth birthday would be the roughest.

One Simple Rule

Hollister, Patch, and Nine Inch sat tight-lipped and stone-faced in the front row as the service ended. A dozen people had spoken, recalling humorous and touching stories, anecdotes, and memories of Angelo. Hollister was sullen and distant over the devastating loss of his father; Patch felt mixed feelings, wavering between sadness and disgust. Whatever idiotic schemes Angelo had cooked up that had cost him his life, he didn't want to know anymore.

The Dire Straits song "Brothers in Arms" played loudly over the sound system. It was time to file out of the chapel and ride off in formation to the graveyard. The newspeople outside filmed eight Infidelz pallbearers hoisting Angelo into the back of a black hearse.

The ride to the cemetery was torture for Patch. He thought about the other guys in the club who had died and the members who had risked their lives battling the 2Wheelers and the Gunners. Their bravery formed a stark contrast to Angelo's hiding in the trunk of some fed's car.

Patch kept to the rear of the mile-long pack. He was more convinced than ever. *It is time to leave Oakland.*

At the cemetery, he remained seated on his bike, away from the graveside crowd. Everyone assumed that he chose isolation because of grief. But it was a lot more complicated. Part of him sorely missed the Angelo that the mourners described at the service; another part of him despised the Angelo that had betrayed him and the club. As Patch sat on his Road King, Eve walked by and squeezed his hand.

301 «

"I'm so sorry, John. I had to come. Charles, my boss, wasn't going to give me the day off. I threatened to quit. I think he's pissed off at me. His little girl asks about you.

"I heard that a cop killed Angelo. That's terrible. I'll always remember him at the house drinking beer, borrowing money, and never paying it back." Eve laughed.

Patch only shrugged. He was lousy at lying to Eve, so he said nothing. He felt her eyes examining his bandaged wrist and the fading bruises on his face. Fortunately, she chose not to comment.

"How much longer you here for?" she asked.

"I leave today, right after this." He pointed toward the gravesite. "It's time I got back. I've got shit to take care of. Check in with the new chapter. Get things hopping down in the southwest. New charters we need to start up. Colorado. New Mexico. Utah. I'll be on the road a lot."

Enough about the club, Patch thought, *what about her?* "How you fixed for dough, doll?"

"I'm okay. Things are going to be fine. I'll find my way through all this, John. I hope you do, too."

"Don't worry about me. I've got my people. I don't want the young guys to think they missed out on *all* the good times or that they just caught the tail end, the death rattle, of the big party."

Eve leaned over and hugged Patch's neck.

"Be careful, be safe," she whispered, and then she kissed his cheek.

As she walked away, she bumped into LiLac and excused herself for her clumsiness. *What a contrast between those two. Two different generations of women. Combine Eve's strength and life experience with LiLac's vigor and youth, and vroom, you've got the perfect old lady.*

LiLac was clad in black leather. Was it because they were mourning colors or because she looked so sexy in tight leather?

"Patch," she said, "I'm so sorry about the loss of your friend. I do have great news, though. Thanks to you, I'm leaving the Blades and forming my own MC. I've hooked up with four other Asian chicks who ride. We're designing a patch. The Mekong Molls. I really wish you would help me put together bylaws and rules of order. Tony's gonna help, too. He loves the idea of us becoming a Blades support club."

"I'm sure he does." Patch pictured Nine Inch frolicking around his compound with a bevy of Asian bike babes.

"Come and visit me in Arizona. But call first. I'm no good with surprises. The boys and I will show you around."

Patch stroked LiLac's hair and admired her long legs one last time. She kissed him on the forehead, the sole extent of any evidence of intimacy between them.

Patch was relieved when they lowered Angelo into the ground. As far as he was concerned, they couldn't put the dirt on him fast enough. Hollister tossed the first fistful of earth onto his father's black metal casket. Then he broke away from the crowd and headed over to where Patch sat on his bike, withdrawn in the day's sunshine, anticipating the ride back to Arizona.

303 «

"Listen, Patch," the boy said, "I'm sorry if I snapped at you. My father's dying certainly wasn't your doing."

Patch swallowed hard.

"What's next for you, kid?"

The boy shook his head. "I spoke with my aunt in Alaska, but I don't know. She said I could move in, though she didn't really sound too keen. Her boyfriend has a couple of kids. I'd be in the way. I'm used to having my own room and I'd be couch-surfing for a while. Dad wanted to settle up there, but jeez, how much of the year would I be able to ride?"

"I wish I could argue that there's more to life than riding, but there isn't," Patch said. "Not for me, anyway." Then, almost without thinking, he blurted out, "Listen, what if you moved down to Arizona and stayed with me, your old god-father?"

The offer caught Hollister off guard. "Move to Arizona? Me? With you?"

The offer had just popped out of Patch's mouth, straight from his heart.

"Yeah, sure, why not? You come down, get your shit together. We might actually be able to help each other out in that department. To be honest, I could use the company."

"I don't know what to say."

"Well, if you're interested, you'd better hurry before I come to my senses. Plus, I leave today." Patch checked his watch. "In exactly two hours. Four o'clock. Sharp. In front of the clubhouse. I ain't waitin' around, either."

Hollister shook his head. "Man, I appreciate the offer, but, really, I couldn't. This is my home. I was born here. I'd miss it too much."

Patch started up the Road King.

"Suit yourself, kid." He mussed the boy's combed hair. "Just thought I'd ask. Ain't no big thing. Anyway, I guess I'll be seein' ya around."

Patch hugged Hollister awkwardly. As he rode off, he felt sort of relieved that the boy turned him down. The responsibility of a kid spooked him as much as the big rumble with the 2Wheelers. Death was immediate, broken bones mended in time, but a teenager in his life at this stage? That meant long-term uncertainty, maybe worse than any prison stretch. Patch could take care of himself inside a penitentiary. Having a high-school adolescent around the house was a total jump into the unknown.

AT THE FRONT GATE OF NINE INCH'S COMPOUND, PATCH said his good-byes.

"Tony, I've enjoyed my stay here. I'm proud to have ridden with your father. Now I'm proud you're my friend. I'll blow in a call to you when I reach the Arizona border. You can stop by on your next trip back from Mexico."

Nine Inch looked at the tiny gym bag Patch packed, the content of a couple weeks' worth of personal effects. It amazed him that anyone could travel so light and live on so little. But if the physical baggage Patch packed on the Mean Machine was scant, the mental baggage he carried back, the knowledge that he'd eliminated a trusted friend, was very very heavy.

It was close to four o'clock when Patch pulled in front of the Infidelz clubhouse. A few members were on hand to see him off, including Ahab, along with Pugsly and Cash.

"Cash just got out of the joint," said Pugsly, a short and stout Canadian who wore gold chains and rings. "I'm helping him find a job and a place to live."

Patch thought about Hollister. No sign of him. *He'll be okay. The boy's bright. He'll get through it.* He had made the offer. He had made an effort and covered his ass.

Ahab toked on a fat joint he'd just rolled.

"Good stuff, Patch," Ahab said, blowing a cloud of smoke out of his long, hooked nose. "Wanna hit? It's DRP."

"DRP?"

"Date Rape Pot."

"No, thanks. I need to at least make it to L.A. with a clear head."

"So don't be a fucking stranger, stranger," Ahab said as he hugged his friend hard. Patch had to take a moment to regain his breath after the brotherly embrace. Then he mounted and fired up the Road King. It produced a hearty blast of exhaust and power. The Mean Machine seemed just as ready and able to log hundreds of miles of highway as its owner was. Patch and the Machine were as one. The roar of the pipes would serve as his road mantra. Today, especially. If his bike was a person, it might finish his sentences. The Mean Machine. His ultimate pal. His other half.

Patch hit the turn signal and inched out onto East Fourteenth toward the 580 freeway and hit the throttle. The sky was sunny and clear and the temperature was just warm enough for a late-afternoon putt, the perfect prelude to a long evening run south. Maybe he'd crash in Berdoo and hit Arizona a day later. Or he could visit that cute bartender in Palm Desert with the nice ass. Whatever. It was all up to him. He had no schedule. He could do as he pleased. Free to roam and be his own boss. A lot to be said for that.

However, Patch's well-earned solitude was about to be short-lived.

Approaching in his rearview mirror was Hollister Timmons aboard his rattletrap Sportster. Patch stopped at the first stoplight as the boy caught up, beeped his horn, and pulled up next to him. The size of Patch's Harley dwarfed the kid's ride. Strapped on the back of the Sportster with bungee cords was a small canvas bag. Just like Patch, the boy traveled light. Both riders slipped off their helmets.

"If the offer still stands," Hollister yelled above the rumble of both motors.

Patch nodded.

"Okay, the offer stands," he replied. "But there's one simple rule."

"Yeah, and what's that?"

"Always remember: I lead, you follow. No exceptions. Any questions?"

"No exceptions, no questions."

"Good."

Hollister took a quick look over his shoulder back toward the clubhouse, and then he pointed at the freeway on-ramp. South.

"Home, James?" he asked.

"Home it is."

Patch and Hollister slipped their helmets back on. Patch looked down at the pavement. East Fourteenth Street. Grimy with plenty of potholes. Oakland. Home of the Silver and Black attack, Everett & Jones BBQ, the swingin' Oakland A's, Jack London, Kasper's hot dogs, and bike riders of all colors, shapes, and sizes. These were the working-class streets both Patch and Hollister had grown up on. The Oakland streets. The light changed and Hollister shifted gears and fell in line behind Patch, onto the highway. They were bound for the desert southwest.